When Palomas Visit

Abel Zavala

For my mother Margarita, my sister Laura,
and my wife Frances.

When Palomas Visit

Abel Zavala

1

P ALOMA F LORES DIED THIRTY-THREE years ago.

Well, thirty-two years and three hundred and sixty-four days ago. Tomorrow, November third, will be the anniversary of the day my mother took her last breath.

It seemed an awful long time to hold on to, but guilt is funny that way.

People like Paloma are not easily forgotten and circumstances like the ones that stole her away from me—they took root. Thirty years had my mother lived inside me, her memory a gentle flame keeping me warm through the coldest winters. Even so, I missed her. God knows a man, just like a boy, needs his mother. These past few hours, I'd been consumed by grief, so lost in memories, I hadn't realized today was Día de los Muertos—Day of the Dead. But the people I drove past down 26th Street in Little Village reminded me as they carried their art depicting Death and their faces painted, embodying it.

How interesting, I thought, while driving toward my father's house on Lawndale, this obsession over the dead on this day. I never understood it, never understood people's hopes for their departed ones to visit them. If that were possible, Paloma would've visited me.

Wouldn't she?

Why hadn't Paloma ever visited me? Sure, she'd been in my dreams, but who hasn't dreamt of their loved ones, living or dead? Was it my fault she never came? I never set an altar for her. My father, Ignacio

"Nacho" Vásquez, never celebrated the day. Most of what I'd known about the tradition came later in life, from TV, movies, and books. Was she still upset with me for her death? I wouldn't blame her.

Parked in front of Ignacio's place just a couple of blocks from the busy street, two girls played a few houses from me. One girl, on the opposite side of the street, radio-controlled a black toy airplane. It was a cheap-looking drone. The toy lifted off the grass and raced for the other girl across the street, but the controller stopped it. The second girl shouted for it to hurry and the first one flew the plane across the street, but it was too late. Before making it all the way, it went down, landing feet away from the second girl.

Had the batteries died?

The second girl, visibly upset, gestured at the first one, a look that said *'look what you did'* on her face as she picked up the airplane. It was wet after having landed in a tiny pool of water.

Stepping out of my white VW Jetta, the girls turned to me when they heard my car door shut. Uttering a quick "hello" at them, I made my way to the backyard and found the hidden key inside the porch.

It'd been so long since I had stepped inside this house. And, God, Ignacio had left it a mess. At least the ambulance had picked him up somewhere on 26th instead of here, saving him the embarrassment.

After a quick cleanup, I headed upstairs to the attic, my old bedroom, where Ignacio had left boxes strewn about the floor.

I checked them, wondering if there was anything worth taking back home to Cincinnati. His old clothes, some movies—they were all junk to me. Although one of the long bottom boxes was filled with briefcases. *Odd.* Ignacio had never been able to hold a job for longer than a few months. What use could he have for so many briefcases?

I opened them and gasped.

Letters.

It only took opening a few to understand what they were. All the time I lived with Ignacio, my sister Sofía had written to me and all along my father had hidden her letters. The bitterness hit me like a whiff of bad cologne. Of course he had. There was nothing this man had not been willing to take from me.

Shuffling around the letters, my hand bumped something hard and I dug it out. It was an old video cassette, a home movie.

The home movie my mother had tasked me with keeping safe when I was a kid. I could hardly believe my eyes. This particular relic had been lost for decades, or so I thought.

I ran downstairs, desperately searching for the old VCR Ignacio had put away because I needed to watch it, to see my mother and sister; she'd been gone from my life just as long as Paloma. Surely, Sofía would be in this movie.

Once I had everything set on the TV, all I needed was the courage to hit Play on the VCR, and when I finally mustered that courage, it was Paloma's face that lit up the screen, glowing as she always had in our old living room, surrounded by faces I'd long forgotten.

When she spoke, her voice was as familiar as my own heartbeat.

"Go, Damián. Sofía is waiting for you."

All of a sudden, my vision blurred and I felt the weight of tiredness dragging me down. *No.* This was *not* the moment to be falling asleep. They'd been gone too long from my life, and now I had them in front of me on the television screen. *No.* I tried to fight through it, but despite my best efforts, sleep wrapped its dark tendrils around me and the fight was done. I couldn't hold on.

WHEN I AWOKE, I was no longer in my father's living room. This room was dark, except for a sliver of light coming through the door. This room felt different, like I'd been here before. But where was *here?*

Conversations flitted in from the other side of the door. They sounded happy, like the people having them were having an enjoyable time. They said my name. "Damián this," and "Damián that." *Damiancito*, they called me. But that was me before, when I was a child. No one calls a grown man by their diminutive. This forty-one-year-old hasn't been Damiancito in so long.

"Who's out there?" I yelled, my voice higher than usual, as if a boy spoke in my place. The music and the voices on the other side of the door must've muffled my sudden child-like sound. As I cleared my throat for a second call, I picked up on the sweet, smoky aroma seeping through the closed door and my eyes lit in instant recognition. *Mole.*

Yes, it was mole, the kind my mother used to make on my birthdays. Drool ran down the side of my mouth as I imagined, for a moment, eyes closed, that spicy chocolate sauce poured over her boiled chicken. Man, the way it flowed to meet the fluffy orange rice she'd make. Even the memory could always bring a smile to my face.

That memory, that nostalgic taste for her cooking, was enough motivation to sit up and try to figure out where I was. A little vertigo set in, but once I composed myself in the darkness, everything around me felt bigger.

The bed.

The room.

My hands touched my chest, then my head, to make sure I was awake. *This has to be a dream,* I thought. But I'd never questioned my dreams before. This seemed too real. Right? Perhaps this was what Alice felt after going down the rabbit hole to Wonderland. What kind of rabbit hole had I gotten myself into?

My feet dangled off the bed instead of touching the floor. Fearing I would fall, I carefully slid down before firmly planting my feet. In the mostly dark room, I extended my hands out to feel my surroundings, hoping not to slam into anything. Yet, I somehow knew where things were placed, through some strange sense of familiarity: a tall, three-drawer chest was on my right; a similar, shorter one with a wide circular mirror on top, to my left.

Once at the door, I placed my ear against it. People sang along to the '80s música grupera I listened to at full volume on the radio every Thursday. *Jueves del recuerdo*, the locutores called it.

The metal doorknob that would usually be at my hip was now all the way up to my chest. With sweaty palms, I turned it clockwise, and, next, found myself blinded by the lights in the other room.

"Where am I?" I whispered, while my left arm shielded my eyes, slowly adjusting to recognize the faces greeting me. These were the people I'd seen on the TV screen moments ago, people decades gone, who'd known me since I was a kid.

But being there with them, it was impossible.

I was sure they were still alive somewhere, but they were more my mother's and sister's acquaintances, and none of them had reached out to me, ever. Then, a voice that only lived in my memory reverberated from the kitchen.

"Mamá?" I said, heart beating so fast I was afraid I'd keel over.

No.

No, no, no. Paloma, you're dead. But the closer her voice got, the clearer it became, and no matter how hard I rubbed my eyes, everything in front of me remained the same.

If this was a dream, this would be the part I'd normally wake up at, confused.

Paloma appeared from the kitchen.

"Stop," I mumbled. "Stop, stop, stop." *Say something in Spanish. She doesn't speak English.* "Mamá, no. Estás muerta." Even in Spanish, my words didn't halt her. Some guests giggled at my words; others gasped.

Then, behind her, Sofía stepped out.

God, what the hell's going on? Am I dead? What other explanation could there be? Had I gone mad? Because one doesn't suddenly arrive at the place one grew up at and converse with their dead mother.

If I hadn't gone mad, then, somehow, I'd traveled back in time and that was entirely too much to consider all at once. All I knew was that here I was, at the old apartment, the same one I'd seen minutes before in Ignacio's living room.

Something pecked at the window. Since my eyes had mostly cleared in the vibrantly lit room, I checked to see what it was. A white dove stood outside the window sill. My wife had just said to me, *a dove symbolizes spiritual love.* The paloma flew away almost instantly when our eyes met.

I then checked my hands. They were tiny, child sized. My suspicions were confirmed in the mirror on my left. I was a child.

"Smile, Damián," someone said. *No*, I shook my head. How could I, when I was suddenly standing in the past with the dead?

"Your cake, Mr. Vásquez," a woman shouted. "On the table." My eyes darted to the table in the middle of the living room, and there it was. A full-sheet cake with an "8" candle. *Eight?*

Yes! It finally came to me. This day... This was July 28th, 1989, my eighth birthday party and months before I'd lose both my mother and sister.

No. I... I couldn't go through this, not again. If I was stuck here, how long would that be? Did that mean I'd lose them again?

It was too much for me. As much as I'd told myself to calm down, I couldn't. My breathing increased in small doses. Still, people focused on me.

Decades, they'd been gone, and now, suddenly, we were together again. For so long I'd needed them, my mother and my sister, and all that time had turned them into strangers.

But they were mine. My family. These people were my friends. So, I took a step toward them. The woman who'd yelled out about my cake called from behind the guests.

"Mijo," Paloma said with a smile, as if she'd not seen me in so long. A tiny wheeze came out of her. Her arms extended, ready to embrace me.

"Mamá," I replied. Tears that had run down my cheek at her words hit my parted lips. I embraced her. Squeezed her. God, thirty-three years, and now, on this Día de los Muertos, it was *me* visiting my dead mother.

As I clung on to her, her ice-cold finger circled the top-back of my head, circling the cowlick that never went away, while humming a John Lennon song I'd forgotten she knew. John Lennon's *Beautiful Boy (Darling Boy)*. My mind raced, trying to decipher this time-traveled encounter.

How did I go from watching a homemade movie in my father's living room to reliving the recorded moments? How did I turn into my eight-year-old self? I did not know.

Maybe that's what happens when doves appear... when palomas visit.

PART 1
BEFORE PALOMA'S VISIT

2

M Y WIFE XÓCHITL HAD already begun to put away the Halloween decorations before I'd arrived from work. Turning down the volume on the car radio, I carefully parked in our driveway in case she came outside unexpectedly. The man on the radio was talking about the world not being a happy place, some crap about how he'd witnessed the pain people left behind. He was a medium of some sort, a scammer, in other words. "We think we're ready to move on with our lives," he explained to the interviewer. "But tragedy waits for us just around the corner, like a lion hidden in the grass, silent, patient, waiting for its prey to come closer before pouncing."

Not knowing why, I found myself listening intently, my hand hovering inches away from the key in the ignition. He was fortunate, the medium said, because he got to assist those who sought truths before moving on. It was ridiculous. His words reminded me of those money-hungry charlatans, who prey on people's grief and offer them empty consolation—card readers, palm readers, clairvoyants...

That was enough for me. I didn't need a spiritualist to tell me the world was full of hurt; I'd seen and experienced it all firsthand.

Xóchitl's frizzy hair peeked out from our side door. I loved that about her, and she knew it, proudly letting her hair loose for the world to see. She didn't demand attention, but she liked to show that off. She wore her hair out proudly. I turned off the car and focused my attention on her instead. She stepped out wearing her favorite sage green long-sleeve shirt with a hoodie, even if the 70-degree temperature required no long sleeves.

"Dami!" The high pitch of her voice immediately put me on edge. She hadn't answered my call when I dialed her on my way home. I figured she was talking to her parents, as she usually did before I'd arrive from work, but her expression was worrying.

"Are you okay?" I asked, stepping out of the VW. "Your parents okay?"

"It's your father. Someone stabbed him."

Her words flew over me. What did I care about what had happened to Ignacio? Without a word, I rushed to kiss her, longing for her soft lips on mine. Nothing else mattered. Xóchitl set down the box on the car's hood, holding on to her phone. She kissed me hesitantly, but it was all I needed. I grabbed the box to finish putting away the remaining Halloween decorations and headed for the door.

"It's bad, Dami," she insisted. "I was just on a call with a lady from Saint Anthony's Hospital near your father's. Amaya? I think that was her name."

"Why'd she call *us*?"

Not even trying to hide my annoyance, I disregarded the first care with which the first set of items had been put in the box and tossed the next round in, cramming them however they fit.

"I have no business with Ignacio anymore. Plus, we're hours away. It's not our responsibility to rearrange our life to accommodate his needs."

Xóchitl's feet remained rooted to the same spot on the ground, while I headed to the front of the house for the rest of the decorations. When I returned to her, she was still there, phone in her hand, not taking the box from me.

"Sorry. I'm a little annoyed." I leaned in to kiss her forehead, holding the box she'd not taken from me. "How'd she get our number, any-way?"

"Maybe he listed you as his emergency contact."

"How? I never gave it to him."

"I don't know. But she said he wants to see you."

I went inside, hoping she'd follow me, and set the box down at the entrance. Xóchitl didn't move.

"Come on," I said.

Why was she so concerned with Ignacio's situation? She knew how I felt about him. Besides, she'd never even met the man.

This time of year, she shined. Her birthday was a few days ago. Halloween had passed, and Día de los Muertos Christmas would come soon. It all brought her immense happiness. But now Ignacio was taking that joy from my wife, which was exactly like him. He had always been good at taking things away.

Shit.

I realized the moment I'd dreaded for so long may have finally arrived. I might finally have to see Ignacio again after twenty years. It was inevitable, wasn't it? The viejo, my old man, who was probably close to eighty by now, would die soon anyway.

Those were the laws of nature, right? You get old and then you die.

I always knew we'd meet again, although I was kind of hoping it would be at his funeral. Always wondered if I'd be responsible for his burial when he died because there was no one else to do it.

Long ago, he'd had another wife and other children, but they were long gone before I was even born. Did they care enough to bring him to mind?

"I spoke to the woman about five minutes before you came in," Xóchitl continued inside our kitchen. "She tried to reach you, but you didn't answer. She said your father insisted you be there."

Why? Did he need something from me? My blood? My kidney? Had his drinking finally caught up to him? Had his body finally given out? Surely it could not take another ounce. Yes, I decided, that's what it was. The old drunk needed my kidney to live.

Well, too bad.

Or perhaps he needed money for his hospital bill. He was never good with it. Maybe he wanted me to pay him back for the money I once asked him for, just over two decades ago.

I took out the frozen meat for the night's dinner and set it on the sink to thaw.

IGNACIO TOOK ME IN when I was eight, shortly after my mother's death. By the time I hit twenty, after years of lies and manipulation, I had to leave. Doubt struck and I questioned whether I could make it on my own. For the most part, I was penniless and hadn't the slightest clue what it meant to be truly on my own. Still, it was time to get away from my father.

If only I'd planned things better, for it was naïve to think that my 30 hours a week waiting tables at a local diner would cover my expenses. The pay was shit, and I knew it: three dollars an hour plus tips. To me, that meant an extra fifteen to twenty percent; to our clients, it meant an extra dollar or two per table. Most times, they only left their change in coins, rounded to the nearest dollar.

When rent or bills were due, I was always short on money. I'd ask for more hours, to work other positions like bussing, washing dishes, even jumping in the kitchen to use my limited culinary skills gained at Ignacio's, not by choice. But my manager often claimed we weren't busy, despite his constant complaints about being short-staffed and in an endless overcrowded rush hour.

I reserved my free days for employment agencies, to look for temporary work. These *chambas*, as many of my coworkers called them, paid better, but were hard labor. Mostly construction or factory jobs. The majority took two or three days at a time to complete.

With limited income and barely any savings, it only took a few months for me to reach out to Ignacio for help; I'd run out of money, and my landlord had already warned me he'd serve me my eviction notice.

After the thirty-minute CTA bus ride, my heart wouldn't stop pounding the last block and a half from his house, beating so hard not even the rumbles of the bus that had dropped me off, or the busy 26th street, could drown out its beat.

Standing at his front door, fist in the air, ready to knock, I debated going inside through the back porch, where he'd hidden a spare house key. Because why should I knock like an uninvited guest? This had been my home too, after all.

Within a minute of biding my time, Ignacio opened the door.

"¿Qué onda?" he said, turning away from me and dragging his feet past his couch, toward his room or the kitchen.

"Hey," I answered sheepishly, taking one step inside. "I need money. My rent's overdue."

"Güey, get in here and close the door," he shouted from afar.

I didn't want to go in, so I stayed at the door's edge. Looking around the living room, it was hard to imagine I had ever lived there. There were absolutely no signs of me anywhere. There were no pictures of me on his walls, no school work displayed anywhere in the house, proudly or otherwise. Nothing but the cruel and bitter memories.

Ignacio returned, handed me some bills, and I left feeling ashamed. I hated the way I'd felt, standing there like a stranger in my own childhood home, and hoped I'd never have to see him again.

"ARE YOU LISTENING TO me?" Xóchitl asked.

"I don't want to go," I said, watching the cold water flow from the sink onto the frozen meat. "I have nothing to say to my father."

Xóchitl sighed. She stood behind me and wrapped her left hand over my left biceps. Her right hand came to rest on my right shoulder and her head on my back.

Did she understand why I refused to go? I'd shared Ignacio's lies with her before, explained how for years he'd made me believe I was undocumented, kept me in constant fear of being deported back to a country I knew nothing about. As a child, the only thing I knew about

Mexico was that they spoke Spanish there and once, long ago, my family had lived there.

"Dami, let's just take time to think about—"

"Look," I snapped, before turning around to face her. "He *lied* to me when I was a kid. You know this. Who knows what other things he kept from me? I don't understand what you expect. Am I supposed to just forget the fact that he was the shittiest of parents just because he got himself stabbed? He probably deserved it..."

"Hey!" Xóchitl slapped my arm and walked away.

Great, now I'd messed up. Shit.

"I'm sorry," I said.

"Now *you* look!" she sighed. "I think you *should* go see him. I understand why you're angry, but perhaps this will finally give you a chance to find closure and move on."

Xóchitl, my analyzer, always helping me rationalize when I hastened out of emotion. Like when I was eager to buy a house, she said we needed to save more. When I wanted a dog, she reminded me we were always working and had no time to care for it. Or when I suggested we open a store, she said we'd need to create a business plan before applying for loans.

But even when I was settled on my decisions, Xóchitl had my back. *I* wanted a house, so we got the house. Now we owed the bank *and* her parents.

"Okay," I said, defeated. "I'll think about it."

"Great. Now, let's go get stuff for dinner."

AS WE HEADED BACK home from our grocery run, a white dove came to stand on my side-view mirror while we waited at a red light.

"Hey, little palomita," I mumbled, turning to Xóchitl. "I love these little guys." Anytime they'd show up, I always assumed it was my mother, checking in on me.

"Oh!" I turned to Xóchitl. "We're a couple of days away from her anniversary."

The bird flew to her mirror. It cooed when the wind attempted to push it off. The dove flapped its wings, digging its claws into the mirror's hard, black plastic. We laughed at the bird, who held on as if its life depended on not being pushed off by the wind. The light that had been red for what seemed like forever, finally turned green, and the bird, as if understanding what had happened, flew away.

"They always remind me of her," I said as it disappeared from our view.

"Who? Your mom?"

"Yeah." I took a deep breath, letting the day's breeze fill me with the courage to talk about Paloma. "I'm sorry I don't talk about her enough."

"Do you want to?" Xóchitl asked, leaning slightly closer.

The wistful look in her eyes made me feel guilty. I should tell her things, share more with her. Of course I wanted to, I just didn't know how. It hurt too much, but I didn't want to say that. I'd shut her out plenty, so I nodded once to let her know I wanted to talk about my mother, and she smiled encouragingly in return.

"She was funny, you know? A corny-joke kinda woman, always making me laugh. There was this one time, on our way to buy shoes, she asked me to translate 'un zapato'. I told her it was 'a shoe', and she replied with 'bless you.'" I chuckled at the memory. "She then pretended to wipe her imaginary mocos on my shirt."

Xóchitl laughed. "She sounds fun. Like this?" She pretended to wipe her imaginary booger on my sleeve, just like my mother had. Then, her expression turned more serious. "I'm sorry you didn't get to have her as a mother for as long as you should have. She should still be here. I wish I'd gotten a chance to meet her."

"Me too," I whispered.

I took her hand in mine, letting the warmth of mine seep into hers. "She would've liked you. I think so, anyway. Sometimes I worry I'm forgetting her, what she looked like, what she sounded like..."

I trailed off and Xóchitl squeezed my hand in sympathy. Forgetting a parent is the cruelest joke. How can someone who mattered so much slowly become a stranger?

"So, why *do you* call her Paloma?" Xóchitl asked. "Did you used to call her that as a kid? I rarely hear you say, 'my mom'. Never 'mamá' or 'mami.'"

"No," I say, smiling at the thought of an 8-year-old calling his mother by her first name. "I started doing it after she died, when her memory started fading. I have nothing else to remind me of her. This is something I can hold on to, something I know I won't forget."

My wife flashed me a sad smile and, for a moment, I wondered why I had avoided talking to her about this all this time. It felt good to share Paloma. It made me feel closer to her.

Xóchitl put her arm around mine. "If you could say anything to her right now, what would you say?"

Her question caught me off guard, but the answer sprung out without me having to even think of it. "I'd tell her, 'I'm sorry, Mamá.'"

Mamá. I hadn't said that word in so long. It felt right saying it then instead of Paloma, but after I let it out, it felt alien, satiated, the way words feel when you analyze them too much.

Xóchitl shook her head. "It was an accident. You can't blame yourself."

She cleared her throat. "Want to tell me more?"

Her encouragement to say more about Paloma was like a jolt that awoke an urge in me. Suddenly, all I wanted was to share more details about her with my wife.

"Paloma had a scar above her eye, just like mine." I pointed to one over my left eyebrow. "Hers was above her right eye. When I got this one, I was bummed out about my stitches, so she reassured me by telling me she got hers when she was a child too, in Guanajuato."

As we drove past a slew of businesses, nothing particularly unique about them, I remembered another thing that always reminded me of my childhood, and more particularly, of my mother.

I parked in front of a Mexican restaurant, a bright yellow and green building with a terracotta roof that, if I were still a child, I would assume was common in Mexico. "You know why I stop here before work?"

"Because you're lazy and don't like making your own breakfast?"

"No." I chuckled. "No. Because of their huevos con chorizo. Before school, Paloma would make them for me, and, I know it sounds dumb, but theirs taste so much like hers."

"It's not dumb," Xóchitl assured me.

"Yeah, but... eggs and chorizo. It's so simple. You and I make them. God, this is so stupid." I turned away from her, a little embarrassed that something so common meant so much to me.

Next to the restaurant stood a small Cuban coffee shop that people constantly bustled in and out of.

"Let's get some coffee," I said.

"We're almost home. We can make—"

I was out of the car before she could even finish her sentence.

The college teen at the counter waved when he saw me. "The usual?" I replied with two fingers up as I held the door for my wife.

Xóchitl stared at the myrtle green wall with white silhouetted palm trees. She checked her phone, then glanced at me before typing. She grabbed one of the pre-packaged coffee bags and squeezed it, smiling as she took in its aroma. It was something we loved doing during our shopping trips. I smiled at her.

After paying for our drinks, a slice of their tres leches cake to share with Xóchitl, and the bag of coffee beans she'd squeezed, we sat at a table near the window.

"When I leave the restaurant, I usually stop in here for this," I said, turning the cup and pointing to where it read *Café con leche*. "I give it a good whiff, like you did with that bag. By now, he doesn't even bother closing my coffee. Anyway, Paloma used to do that, too, before drinking her coffee."

My fingers circled the cup as I thought back to the Saturday mornings when Paloma would chat with me about random stuff—her life in Mexico, Sofía, my older brother Moisés (whom I'd never met), my school—while she drank her café and I ate my huevos con chorizo; or how she'd sit with me on our old as hell couch that used to pull her in until she almost touched the floor and she'd hold on to her hot coffee the way the white dove had held onto our car's side mirror.

My mother drank *a lot* of coffee.

On the other side of the parking lot, we watched children play inside the McDonald's. Through the restaurant's giant windows, we could see them running and jumping, while some parents forced their crying children to eat. Xóchitl and I quietly gazed at the mostly blissful families, but I knew better. Like that medium on the radio had said, tragedy could strike at the most unexpected moments.

"You still remember what she looked like?" Xóchitl's chilly hands sat on top of mine. Her voice was enough to distract me from my temporary trance.

"Yes. Well, I think so," I answered. "She was tiny and a little morenita, like you. Too bad I don't look much like her, though." When I was a child, everyone always said I took after Ignacio more than Paloma.

Xóchitl looked up at me, surprised. "My mom's tiny," she said.

"Maybe they'd see each other eye to eye. Anyway, I just know that I was almost as tall as her, even at eight years old."

"And your dad?"

My eyes rolled. "He's tall," I said. "I'd guess she was just over five feet tall and he's around six feet. He always seemed bigger, too. I guess I slouched a lot as a kid, so..."

I let out a loud sigh. "Ignacio was fit too," I said, pinching the fat on my side.

Xóchitl laughed a little. "Stop it."

"Well, he was a boxer. When I lived in his house, he'd do push-ups in the middle of the living room while I watched TV. He also had a boxing bag in the basement. But he never took the time to teach me anything about it. How to fight, how to defend myself, how to train. Nothing. That's why I'm fat now." She scowled at me. "Okay, *fine*. I got *lean* fat," I said smugly.

It had taken me years to lose weight, but in the last year, we'd committed to eating healthier, and we'd done well. Stuck with it. My weight dropped from two-fifty to one-hundred ninety pounds. Hated exercising, though. Hence the fat rolls around my waist. At least, that's what I attributed them to.

Physically, I felt the best I had in a long time.

Emotionally, well, talking about my parents probably wasn't helping.

I slid the cake in her direction.

"WE'LL BE HOME SOON," Xóchitl promised her mother, Doña Mari, in Spanish. She turned to me, waiting for my confirmation to drive to Chicago, but I gave her no indication. She stepped away to another room while I put our groceries away. Then prepped the thawed meat for a caldo de res, trying to eavesdrop on her conversation from afar, and wondered what conversations Paloma and I would have had if she were still alive.

Tell me about your job, I imagined her asking.

I'm an interpreter for undocumented immigrants.

Good. I need you to translate these letters, por favor.

After forty years in this country, she'd probably barely speak or read English, and I'd roll my eyes and complain to Xóchitl after, but I wouldn't deny my mother help. She'd then tell me about my tíos and primos in Mexico.

¿Y mis nietos? she'd also ask.

We're not having kids. They'll end up like me. No thanks to Ignacio.

"Shit!" I shouted when the knife's blade chipped my fingernail instead of cutting the meat. My make-believe conversation about the make-believe grandchildren Paloma might've hoped for had stressed me. Xóchitl rushed into the kitchen.

"I'm fine," I said and waved her off.

"See you soon, Mami." She ended her call.

She got a text, the second one in a short while, and replied quickly before sliding her phone into her sweater pocket.

"I'll take it from here," she said.

AFTER DINNER, WHILE WE watched our usual late-night shows before bed, I texted my boss, explained Ignacio's situation, and asked for the rest of the week off.

Of course he said it was fine and to take all the time I needed.

"Fuck."

Xóchitl shot a look at me.

"He had to make this about him, right when my mother's anniversary is coming up," I said, typing back a reply.

"I don't think he planned to get stabbed," she said.

"All I know is that he's selfish. Maybe that's why his parents abandoned him when he was a kid and he later treated me the way he did."

God, I hated myself for justifying his behavior.

"But my father got what he wanted. Paloma died, Sofía left, and he got me. No responsibility after. Sometimes I think I was like a trophy to him. He wanted to be a boxer, but never made it big, so maybe I was his consolation prize—the one thing he could actually win."

The TV played a scene from a TV show we'd watched countless times. I stared blankly, not paying attention. I didn't need to; I knew what was coming. The scene cut to a commercial and I checked my phone. It was 9:30 p.m.

"Let's just go," I said, letting out a sigh.

"To bed?"

"No. Let's go home, I mean. Let your parents know we'll be there for a few days."

Xóchitl immediately pulled out her phone and called them. While she talked to her mother, I headed upstairs to our bedroom to pack my bag, a task that only took five minutes.

She packed a week's worth of clothes, still on the phone with her mother. Watching her, I couldn't help but laugh to myself. She had always been an overpacker.

Xóchitl ransacked a pile of clothes on a chair that contained our work shirts, her pants, unmatched socks... stuff she'd asked me to put away days ago. She mouthed that she was searching for a floral dress. I shrugged to let her know I had no clue what dress she meant, but then she found it and glowered at me.

"Ugh, it's wrinkled now," she mumbled.

"I'm sorry," I mumbled, hoping her parents hadn't heard her discontent. Xóchitl shook her dress, folded it neatly, and packed it in her travel bag. I considered helping her, but figured it was best to avoid doing anything that might upset her further.

I went back to my phone and set my alarms early so we wouldn't leave late the following day.

"What time are you setting it for?" Xóchitl asked, throwing her phone on the bed that almost grazed my face.

"8 a.m."

"So, you'll wake up at 10?" Xóchitl winked. I rolled my eyes and showed her my alarms set for 7, 7:30, 7:45, 8, 8:30, and 9 a.m.

Xóchitl would need no alarm. She'd be up by 5 a.m. She would always wake up first and keep herself busy on her phone instead of trying to get more sleep. Me? I was more of a turn-them-off-one-by-one-and-go-back-to-sleep guy.

"My parents asked about our kids again."

Xóchitl snuggled close to me. She kissed my lips, distracting me from the social media posts I was catching up on. "Imagine," she said, peppering my cheek with gentle pecks here and there, before moving down my neck. "A little Damián or Xóchitl running around, watching movies with us, breaking stuff that we'd laugh about after scolding them."

"Yeah." I tittered. "Watch me yell at them after behaving like a dick, just like Ignacio."

Xóchitl stopped kissing me. She punched my arm lightly, then scooched to the other end of our bed.

"God, Damián. What's wrong with being your own man? Change the story. You're not him. Close his chapter in your life and move on. Or let me move on."

Let me move on? She'd never said that to me before. Shit, I'd never considered her feelings toward starting our own little family. Could I lose her if we didn't move forward? If I didn't get my shit together? Ignacio's shadow was always hanging over me like a dark cloud. But we weren't all cursed to become our parents, were we?

"Babe, I'm sorry..."

I turned to her, hoping to get close to her again, but her back had turned toward me. She had edged further away. I wrapped my arms around her, but she shrugged me off.

Fuck, I'd hurt her feelings, and I hated that, but it was too late. The damage had been done.

"Xóchi," I whispered.

She replied with a cold, "it's fine. Go to sleep."

I HADN'T MEANT TO fall asleep and only realized I had when a text startled me awake.

Hola Mijo. I hope you're well and good luck with your dad. Call me when you can, please.

Odd. Who had texted me so late at night? And how did they know about Ignacio? And why did they call me "mijo"?

I opened the message app and saw another message being typed. Suspicious, I blocked the number and set my phone on silent.

Xóchitl turned to me. "Who was that?"

"I don't know. A wrong number, probably. Don't worry, though. Get some rest. Good night."

My mind raced while I tried to go back to sleep. Suddenly, I was flooded by memories of our talk about Paloma and Ignacio. He had often asked, *Damián, ¿pa' qué no te fijabas por 'onde ibas?*

Though I hated to admit it, it was a fair question and one I had asked myself many times since Paloma's accident. Why hadn't I been more careful? Would she be alive today if I had?

A tear ran down my face and seeped into my pillow.

3

NOVEMBER 02, 2022
THE MORNING BEFORE

*M**E VOY A MORIR.*
I'm going to die.

Paloma had said that to me the day before she died. Why did she have to say that? It felt like tempting fate to announce something like that.

"Careful!" Xóchitl shouted, her warning snapping me out of the memory. I slammed my foot on the brakes. If it hadn't been for her, I would have rear-ended the car in front of me. That driver honked and rightfully flashed me his middle finger.

"I'm going to die," Xóchitl mumbled while clutching her seatbelt, and I shuddered, remembering my mother's augury.

"I'm sorry," I muttered, scowling at the driver in front, as if it was his fault my mind had wandered. "Are you okay?"

Xóchitl let out a long sigh. "Yeah. *Please* be careful. I don't want to die before seeing my parents. What's going on?"

"Nothing. This drive and us talking about my parents yesterday, it got me thinking about when she told me she was going to die."

"She said that? You never told me that. That doesn't sound like something she'd say."

Xóchitl was right. It was completely out of character for a woman who always looked at the bright side of life. Everyone who knew Paloma loved her positivity.

The road was lit up by the brakes of other cars, blinking in and out like Christmas lights despite it being weeks before the holidays. Cars merged carelessly onto our lane, the only one on I-275 that would be open for miles before we'd cross into Indiana. Already, I doubted the trip was worth the risk of getting hit by a reckless driver swerving into our lane. For Ignacio? Definitely not. To appease Xóchitl, however... That was a different story.

At the last possible second, I swerved and took the next exit. The guy behind me honked, throwing me the dirtiest look as he passed us.

"What are you doing?" Xóchitl asked.

As I pulled into the first gas station, she peeked at the dashboard. "We don't need gas."

I didn't answer immediately.

"Hey," she said, "if this is because I freaked, don't worry. I'll be fine. Just drive more carefully, please."

"It's not you. It's me."

"Excuse me?" Xóchitl backed away. "Are we breaking up?" She joked. Xóchitl was always great at lightening the mood.

I wanted to drive back; hoped the nurse who'd called her would pick up the phone again and confirm Ignacio's departure from this world, so we wouldn't have to make this dreadful trip. The last thing I wanted was to see my father. Time didn't heal all wounds; this one was as fresh as ever.

Alas, all I could say, chuckling, was, "No. What I mean is—" I paused, tightening my grip on the steering wheel, unsure how to tell her I wasn't ready.

"Well, we're packed and driving. Let's drive to Indianapolis and see how you feel then. We can spend the rest of the day there instead. Stay the night and enjoy the city tomorrow."

We'd said we'd visit the city, but never made plans for it. Xóchitl continued suggesting restaurants we could eat at, places she'd wanted to visit, and so on, and so on, and so on.

As she continued rambling on about Indianapolis, I smiled and felt thankful and lucky to have her in my life. On this trip. If it had been me driving alone, I'd have turned back home and let fate take care of Ignacio.

I can get through this, Xóchi, as long as you're by my side.

But that crude bitterness toward my father lingered deep within me, and an affliction for my mother filled my heart.

My smile at her changed quickly.

"Or not," she said in a way that sounded like a question. "Are we going home?"

I turned from her, disregarding what she'd said. Not on purpose, I just didn't want her to see me cry. The quick fluttering of my eyelids told me I'd be doing so soon. I bit my bottom lip with my top teeth and hoped the pain would keep me centered and ward off the tears threatening to spill. Placing my fist over my mouth, I thought about the decision I had to make. Drive to Chicago or go home.

A scraggly kid was leaning against the wall of the gas station store, snacking on what looked like a muffin. He was ripping off little bits of it and feeding a small flock of birds that were gathered around him. He had gathered quite a crowd, some house sparrows, Carolina chickadees, crows...

"A palomita!" Xóchitl pointed.

Sure enough, a small white bird looked up and gazed right at us, tilting its head as it surveyed us sitting in the Jetta. A few seconds later, a piece of the worker's pastry bounced off its head and the dove flew away.

"I heard or read somewhere that a dove symbolizes spiritual love, so when you come across them in the world, it means someone you love has sent them." Xóchitl said.

I wasn't sure if she'd meant that to be motivating or if what she'd said was true and it meant that my mother was nearby. Reluctantly, I replied, "Ugh, fine," and I set the car in motion to continue our trip.

Driving down the busy highway, saying nothing, gave me time to think about Ignacio. Would he ask me about my life in Cincinnati? Would he want to know Xóchitl or about her? Would he scold me for not calling or visiting him?

Once the eternal silence felt tiresome, I scanned the radio stations and stopped when I heard the man from the day before discussing what he described as "otherworldly beings guiding us in our life and sending us on quests from the afterlife."

What the hell was he talking about? I turned to Xóchitl and laughed.

"Why are you listening to that?" she said. "You don't even believe in it. Remember, you once said, 'It's all *malarkey.*' I remember you specifically said that. Malarkey." She smacked my hand, plugged her phone in, and hit play on one of her playlists.

To a certain extent, gods and divinities and the afterlife sounded interesting to me, but I had stopped believing in them long ago. I had asked God to answer my prayers and he never had. Books, comics, TV shows, and movies were now the extent of my fascination with them.

"How about you focus on the road?" Xóchitl said. "I'm not ready to discover if there's something else after this world, or if it's *malarkey.*"

Xóchitl found a Halloween playlist she'd often enjoyed jamming to, and because she'd always preferred to listen to her playlists in order, we ended up singing along to *This Is Halloween.* She dropped her voice, mimicking the characters in the movie, like she always did.

When the song finished, she lowered the volume and turned to me. She was quiet for a moment, thinking, and then she said, "Love, I'm sorry to ask, but..." she paused. "Do you think, with all that's happening now, you could tell me what happened to your mom?"

"Um..." What was I supposed to say to her request? She was my wife; I should be able to tell her anything. She was my greatest confidant and yet I'd barely touched on the subject. It'd been over thirty years since it happened, but it still hurt, no matter how much she'd assured me it wasn't my fault.

I suspected part of the reason it was difficult for me to say anything was, perhaps, my jealousy in regards to our different upbringings. We'd had differently opposite childhoods. Xóchitl had family gatherings and parents who gave her money to spend with her friends at the mall or at the movies. She had people who'd take her places to keep her safe.

I had none of that with Ignacio. He constantly reminded me that I only had him and wouldn't let my friends visit. When I worked, he'd keep my earnings and make me do housework anyway. And who would keep me safe when I'd go out? No one.

I'd take lonely walks around my neighborhood and see homeless people and drug addicts stepping out of the shadows of abandoned houses. Even though I'd keep my distance, they still always asked me what the fuck I was looking at. Back then, I never faced them, but I also never ran away. I knew too many people who'd been chased and killed. Instead, I had learned to keep to myself.

Until now, the few details Xóchitl knew about my past were these: Paloma died because of me, Ignacio raised me after she was gone, and he made me think I was undocumented. She knew I had an older half-sister named Sofía, who lived with us in Pullman after Ignacio left Paloma, and now lived in Mexico with our other brother, Moisés.

It was easier to escape giving her more details when we weren't locked in the car together for four hours. If Xóchitl had planned on me opening up to her about what had happened, she'd played her cards right.

"Forgive me," Xóchitl said. "I didn't mean to pry. I know you don't really like talking about your past, but I love when you tell me things. And from what you've told me about your mother, she sounds like an extraordinary person."

I simpered after her words.

As we slowed down, merging onto another one-lane road, she turned my face to her.

"I'm sorry," Xóchitl said. "I shouldn't have thrown that at you. I'm also sorry that I never got a chance to meet your mom. But you need to understand that I know her through you, and even if you don't say any more than what you've already told me, that's enough to know what a wonderful person she was, because *you* are wonderful."

Whatever wonder lay dormant inside me woke up the moment she spoke those words and, once again, I was moved to tears. Her eyes followed them as they ran down my face, until their salty taste hit my mouth. Xóchitl delicately wiped them off.

We had four hours ahead of us. Maybe close to five, considering the stop-and-go traffic; this wasn't the first time we'd experienced heavy traffic on account of the never-ending construction work.

It was time for me to say more.

We'd promised to be truthful with each other even before we married. So why should I keep my past from Xóchitl? Why should I keep Paloma from her? She'd allowed me into her family, so why shouldn't I allow her into mine, even if they were nowhere near me? Except for Ignacio.

I felt it in my bones. It was time to tell Xóchitl what happened to Paloma Flores on that early November morning. It was time to divulge the moment that had ended her life and forever changed mine.

4

T HAT WEDNESDAY EVENING, BEFORE bed, I asked Paloma for my Halloween candy. She refused. She'd already allowed me a few bite-sized Snickers and Twix pieces after I arrived from school, and now I'd already brushed my teeth. Knowing that I had a strong sweet tooth, she had hidden the candy.

But I wanted it. Demanded it. It was *my* candy. The way I saw it, I'd earned my candy the way she and Sofía earned money at the factory they worked at. So I took it upon myself to refuse her last piece of the day just as she was refusing me my hard-earned candy.

"¡Que no, Damián!"

"But it's mine!" I screamed in Spanish, petulant the way children often are when they don't get what they want. Anything within arm's reach was thrown to the floor in the heat of my tantrum. Spoons, napkins, the napkin holder, a green and white handmade placemat her sister, Tía Soledad, had gifted her from Mexico... they all found their way down to the kitchen tiles.

"Niño, stop!" My mother slammed her hand on the table just as I was going to throw her evening coffee. "You're going to get sick if you eat it all."

Whatever consequences awaited, they were future Damián's problem. Rotten teeth? Whatever. I'd had cavities before and they'd never bothered me. Were they supposed to hurt? It didn't hurt when I scraped my tongue over and around the holes in my teeth. I enjoyed doing that.

I continued nagging her, testing her limits. She'd tire of me soon enough, she always did. It went like this: I'd act like a brat and it would come down to my wants or her nalgadas, be it with a belt, a chancla, or her hands. No matter what, I knew the odds were in my favor. Paloma was much more likely to give in than to hurt me.

When she finally gave in to my incessant pestering, she slammed a couple more bite-sized chocolate pieces in front of me. Was that enough? No. My bucket contained full-sized candy bars. I'd seen them and now I wanted them... No. I needed them.

Chewing my candy, I spotted the bucket in the pantry, behind the bread and rice bags. I chewed slowly, watching her like a hawk, waiting for her to leave the kitchen. The moment she was out of my view, I dragged my chair to the pantry. It scraped its worn-out rubber leg caps over the black and white tiled floor, marking my path.

The loaf of bread was in my way, so I shoved it aside, not concerned with gentleness even though I knew Paloma hated squished bread. A bag of rice and cans of refried beans and veggies dropped like bombs on the floor, but I didn't care. I found and pulled the bucket out, checking behind me for any sign of Paloma.

Before I could make it to the floor, she rushed in, belt in hand, but she snatched the bucket first.

"Give me my candy!" I griped.

"Damián, ¡ya! Por favor."

"¡Tú, ya!" I jumped off the chair. "It's not yours. It's mine. You didn't get it. I did. It's mine!"

"¿Sí? Here then." She set the bucket on our table and beckoned for me to approach, pulling me by the ears the last few steps. Her belt hit the table, and I flinched. "Go ahead, then. Eat them all! I don't want to see anything unopened, got it? And if you get sick, don't cry to me, ¿¡entendiste?!"

Yes. I understood that I'd won.

Paloma left the kitchen. The apartment's front door slammed closed. And I happily ate my candy.

She returned many minutes later and sat with me on the table, a concern on her face. I wanted to ask her if she was okay, but I was still upset at her. Huffing, I chose the best pieces—the boring ones would have to wait to be thrown away when she wasn't looking. Her foot tapped the floor. Surprisingly, she hadn't asked me to stop eating. Candy wrappers continued to pile next to the candy bucket.

My mother shouldn't have allowed me to eat that much candy, but she was teaching me a lesson. I slowed down before finishing the rest, never even making it to the full-sized candy bars.

"I don't want any more," I admitted.

"You said they were yours and I told you I didn't want to see—"

"No más, Mami," I cried, not daring to look her in the eyes.

"Pick up your mess and go to bed," she instructed.

I slid the hard candies back into the bucket and threw the chocolate wrappers in the garbage can. Paloma grabbed a caramel piece before pushing the bucket toward the middle back of the top of our refrigerator, away from my reach, and hers.

"Good night, Mami." Sheepishly, I kissed her on the cheek.

"Good night," she said.

NOVEMBER 02, 1989

THURSDAY MORNING WAS ONE of consequences.

My head ached, my saliva felt sour, and every time I swallowed, I tasted the bile burning its way back up my throat.

Paloma's voice came from the other side of our door. Confused, I got up to check why she was still there. The sun had already risen, so she should have been at work with Sofía. Usually they'd leave together by 6:30 a.m. and I would get up shortly after, dress, grab my backpack, and head downstairs to our neighbor, Cecilia's place. She would feed me and take me and her daughter, Jenni, to school.

I didn't feel like going, though, so I laid back down and tried to go back to sleep. Seconds later, I had to run to the bathroom and kneel over the toilet to throw up. Nothing came out, only my runny spit.

Next, I lumbered into the kitchen, hands over my stomach, and dragged the chair out from under the table.

"Buenos días, Damián," Paloma said, kissing the top of my head and sitting down. She then ruffled my hair. "*Ya*. Don't be so dramatic."

The acidic taste in my mouth felt the same as it had the day doctors had removed my appendix. So, I asked if it had come back. Paloma only chuckled.

"No, niño. But I told you you'd get sick eating all that candy." She placed a cup of Pepto in front of me, but I pushed it away.

She continued beating the eggs with chorizo and added the mixture to the hot pan. Usually, the sizzling of the huevos hitting the oil made me smile, but this time, despite my stomach growling, I wanted none of it. Too soon that growl in my gut had turned to sharp pains.

Paloma served refried beans next to her huevos con chorizo, placed hot tortillas and chiles en vinagre on the table, and sat down to eat with me.

I could hardly swallow a single bite before my body begged for me to let it all back out, but in some cosmic sort of punishment, I gagged and...nothing. Wanting no more food, I pushed my plate away and my head took its place on the table.

"Let's not do that again, okay?" Paloma said. I loved the way she pronounced *okay*. 'O-kei'. That's how it sounded with her accent.

"Next time," Paloma continued, "have what I tell you and no more. Or you'll be sick like right now." She poked at me to look up and make a note of how much her fingers measured. I nodded and set my head back down.

Paloma finished her food, then called my school to let them know I wouldn't be in that day.

It was 10 a.m., and I remained in my chair, alone in the kitchen, food still near me, completely cold and untouched except for my first bite. My chin rested over my left arm while my right hand played with the food. My headache remained, mild though, and with each pounding knock, I fantasized about having mind abilities. Telekinesis, they called it on TV. Pretending to use these imaginary powers, I imagined opening the tortillero and throwing it across the kitchen, moving the saltshaker from one end of the table to the other, but nothing happened. Instead, I'd shaken my hand so much around the saltshaker, I'd accidentally spilled it. My head only throbbed harder.

Surely my mother would scold me for spilling it. *No tires la sal,* she'd probably say, a reminder that spilling salt was bad luck. Instead, she reappeared, poured herself the hot water she'd boiled for her next helping of coffee, and humphed at my small mess. She cleaned the salt off without another word.

I turned to the candy bucket on top of the fridge and pretended to use my imaginary super-mental powers to push the stupid bucket into the garbage, which only increased the ache in my head.

Obviously, nothing happened. Only the superheroes I admired had superpowers like the ones I imagined. *I* was powerless. They were heroes and society rewarded them for their heroic deeds. I had been a brat the night before and my body had punished me for my unheroic behavior.

When Paloma sat down with her fresh café con leche, she made funny faces to attempt to cheer me up.

"Hungry now? I'll heat this up for you." She combed my hair with her fingers, then proceeded to circle my cowlick, humming Lennon's *Beautiful Boy.* I shook my head. "Let's go outside, then. We can go see what new toys they have at *Las Hamburguesas.*"

Las Hamburguesas, that's what Paloma called the McDonald's down the street. "¿Sí, mi chiquito?" she asked in a soft voice.

My stomach agreed with Paloma, grumbling at the thought of the cheap fast-food, so I forced a thumbs up, gave her a crooked smile, and left the kitchen to change out of my PJs.

Las Hamburguesas was a rare treat, especially when it was just the two of us. And I couldn't be happier at that moment. No more stomach ache. Barely a hint of my headache. *And* I was there on a school day.

While Paloma waited for our food, I asked to go play in the quiet indoor play area. She gave me her *okei.* There, a girl I'd never seen appeared out of the slide. Her giant hair stood up, touching the hard plastic.

"Hi," I said, giggling at the girl. She walked up to me and courteously extended her glistening bronzed arm to shake my hand. When our fingers touched, they sparked. "Oh," I said, a little taken-back. "You have superpowers?"

"Nooo," she giggled.

"I *know*," I followed sarcastically. "What's your name?"

The girl whispered her full name so softly and so fast I couldn't make it out. Her eyes flashed before she looked away, blushing.

I told her my name and asked where she lived.

"Indiana," she said, peeking over my shoulder.

"Is it fun?" I asked because I knew no one who lived there. All I knew about Indiana was that it wasn't far. I'd never been. In fact, the only places I knew were my neighborhood, Pullman, and South Chicago, where, at Christmastime, Paloma, Sofía, and I would take the bus to *La Comercial* Street to buy masa for tamales. I supposed I also knew *of* Roseland, where some of my school friends lived.

The shy girl shrugged her shoulders.

"My dad took me out of school today," she said. "He took me to see where he works and then we came here."

"Hija, let's go," her father interrupted.

The girl whispered her name again and this time I understood 'Oli' and 'Luna,' and I imagined her place over a rocky terrain, the same as I'd seen in images of the moon. *Fun.* She waved goodbye and walked out with her dad.

"Mami, did you see the girl?" I asked my mother ecstatically, gasping after running from the slide to the booth she'd chosen close to the play area.

"Yes, mijo. Did you ask what her name is?"

"Se llama... Oli! And her last name is... Luna."

"And what did you and Oli Luna talk about?" Paloma asked, taking our food out of the bag and separating her number one from my Happy Meal.

"She lives in Indiana. Mami, did you see her dad's mustache?" I laughed, then coughed, choking on the large pieces of the burger I'd bitten off. "It's bigger than my dad's."

"Like this?" Paloma tickled my upper lip, making me cough more. "Ya. Drink your juice and eat your food, carefully."

"But the girl..." I rambled on, choking plenty of times. Since I was more interested in talking about her than finishing my food, Paloma packed what I hadn't eaten, helped me with my jacket, and we left to go back home.

Clouds covered the midday sky completely. Bursts of the cold fall wind punched my face as we walked toward our building at the other end of Champlain Street. Before the end of the parking lot, I realized in all my excitement about the girl, I'd forgotten to play with my new toy.

I tugged on Paloma's sleeve. She stopped at the end of the lot, handed me the box with leftovers, ripped the toy's plastic bag with her teeth—growling playfully—and, once the toy airplane was free, gave it to me. The wind snatched it from my fingers and sent it flying into the street, a wing damaging as it hit the pavement.

When I picked it up, the toy's wing was bent, but still holding on. Paloma told me to leave that part alone and that she'd glue it once we returned to our apartment. She also warned me to be careful when running, despite the sidewalk being quiet and no cars approaching down our street.

The airplane balanced on my hand as I pretended it was gliding on an air current, the wind turning its rotors. Halfway down the block, I stepped onto the road, ready to cross to our side of the street. Much too engrossed by my game, I didn't bother to look both ways, or even a single way. I'd crossed the street alone since I was younger. This was my street. I had grown up on it.

A white bird flew past me, landing on the sidewalk I was headed to.

"Look, hijo, una palomita blanca," my mother said behind me.

This was my first time seeing one. The brown ones—*mourning doves*, according to what I'd seen on TV—were common. But this white bird, it was a rarity, and it was precious.

I stood in the middle of the road, admiring how black its eyes were. The dark little orbs contrasted with its plump white body. Hoping not to scare it, I continued carefully toward it. "¡Damián!" Paloma shouted.

A brown car sped down the street toward me, close to colliding with the parked cars. Paloma dropped the food, and rushed after me, pulling me out of the way and shoving me behind her, where I landed next to a puddle. My toy plane splashed in the water, its wing now broken. Everything that came after, happened too fast for me to process it. All I knew was one moment Paloma was on her knees before me and the next she was meters away, crumpled on the pavement. Turning to my mother, who was on all fours, she slowly picked herself up, but the car approached her too fast. The driver swerved to the right, the back of the car scraping against a parked car, which took my attention away from Paloma. Seconds later, I heard the tires' high-pitched squealing as it tried to stop.

Everything was silent after that. The only sounds were the hums of the stopped car's engine and my own breathing.

"Mami?" I mumbled.

Tears filled my face. Everything went out of focus. I got up, wiped my face hard and looked at the car, trying to make out the face behind the foggy windows. Two sets of eyes were staring back, but as soon as they locked on mine, they turned away. The brown car reversed and sped away.

Paloma never got up.

Instead of running to my mother, I chased after the car, but too quickly, it turned down the street it had come from—114th—and vanished. Even so, I caught enough of a glimpse of the back of the car to recognize the make and model. It was an Oldsmobile Cutlass Supreme. I only knew that because my father had seen it in a commercial once and mentioned it to me.

5

COWARDS. WHAT ELSE COULD I call them? There was no other word for whoever slammed into my mother and fled the scene. I didn't know what to do. I couldn't leave Paloma there alone, not when there was a risk that another car could come and hurt her more. Most people on our block were probably working anyway, and if I ran to my neighbor Cecilia's, surely she'd be mad at me for crossing the street with such little care. She was scary when she was upset.

I could have run home and called the police, as I'd been told in school, but Paloma had our keys, and her broken body on the ground frightened me too much. I couldn't bring myself to move her and look for them.

"¿Mamá?" I whimpered, approaching her slowly, wiping my tears with my sleeve. "Mami, ¿te moristes?"

I stopped at the edge of the pool of her blood. Her eyelids moved in quick, tiny flutters. Then, her fingers moved. When her body twitched, I jumped back.

¿Te moristes? I wondered again.

In my mind, she corrected me. *Moriste*, she said in my thoughts, just as she'd taught me before. *There's no S at the end.*

"¿Mami?" Still no response.

Just as I finally considered running to someone's door and asking for help, a stranger parked close to our building and ran toward me.

"What happened?" the man asked in a pressing tone. "Boy, what happened?" My mouth opened, but nothing came out. It wasn't until I started hyperventilating that I let it all out.

"I didn't watch where I was going... and... and... a bird... my mom. Someone hit her."

The man grabbed my shoulders with both his heavy hands, his grip dug into my tiny shoulders. "Why didn't you *knock* on their doors?" He searched around the empty street as neighbors began to peek through their windows. "Stay here. I'm going to call the police."

The man knocked on the building's door behind me, then ran inside. I waited as the man had asked. Stood there, in the middle of the street, close to my mother's body. Nothing would move me until he said otherwise, not even the next oncoming car. I had to obey. Be vigilant. Aware.

Soon, the man returned.

"What's your name, young man?" he asked in a calmer tone.

"Damian," I answered, the way a non-Spanish speaker would have said my name.

The man extended his hand to me. "Hello, Damian. I'm Derrick."

Derrick asked where I lived and I pointed to our building near his car. The door to the building he'd run into opened and we both turned. An old Polish woman stepped out and carefully made her way down.

"Listen," Derrick said, kneeling in front of me and gently wiping my face with his handkerchief. "I called 911, so they should be here in a moment to help your mommy, okay?"

Nodding in agreement, I noticed the roughness on his face. It was thin and scarred and covered in a graying stubble. He smelled of copper and I wondered if he worked at the paint factory across from the McDonald's.

"Hey," he said, voice soft, "go over there and wait with her." His eyes looked at the old woman. "I'll go down the street to stop cars from coming this way and direct the ambulance to your mom when they arrive."

Derrick helped himself up, pushing down on my shoulder. Once on his feet, he tapped my back and walked away.

"Oh, God," the woman said with a thick Polish accent, waddling to me. "I'm very sorry this happened. I'm Anna. You?"

"Damian."

"Nice to meet you, Damian. Come sit with me. Tell me what happened." Anna led me to her building's steps. I briefly turned back to look at my mother, anticipating the trouble I'd be in for not listening to Paloma. Trouble with Sofía. Ceci. My dad.

"How are you, Damian?"

I said nothing. My tightened lips trembled and I felt close to crying. A tear formed in my left eye.

Finally, the sounds of nearing sirens distracted me from my anguish. Derrick jogged toward us, directing the approaching ambulance, even though Paloma was visible on the ground. Once the ambulance positioned itself close to her, the mostly older Italian and Polish neighbors stepped outside. They stared and pointed at my mother. Their heads moved like bobbleheads as they tried getting a good look at Paloma.

Those that knew me from our brief encounters when I walked the block, waved at me. Some covered their mouths with their hands, whispering to each other. Were they saying something about me? Blaming me already for Paloma's injured body?

If it were Paloma or Sofía talking amongst themselves like my neighbors, they'd probably say, "Ay, pobrecita, and the boy she's left behind." Had she left me behind? I still didn't know.

Cops arrived, and Derrick talked to them, pointing in all directions. My eyes followed his movements: to his car, the end of the street, to where a different cop ran yellow police tape from one light pole to the other, one end of the street to the other.

POLICE LINE DO NOT CROSS.

Clicking sounds startled me. One paramedic prepared a gurney for my mother while a couple more placed a blanket on the ground, turned her to the side, and slid her onto it. Together, they lifted my mother's body and secured it with the stretcher's black belts.

When they rolled the gurney to the ambulance, I wanted to run after my mother, to be with her. I wanted to cry next to her, but Anna held me down.

"You see," she said, her finger following the paramedics. "They didn't cover her. That means she'll be okay. I'll find out where they're taking her and then we'll walk to your home. Stay here."

Through grunts, Anna pulled herself up by the railing. She shouted at the paramedics while sauntering up to them. Whatever conversation they had, all I got was intermittent sidelong glances.

Lifting my head to peek at Paloma inside the ambulance, I thought back to my favorite superheroes, going over what they'd do in this situation. Superman and Batman's world had changed when they lost their parents. At least I still had a father. And my sister.

If my mother died, would that mean I'd have to look for that driver and avenge her death? But... But... I'd never been one for confrontations, always cowered at the first sign of danger, unlike my heroes. *They* were fighters. I was not. Stupid eight-year-old thoughts. Guilt came over me for thinking Paloma would die. They hadn't covered her up, Anna had confirmed so, and that meant she was still alive. Unlike Superman and Batman, *I* still had a mother.

After the guilt, the worry came. I worried about the spanking that awaited me for what I'd done to Paloma. If not from Sofía, certainly from my father. They had all hit me before for misbehaving. Paloma, Sofía, Ignacio, even Ceci. They'd used belts and shoes. They'd slapped my hands and pulled my ears for disobeying and talking back to my elders, for not doing my homework or helping clean the house, and for not eating what they'd cooked. So why wouldn't they punish me for what I'd done to Paloma?

Scared again, I cried. Closed my eyes, covered my ears, and swayed back and forth, because that's what I'd seen people on TV do to calm their worried minds.

"Oh, young man. Don't cry. It's going to be okay," Anna said, surprising me upon her return. She extended her hand again. "¿Vamos, Damian?" she said, and I smiled at her but also at the way she'd said it. Her accent made her 'v' sound like an 'f' and that brought me a little joy during this terrible moment.

At my building, Cecilia stood just outside the building's door, watching. "¿Qué está pasando allá?" she wondered. She was a woman in her late thirties, with long hair that almost reached her knees. I wasn't sure if the question had been directed at me and she didn't seem quite sure either.

Before I could answer, she instructed me to go inside and wait with her daughter. She hugged me, never looking away from the scene ahead. Cecilia and Anna spoke using their best broken English, emphasizing through their inflections. As I pushed apartment #102's door open, I heard Cecilia say from afar, "¡Ay no! Dios mío. Poor Paloma." Even without seeing her, I knew she probably did the sign of the cross as she often did in harrowing situations.

When I walked in, little Jenni jumped off her couch near the window. She covered her mouth after uttering, "Oh shit."

"Don't worry, *chismosa*. I won't tell your mom you said a bad word."

Jenni giggled, then ran to hug me. She was one of my first best friends, though she was a few years younger than me and still in kindergarten. She was a gaunt-looking girl with straight hair that barely reached her shoulders. Like me, Jenni was from Chicago, her father was mostly absent, and we were the only English speakers in our entirely Spanish-speaking homes.

"Oh, shit!" I exclaimed when her older cousin, Carlos, a boy a year younger than me, startled me after coming out of the kitchen with a stack of chocolate chip cookies in his hand.

"Look, Jenni, tía's outside," he mocked. "She can't see me. I'll finish these before she comes in." I rolled my eyes at Carlos and sat on the couch.

"Why are you here?" I asked.

Jenni sat next to me. Carlos joined us, burrowing himself between us. I moved away from him. He extended his hands to balance himself, dropping a couple of cookies. My foot covered them fast and I slid them under the couch.

"My dad let me stay over," he said, searching around the sofa for the cookies. "He said I could eat my Halloween candy if I want."

"You're going to get sick," I said, remembering my aches that morning and Paloma's words the night before.

Carlos shrugged. "He lets me do what I want. He says that if I'm not happy, I won't reach my full potential."

"What's that mean?" I asked him.

Carlos shrugged again. "I don't know. I guess that means I can do whatever I want when I'm big."

I rolled my eyes a second time and walked away.

"Damián, what does 'hipócrita' mean?" Jenni asked, following me.

"I don't know. Why?"

"Mom said it to tío—"

Carlos interrupted. "She said it..." Carlos slowly swallowed the dry, chewed-up cookies he'd stuffed in his mouth. "She said it when my dad was leaving to go to church. He didn't want me to go with him because..."

Carlos bumped his chest as he finished swallowing the last of his mouthful of cookies.

"...because God doesn't like Halloween. He said it's the Devil's day."

Carlos got up from the couch and dropped to his knees on the floor, searching for the fallen cookies. Within seconds, he found the two I had pushed under the sofa, pulled them out, and brandished them to Jenni and me with a victorious smile. He blew the dust off of them and stuffed the cookies in his mouth.

"Gross, man," I said.

His knock-off Transformers costume was on a chair by the TV. On top of it, a camcorder.

"Damián." Jenni pulled on my shirt and got on her tiptoes to whisper in my ear. "He got in trouble." She paused and looked at Carlos before turning back to me. "Mom yelled at him because he was pulling the tape from the cassette."

Good, I thought. To Cecilia, we were all fair game. She punished or scolded us, no matter whose children we were.

"I was bored," Carlos said, moving his costume to reveal a VHS tape underneath. "But I was trying to put it back in."

"Why did you pull it out?" I asked him.

"I wanted to see what was on the tape."

"Stupid. You have to put the cassette in the VCR."

Jenni's eyes widened at the insult. Carlos, though, kept talking.

"I saw someone on TV put a tape over the light to see the images. I wanted to see if that was true, but tía caught me."

"What movie is that?" I asked. Carlos grabbed the cassette, opened the top flap, and pulled the tape, leaving his fingerprints on the film. There was a tiny rip where he'd creased it.

"It's from last night. Remember? Your—"

He didn't get to finish his sentence because I caught sight of the name on the white label: *Paloma*.

"Give me that!" I yelled, furious at what he'd done to the tape, *my* tape. I was concerned I'd be punished for the damage *he'd* done to it, which would only add to my list of troubles.

I reached for the movie and Carlos swung it away from me. Exasperated, I pushed him to the ground. Just as my fingers touched the ridges of the hard, black plastic, Cecilia pulled me away from Carlos.

"¡Se calman o los calmo!" she warned, digging her fingers into my arm.

"But it's—" I turned and cowered when I noticed her bulging eyes.

Cecilia sighed. "Forgive me, Damián. I forgot." She released her fingers and rubbed the spot where they'd been. She shot a look at Carlos and pointed to the sofa. Carlos gave me the cassette and walked meekly to the sofa.

"Damián," Cecilia continued, "I'm going to call Sofi at her job. Once she's home, we'll figure out a way for you to see Palomita. Okay?" I nodded. "¿Tienes hambre?"

Of course I was hungry. I rarely turned down anyone's cooking. My stomach even growled to punctuate my statement. Jenni giggled.

"Want some huevito?" Cecilia asked.

Eggs always sounded good. "¿Con chorizo?" I suggested.

MY EYES ROLLED BACK as I savored the eggs with chorizo Cecilia made for me. I moaned, forgetting the day I'd had for a second. My feet dangled from front to back as I wiped her plate clean using her warm, handmade flour tortillas. I ate as if no one had fed me in days.

"Hi, mijo," Sofía's voice echoed from the other side of the kitchen. I gobbled the last of my eggs and chorizo taco and ran to her, hugging her tightly.

"Gracias, Ceci. Here." Sofía tried handing Ceci some money, but she rejected it. "No, Comadrita," Cecilia said, a term of endearment she often used with my mother and sister. "Once you know more, let me know what's going on with my comadre, so that we can go see her. Dios la cuide."

Cecilia made the sign of the cross, first over herself, then over my sister, and finally over me.

Halfway up the stairs to our apartment, I remembered the video cassette and ran back for it before Carlos could ruin it again.

"Psst. Jenni."

Jenni didn't question my return. She knew exactly what I needed. She snatched the movie from Carlos's greedy hands and brought it over to me.

"Thank you." I hugged my dear friend and ran back upstairs.

Sofía stood in the kitchen, talking to someone on the phone. I handed her the cassette, hoping she would fix it.

"Siéntate," she instructed, covering the mouthpiece with her hand and pointing to our kitchen table. When she finished her call, she sat with me, butter knife in hand, and turned the white spool to finish rolling the tape in.

Our wall clock indicated it was now close to 2 p.m. If I'd gone to school, we'd probably be going over our spelling words.

"Oye," she stared into my dark brown eyes. "Remember why I came here to help mamá?"

I did.

SOFÍA HAD ONCE TOLD me that after her father died and Paloma met my father, she had followed Ignacio to Chicago and left Sofía and Moisés Jr. behind. Sofía had been fourteen at the time and little Moisés had only been eight.

Years later, Ignacio had left Paloma and Sofía had left Mexico to help her raise me. I was four when she first came to the United States.

The hope was that they would eventually raise enough money to bring Moisés too, but until then, they'd send him money, clothes, and gifts.

I loved Sofía. She was kind, like Paloma, but stricter. Sofía laid down the law. When Paloma allowed me to get away with things, Sofía disciplined me.

When our mother made expensive, long-distance calls to Mexico, I'd sometimes pull a kitchen chair over to the wall and end her call by pushing the button on the phone's receiver or unplugging the cables. Paloma would simply turn to me and yell, "Ay, pinche niño. ¡Bájate de ahí!" Sofía, though, would bring me down from the chair herself and pull me away by the ear.

"Sit there, face the corner, and don't get up until I tell you to," Sofía would instruct.

Anything Sofía cooked, I'd have to finish. When she wasn't looking, Paloma would pull the chiles that made my food spicy and transfer them to hers. "¡Mamá!" Sofía would say before giving me a stern look, one that would make Agatha Trunchbull herself tremble in her boots. And I would eat my food, but without enjoyment.

Homework was also a priority and Sofía made sure not to let me leave our kitchen table until I'd finished it all. She'd also check my work to make sure I'd done it correctly, and when I hadn't, Sofía would force me to recite multiplication tables, from zero times zero to twelve times twelve. The sevens were the worst.

Still, despite her strictness, I loved Sofía, and knew that, like our mother, she loved me too. She'd watch cartoons with me and, in turn, I'd watch telenovelas with her. Through my cartoons, she'd learned about Superman and would gladly watch me as I put on Paloma's work glasses and pretend to be him, ripping my shirt open to reveal the red bath towel underneath. I'd learned some things from her telenovelas too, mostly things about overbearing mothers, Hellish mothers-in-law, and greed.

SOFÍA DROPPED THE FIXED cassette and asked me to watch TV with her while she waited for a friend from work to pick us up. Since neither my mother nor Sofía owned a car, we had no other way to get to the hospital. We often relied on others to take us places or took the bus on 115th Street.

I ran to the TV, turned the bottom dial to find something enjoyable but was disappointed by the boring programming. The good stuff came on after school.

One channel, though, was playing *La Bamba*, a recent favorite movie of mine. I leaned back to watch the scene where Richie Valens, who hated flying, called "heads" on the coin Buddy Holly flipped. Sadly, we knew what followed.

"Change that," Sofía said. "I don't like how that ends. That's why I'll never fly." I switched the channel to avoid causing us further pain in an already distressing day.

Then, I found my favorite TV show. *Batman* with Adam West and Burt Ward.

"Can I watch this?" I wouldn't wait for her answer; my eyes were already glued to the TV, relishing in the ZOCKs, POWs, and WHAPs playing in the animated opening credits, as Batman and Robin punched their way through Cesar Romero's Joker, Burgess Meredith's Penguin, and other Gotham City hoodlums.

The phone rang. We had no caller ID or answering machine, so Sofía ran to answer it. We couldn't afford to miss any updates on our mother's condition.

"What do you want?" Sofía's voice was tense. She sounded annoyed at whoever was on the other end of the line.

"No. You know very well what she said, so it's best you don't call or visit. Once she's better, we'll see." Sofía slammed the phone on the receiver.

"Who was that?" I asked.

"No one, mijo."

Someone honked outside, drawing Sofía's attention. She checked who it was through the window and asked me to grab my mochila. "'Amonos, Dami. He's here. Let's go see Mamá."

I rushed after her, grabbing my backpack on the way and stuffing Paloma's video cassette inside.

6

THE AIR INSIDE THE stranger's car was colder than the chilly November outside temperature, yet I was sweating profusely. "¿Estás bien?" Sofía asked, wiping sweat off my forehead. She checked my temperature with both sides of her hands. I felt fine, I assured her, and since I didn't have a fever, she believed me, but the bullets of sweat kept sprouting from my skin. Every time I moved, my arms and backside squeaked as they rubbed against the leather seat.

"I don't want to go," I confessed, thinking back to my previous hospital visits.

"Ey, this isn't for you. We're going to see Mamá." Sofía leaned in to kiss the top of my head, then whiffed around the car. "It's a little *apestoso* in here," she whispered close to me. Her friend must've heard because he cleared his throat, cracked his window open for a second, and then closed it to blast the heat.

But it wasn't the car that smelled.

"Ay, Damián." Sofía pushed away from me. "You have to shower tonight." I frowned in annoyance at her judgment and how loud she'd said that. Her face turned red. She placed her arm behind my back and pulled me back toward her.

"Perdóname," she whispered.

We arrived at the hospital minutes later. Sofía's friend dropped us off at the entrance and said he'd return after running an errand.

"Damián, tell the woman we're here to see Mamá." But the woman at the front desk wouldn't look at us, she just asked for a name.

"Paloma Vásquez," I said to her, lifting to my toes to see the woman better.

"*Flores*," Sofía corrected me. "Paloma Flores."

"Sign your full name and go sit over there, please."

Sofía Laura Alonso Flores, my sister wrote. The receptionist, still refusing to acknowledge us, waved us off as she checked the sign-in sheet before leaving her spot.

We waited.

Waited and waited and waited. To calm my nerves, I walked around the cold waiting area, riffling through magazines and grabbing as many pamphlets as possible. Perhaps Paloma would need those medications or that care, whatever they all meant. It seemed like a lot of the same stuff—new meds, what to do in case of a heart attack, how to protect yourself against the flu. There was an old National Geographic magazine, older than me, and it read: *Living with Orangutans*. It was from June 1980.

When I got bored of going through the magazines' pictures, I joined Sofía again. Resting my head on her arm, I thought back to the times my parents had taken me to the hospital before, every one so anxiety-inducing.

MY EARLIEST MEMORY OF a hospital was from a few months before Sofía arrived in Chicago. My parents had enrolled me in our local preschool, but there was a problem.

"I'm sorry," the man at the school said. "His vaccinations are not up to date."

My parents took me to the hospital's clinic. When we saw the doctor, he asked me to look up and wave at the monsters above, at Big Bird and Grover, who waved back at me. But the doctor had tricked me. He stabbed my non-waving arm. Shot after shot. Stab. Stab. Stab.

I received ten shots that day, maybe a few less. All I knew was that the doctor was the only real monster in the room.

My parents successfully enrolled me in preschool the next day and I missed Sesame Street the next few days. It didn't matter, though. After that vaccination experience, I'd had enough of Big Bird and Grover for a while.

Two years later, I had tripped and banged my head on a table, slicing my eyebrow. It happened while navigating the darkened living room. Paloma had cleaned me up with paper towels, but the blood continued pouring out of me. Through the pain and the stinging, I felt like one of those monsters in the horror movies Paloma allowed me to watch. Like David Kessler transforming into the werewolf in *An American Werewolf in London.* Paloma called Ignacio, who arrived within minutes. He took off his shirt and pressed his heavy hand on my head, which had only intensified my pain and my cries.

"Ya, Damián," he said as I wiggled, leaving our couch bloodstained. "Boys don't cry. *Men* don't cry."

Paloma held Nyquil in her hand, and Ignacio forced a tablespoon into my mouth. At some point after we arrived at that same hospital, I awoke to a pulsating sensation on my head. Doctors had stitched my cut. I let out a big scream and Ignacio came into the room.

"¡Chingado, Damián!" he said, leaning close to me, He placed his hand over my mouth and through gritted teeth uttered, "Stop crying! I *told* you. Men... don't... cry."

An attendant came in. "Let the fine lady take care of you," he said, winking at the woman, who then scolded Ignacio for giving Nyquil to a child. Ignacio rolled his eyes and told the attendant to talk to my mother. Then, he walked out of the room.

My most recent visit was about a year and a half ago. I felt a gut-wrenching pain in my stomach during class and my teacher sent me to the nurse's office. When she asked what was wrong with me, all I could specify was, "My stomach hurts."

Ignacio had picked up Paloma and dropped her off at my school. She and I walked the two and a half blocks back to our apartment, taking our time to get there. When we arrived, Paloma sent me to bed. She checked my temperature, declaring, "Ay, Dios. Ninety-nine degrees, hijo." She left the room and returned with a green bottle.

Nyquil.

"Take it and go to sleep. You'll feel better after."

She'd lied. I felt worse and worse. I wormed around the bed, writhing and crying at what felt like something intensely pulling at... my guts, maybe. It was like tiny hands held the inside of my stomach and were slowly tightening their grasp.

Was I imploding?

Paloma waited by the window while I cried for her. "Mami, mi panza. Me duele."

"¡Mamá!" Sofía, who had arrived unexpectedly from work, exclaimed coming into the room. She placed a cold, damp towel on my head and patted it. "I told you, we can't rely on him. Ever."

"I know, mija. But he's just around the corner."

"Ma, he probably stopped for a drink. He should have been here by now. Go there and tell him to hurry."

Did he live nearby? No one had taken me to my father's place yet.

Sofía left the towel on my head and stepped out, letting us know she'd call an ambulance. "They'll be here before *he* arrives."

"He's here," I heard Paloma say. "But I don't see—"

There was a pounding on our door and Ignacio's voice drummed outside. "A ver pa' cuando," he said, as the door creaked open. "I've been waiting outside."

"Nacho, he's in the bedroom," Paloma said, but Sofía came in the room first. She picked me up—her hefty, six-year-old brother—and rushed out with me in her arms.

"What's wrong with you?" she scolded him. "He's your son. This is urgent." Ignacio reached for me, but Sofía brushed him off and got into his LeSabre.

Once at the hospital's entrance, Sofía carried me inside. Ignacio took off. The hospital staff asked Paloma and Sofía questions in English. I watched from a nearby chair, drowsy from Nyquil, as they replied with small words and hand gestures.

The transition from the waiting area to my new room didn't register. One moment I was out there, the next, I was lying on an exam bed. Paloma and Sofía laughed amongst themselves, unaware that I'd woken up. A doctor came in and asked how I felt, to which I groggily nodded and gave him a thumbs up.

"Well, young man, they brought you in just in time." The man turned to my mother and sister. "Luckily, his appendix didn't burst before his surgery."

He turned to me as I looked at my patched tummy.

"Don't touch it," my mother warned. "Or your tripas will come out."

The doctor, who'd understood the Spanish, agreed and walked away. But I wanted to see my guts, so I pulled the patch off.

SOFÍA SHOOK ME, SNAPPING me back from my memories. A doctor approached. How long had we been sitting there? Minutes? Hours?

The doctor, a tall, slim white man, resembled Christopher Lloyd's "Doc Brown" from my favorite time-traveling movie, *Back to the Future*. He talked just like the actor, too.

"Sofi, that's the guy from the movie," I whispered, while the doctor checked his chart.

"It's not him," Sofía said. "This guy's bald and has a beard."

"I know, but that's him."

It wasn't.

"Young man," the fake Doc Brown said to me, "tell your sister that your mother will be okay. Ms. Flores will need to take it easy for a while, though. She lost a lot of blood and will have lots of headaches, but we're certain she'll recover in no time." He looked at Sofía and said, loud and slow, "*No trabajo.* No work until we say it's okay, *¿entiende?*" Sofía nodded. "We don't want her to get dizzy and hurt herself."

"Ask him if we can see her."

Just when Sofía pointed to the rooms, a pale nurse with hypnotizing blue eyes and short permed black hair walked through one of the doors, stuffing what looked like a bookmark in her pocket. She froze when her eyes met Sofía's and for a moment we all just stared at her, unmoving. Her beautiful eyes made it hard to focus on anything else, but eventually, my eyes settled on her swollen, bruised neck. When the nurse finally snapped out of her trance, she must've realized we were all staring, because she cleared her throat and lifted a neck cover from under her top of her scrubs.

The nurse translated Sofía's request and, at the doctor's approval, answered in Spanish, "Yes, you can both see her right now, but only for a few minutes. The doctor needs to keep monitoring her closely these next few hours—"

Cecilia's voice resonated from afar for all to hear. She must've taken a bus to the hospital.

"Ay, Dios mío, Comadrita. How is Paloma?"

"Go, see Mamá," Sofía instructed me, handing me my backpack. "I'll be right in."

The young nurse, who looked to be around Sofía's age, led me away.

Out of the corner of my eye, I read the nurse's name tag: *Amaya Quintero*.

"What happened to your neck?" I asked her.

Amaya rubbed it, lifting the cover again.

"Does it hurt?"

"Yes... No... No, it's fine. It's nothing."

It didn't seem like nothing. In fact, it looked red. Amaya cleared her throat again. "I accidently hurt myself, but that's not your concern." She knelt in front of me and her voice got softer. "Now, Mr. Vásquez, if you need anything, call for me or come on out there." Her head and eyes motioned to a station behind her.

"Where's my mom?"

Amaya stood behind me, pointed to a door past her workstation. "She's right over there." She walked me there and stopped just outside my mother's room's entrance, nudging me to go in. "Go on, jovencito. Just be careful when you close the door, it'll—"

The door closed before she could finish warning me. She wiggled the handle, and after a few struggles, cracked the door enough to give me a thumbs up, then left it cracked just enough to let a sliver of light in.

Inside the room, my teeth shivered, and goosebumps raised the little hairs on my arms. Why was it so cold? Couldn't they have turned up the heat for my mother?

Paloma rested peacefully on the bed, and I wondered what she was dreaming of. She'd often tell me the weird dreams she had. Perhaps this time she was replaying what had happened hours ago. Had she seen the same eyes I'd seen, staring out at her from behind the foggy car window?

A draft hit me, and I wished I had brought my jacket instead of standing in the cold room with a light t-shirt. I rubbed my left arm with my right hand and wondered if she was cold like me. If she was cold, did that mean she was alive? Or not? Because I'd heard people went cold when they died. Where was that draft coming from? There was no window to close, so my mother would be less cold.

Where was Sofía? Why was she taking forever to be with us? Though I was safe, I needed her protection, her comfort.

I switched my backpack from my back to my front, just to have something to hug. There was a void inside me, but I couldn't tell where it was coming from or how to make it go away.

Sofía, hurry.

4:37. That was what the wall clock above her head said: the time was 4:37 p.m.

My breaths became shorter, coming in quick hiccupping gusts. Anxiety hit me when I realized there was hardly any light in the room. The only glimmer came from a small table lamp on Paloma's bedside, right under the clock that still read 4:37 p.m. Why wasn't there more light? My mother needed more light.

Paloma's sleeping body frightened me so much I froze. I walked backwards. For some reason, I couldn't bring myself to turn around, so I edged backwards all the way to the door.

There was no logical reason for me to be this scared. After all, she was my mother and she was doing nothing but rest. Perhaps it was the guilt that was tormenting me.

When I hit the wall, I tapped it desperately, searching for a light switch. The blue machine behind Paloma beeped and whirred, indicating she was in a fragile state and it was all because of me. I looked at the clock again and it was still 4:37. Time was standing still, punishing me by making the worst minute also the longest minute of my life.

The almost-closed door clicked shut and I was left alone, locked in the unnerving room. I finally turned around, grabbed the handle, and shook it to open it. "Amaya!" I called because she'd told me to do so when I needed her.

"Amaya!... Sofía!" I shouted again, and again, and again, and... and then Paloma spoke. She said my name, softly.

I turned to face my mother. Took a few steps toward her, but she only seemed to slip further away.

Stop. Relax. But don't cry in front of your mother. Dad said boys don't cry. Men *don't cry. Be strong for your mother. Brave.*

I walked up to her bed, meekly. Her eyes remained closed.

Mami, ¿despertates? You called my name.

Des-per-tas-te, she corrected me in my mind. She'd done that multiple times, calling me her Pocho... her "Pochito". Said it was because of the way I spoke Spanish. Very broken. Americanized. But that's how most of us spoke in school.

Paloma opened her eyes as I reached for her, and when she did, I jumped back. Paloma closed her eyes again and mumbled something, like a prayer. When she finished, she opened them again and smiled.

"Mi niño," she said. "Come closer."

I refused. What I wanted instead was to run back to the door and get Sofía, but that stupid door had locked us in.

"No," I whispered.

"Hijo, don't be scared. Soy yo, tu mami."

Fear overwhelmed me. It made me move backwards again, away from her. Back, back, back until my leg bumped into a chair and I fell into it. I lifted my feet onto the chair, afraid that something lurked under her bed, ready to grab my feet and drag me under. Placing my mochila before me on my knees, I wrapped my fingers tightly around the straps.

My mouth opened to take in tiny gasps of air.

Why was I so frightened? Was it seeing her so weak? With barely an ounce of joy in her? Bandaged in the head? Attached to the hospital's machines? Why was I so scared of my mother in that bed? Paloma would never purposely hurt me. *¿Por qué te tengo tanto miedo, mami?*

"Close your eyes, Damián," my mother said in a dry voice. "Give it a moment. You'll be okay."

Trusting her, I did as she asked. With my eyes closed, I focused on my mother, the one from before. The strong one. The one that was filled with happiness, who wasn't supposed to be in the hospital. Those thoughts calmed me. That image of the healthy Paloma helped me accept the woman in the bed, because regardless of what had happened, the woman in the bed was still Paloma, my mother.

"Damián," she said, voice clearer. "Where's your sister?"

I got up from the chair, letting the mochila slide off my legs and kicking it after. Warily, I inched toward Paloma.

"She's coming," I said, barely raising my voice. "She's outside talking to Cecilia."

"Oh. Did Jenni come too?"

"No."

My foot caught on the bag's strap, which reminded me of the videocassette in it. I pulled the movie out. "Mami, Carlos was playing with this. Mira, it has your name." I handed her the movie, which she studied carefully. Putting it over her face, she whispered something that might've been another prayer. She handed it back to me.

"Hold on to this, okay? This movie is special. Don't lose it," she instructed, so inside my backpack it went again.

"Remember how much fun you had at your birthday party?" Her voice grew more joyous. "Oh, and how *excited* you were about your first day of school? You didn't even look back at me when you went in. And Halloween, you were so happy, mijo, with Jenni and Carlitos, running together and knocking on everyone's door, asking for candy."

That was the Paloma I knew, not the dreadful one from seconds ago. My heart was happy again.

"That's all in there," she continued. "Now, when Sofía and I are not around, you can watch this, and you'll have us with you. So don't lose it," she warned again. "Most importantly, *never* lose that love inside of you. You have a big heart, mi niño."

"Sí, mami."

In all that time I spent locked inside the room with my mother, I never asked her how she felt. She seemed to be in better spirits, but I needed to know.

"Mami, cómo—"

Paloma screamed. Bellowed like I'd never heard her cry. If the room had windows, they certainly would have shattered. I let the bag go to cover my ears. Her arms covered her head. Her body curled.

"Sofía! Amaya!" I called again. *Amaya, you said you'd be right outside. Where* are *you, Amaya?*

Paloma moved her hand, as if searching for something. Instead of helping, I ran away, back to the door. I jiggled the handle, but it didn't budge. Ear against the door, I hoped to hear Amaya's voice... hear anyone's voice. All I heard was silence. Never, in the countless times I'd been to this hospital, had it been so quiet.

Paloma frightened me again. I didn't dare run to her. My body stayed glued to the door.

I didn't know what to do. I felt as helpless as when she had lain on the ground after being hit. *Mami, what do I do? Can I hug you? Will that help you?* My mother's embrace had always helped me when I was in pain; perhaps mine would do the same for her.

The glimmer of courage inside me told me to let go of the door handle and go to her, so I did. I jumped on the bed and wrapped my short arms around her, squeezing my mother hard. *Is this helping, Mamá?*

Tears rolled down my eyes as I begged her to stop, but Paloma shook her head. She was hurting. Paloma didn't deserve this. I'd been the one to cross that street before that car sped through.

Seconds later, everything went silent. Paloma calmed down.

Her exhales became heavy, her breathing brushed my hair. She kissed the top of my head. I looked up at her and felt the tears from her tired eyes rolling down to me.

"Me voy a morir," she whispered.

"No," I pleaded. "Mami, ¡ya párale!"

I wanted to tell her to stop being so dramatic, like she'd told me that morning. But my instinct was to hit the top of her arm as I begged her to stop telling me she was going to die. Why would she say that? The doctor had said she'd be fine.

Paloma held me tighter. "Don't worry, hijo," she whispered. "But I need you to do something for me."

"¿Qué mami?"

"Listen to Sofi, okei?"

Of course I would. It was an odd request. She had no reason to think I wouldn't. She needed to stop talking to me like she'd be dying soon. She'd been fine earlier in the day. Days before. I couldn't remember the last time she was sick. Sure, she was in the hospital right now, but she'd recover in no time, the fake Doc had said.

Paloma kissed my head again and I closed my eyes, falling asleep to the rhythm of her calming heartbeat and the tune of her humming *Beautiful Boy*.

Moments later, the door finally opened. Half asleep, I recognized Sofía walking in with Amaya.

"I tried to warn him about the door," Amaya said in Spanish. "Do you want to take your little brother?"

Someone lifted me off my mother. It was Sofía. I cuddled into her.

"Can I stay with her?" Sofía asked.

"Sure," Amaya confirmed.

Sofía's arms trembled and I probably should have given her a break, stand on my own, but I couldn't let her go. She'd finally rescued me.

Sofía told Amaya she'd return. She walked down the long hallway with me in her arms, then handed me off to her nameless friend. She asked him to take Cecilia and me home, and asked Cecilia to watch me for a few hours, assuring her she'd update her once she had more information on our mother.

As Paloma had done minutes ago, Sofía kissed my head and walked back to our mother's room.

7

NOVEMBER 03, 1989

"**D**AMIÁN, COME ON. MOM'S waiting for you," Jenni said, shaking me awake the way annoying little siblings do. My head shot up fast from the sofa pillow, only one eye opened. Jenni stood in front of me, fully dressed, ready for school.

"What time is it?" I asked her, confused by the room I'd woken up in.

Jenni shrugged. "We have to go to school."

"Why? Your lights are on."

Jenni turned off the living room lamps, squeezed herself between the sofa and the front window, and opened the blinds, letting the morning light in. She stood in front of me again. "There," she said and pulled my arms to get up.

My eyes caught the wall clock. The small hand was on the eight; the longer was past the five.

"Damián, ¡apúrale!" Cecilia called from the kitchen as Jenni poked my arm, like the pesky little sister I'd never have. I wondered if she thought of me the same way, like her big brother.

"Stop," I said, pushing her hand away. She immediately sat on the floor facing her TV to watch her morning PBS cartoons.

Breakfast awaited me in the kitchen: a box of Lucky Charms, milk, and orange juice in small glass jugs. There was a banana between them and the empty bowl for my cereal, along with a few empty glasses for my drinks. It was like a scene from the TV breakfast commercials I knew well. The only thing missing were the two slices of toast with butter on top and Lucky the Leprechaun saying his cereal was magically delicious.

DING.

Well, the toast was ready. Now, where was Lucky?

"Buenos días, Damián," Cecilia said.

Still partly asleep, I groggily answered her and waved. Cecilia plated the bread and set it in front of me. She urged me to hurry, otherwise we'd be late for school. She then called out to Jenni to hurry as well, even if she was already ready. Cecilia continued washing their breakfast dishes.

It was 8:28 a.m., according to her kitchen clock, just over thirty minutes before school started. I poured the cereal into my bowl, then added the milk and thought about Paloma as the cereal rose; wondered how she felt. Sofía? Was she still there at the hospital? Had she gone to work?

My arm shook as I drowned the cereal. Fortunately, nothing had spilled, otherwise Cecilia would have scolded me.

"¿Y mi mami?" I finally asked.

Cecilia stopped scrubbing her dishes. She let out a sigh and I wondered if Paloma was *not* okay. She turned to me, shaking the water off her hands. Maybe I had poured my milk and cereal wrong and she'd give me a good regañada.

"I don't want you to worry," she said, her tone soft, and *that* worried me. She smiled. "Sofi and I spoke before you woke up. There's a chance your mom will leave the hospital today."

I dug the spoon in the bowl, letting the milk fill it, and hoping to only catch the marshmallow pieces, not the boring oat ones. I got a red balloon.

"I don't want to go to school," I confessed. "Can I go with my mom?"

"You must go to school. You already missed a day, and I can't have you here while Jenni is at school. Plus, I can't take you to see her and Sofi can't pick you up right now."

"Mi papá," I suggested.

"No. Your sister said she doesn't want him around without your mom. If Paloma isn't out by the time you're out of school, Sofi and I will figure a way to pick you up and take you to the hospital to be with her. Now, ¡apúrate! We have to go."

I sighed hard at that. If Cecilia hadn't been watching me, I would have taken the bus to the hospital. Paloma had taken me a few times for checkups, so I knew the route. Disappointed that I couldn't be with her, I still smiled at Cecilia. She was truthful. A matter-of-fact person. I liked that about her.

"Okei," I said in my household Mexican accent and chugged the milk in the bowl, letting the wet cereal slide down my throat. The toast would have to wait until we walked out the door, to be eaten on the way to school. I chugged a glass of OJ next.

I brushed my teeth with a new toothbrush Cecilia told me to use. Then, I took off my day-old shirt and shook it so it wouldn't look too wrinkled after I'd slept in it, and headed back to the living room to grab my backpack.

"Where's my mochila?" I asked Jenni in an accusatory tone as I searched all over her couch and around the living room. Jenni remained in front of the TV, her Rainbow Brite backpack was ready on her side (mine was a boring blue one with black straps). She turned to me.

"Mom said your sister has it and will take it to school when she's back."

I stopped. Jenni was right. I had dropped it in my mother's room when she had screamed.

Jenni opened her backpack and pulled out a notebook and a pencil. "Here. You can have this."

As she had every morning while Paloma and Sofía worked, Cecilia walked Jenni and me to our elementary school. Usually, Jenni walked in front of us, I'd be close to her and Cecilia would be behind us both. This time, I took up the rear.

My mind spun concerning scenarios: One of my teachers would be upset because I didn't have my homework; the movie my mother tasked me with not losing had been left behind; my mother... she could be dying. She'd said it. God, I hoped that wasn't true. I sent up a prayer for her.

God, please don't leave Sofía and me without our mamá.

"Ceci," I called out, teary faced. She stopped to wait for me. "My mom said she's going to die."

"No, Damián." She opened her arms to receive me. "Don't think about that. Si Dios quiere, you'll see her again."

But what if God doesn't want her to get better?

"But it's my fault," I sobbed. "I wasn't paying attention and now she's going to die and it's my fault. She saved me. She's going to die." Jenni stood watching. Her enormous eyes looked at her mother, then at me, then back at her.

Cecilia knelt in front of me and gently cleaned my face with her sweater. "No, mijo, it's not your fault. It was that driver, ¿me entiendes? That person is the reason your mother is in the hospital. That person is a coward, because cowards, you know what they do? They run away. So, no, it's not your fault. Ese estupido, he'll pay for what he did. ¿Entiendes?"

I nodded, though I was still convinced it was my fault.

"Good," Ceci said. "Now, help me get up because I'm an old woman."

Late thirties were old to me, but Paloma, who was older, said it wasn't. So, I laughed at what Ceci had said. With all my strength, I helped her up, then wiped my face the rest of the way to school.

When we arrived, I stopped halfway down the hallway and turned to wave goodbye to them. Jenni waved back and pulled her mother's arm. Cecilia yelled, "Bye, Damiancito."

Mrs. Gómez reviewed her daily attendance list and checked off my name when I stood in front of her. As I explained why I didn't have my backpack that morning, only Jenni's notebook and pencil, she raised a hand to stop me.

"It's fine, Damián. Your sister called and said she'll bring it later." She paused, looking up from her list. "How's your mom?"

I shrugged.

"I'm sorry. I'm sure she'll be okay soon. Are you okay?"

"Yes," I answered.

"Good." Mrs. Gómez smiled at me. "Go on and have a seat, then."

Mrs. Gómez continued marking her list and calling out names. A knock interrupted her. Our principal peeked in.

"Excuse me, class," she said, and instructed Nancy, our tattle-tale classmate, to watch the class while she spoke with our principal.

Four third graders, including Nancy and me, had transferred from Mr. Adams' second and third grade class to Mrs. Gómez's fourth and fifth grade class, supposedly because we were the brightest in our grade. But we suspected Nancy came along because Mr. Adams didn't like Nancy for her... overly honest disposition. So, he sent her with us, adding to Mrs. Gómez's already packed fourth and fifth graders' world.

"Where's your homework?" Nancy asked bluntly, holding a stack of papers from other classmates.

"I don't have it," I answered, suddenly feeling queasy. "Mrs. Gómez knows. You don't have to tell on me."

Nancy stared at me like I'd wronged her, like she had a deadline and there would be no compensation because of my lack of commitment to the team.

"You know, my dad doesn't get paid when he doesn't turn his work in on time. That's what happens when you grow up and have to work. You don't do the work, you don't get paid, and you don't put food on the table. That's what he says, Damián."

Ugh. Stupid Nancy, right?

I stared at her shoes and gagged. A few weeks ago, I had thrown up in class and Nancy had stepped in it. Of course, I never came clean about it being me who threw up, so I hoped my sudden bout of nausea would not be the thing to give me away.

"Ew! Damián." Nancy walked away.

My head rested on my desk. On Jenni's notebook, I drew squiggly circles, thinking back to that day I was sick in class. It was October 13th, when Mrs. Gómez had planned a Hispanic Day celebration ending President Reagan's month-long celebration after he'd expanded it a year before. President Johnson had begun the celebration in 1968, but only for a week.

"Mrs. Gómez!" Nancy had cried after stepping in my vomit. "Ew!" She waved her hands and wiped her shoe on the floor. "It's on my shoe. It's on my shoe!" The whole class laughed at her misfortune. The memory brought a smile to my face even now, but it was wiped away when I remembered how Mrs. Gómez had lined us all up and sniffed our breaths to find the culprit. I escaped, but barely. I didn't think I'd be that lucky if it happened again.

Mrs. Gómez returned with red and puffy eyes. The entire class quieted down.

"Mrs. Gómez?" Nancy asked, returning to her desk after dropping off everyone else's homework on our teacher's desk. Mrs. Gómez opened her desk drawer, pulled out some tissues, and stared ahead. She sniffled and didn't say a word.

"Who died, Mrs. Gómez?" shouted Albert, a fourth grader who really should have been in fifth grade, but his only two brain cells were not enough to get him there. The class laughed, including me, but the memory of Paloma writhing in the hospital bed stole my smile away and I immediately felt guilty.

"Dude, shut up," I said, changing my stance on Albert's joke.

Nancy followed. "Ya cállate, Albert," she said through her teeth. She eyed him scornfully, giving him one of those looks that could start a fire. Albert calmed himself.

Mrs. Gómez's gaze remained on us. We whispered, but she kept quiet. What had the principal said to her? In a matter of seconds, our whispers turned dead silent. She had our undivided attention, which didn't happen often. We couldn't pull our eyes away from Mrs. Gómez.

"Kids," she finally said. Something caught in her throat. She cleared it and composed herself. "God, I have no clue how to say this. I... I never considered my students would have to hear this from me."

Mrs. Gómez rambled on about kindness and talking to her if we had questions. Honestly, I'd stopped paying attention, not because what she said didn't interest me, but because my stomach kept churning.

The wind outside whistled through the trees, distracting me from Mrs. Gómez's discourse. Leaves danced to the tune of the whistling wind and even through the heavy winds, birds traveled from tree to tree.

A white bird appeared on the window's ledge, digging its clawed feet into the stone. The gusts of wind tried to push it off, but the stubborn bird, a dove like the one I'd seen the day before, hung on, flapping its wings.

The dove seemed to bob its head, as if exploring our classroom, searching and searching. When our eyes met, it poked the window with its beak.

The pressure inside of me intensified, and it didn't help that the bird's presence reminded me of the incident the day before. It reminded me of Paloma's body on the cold street and her blood making its way toward me, slow like molasses, but scary as hell.

The bird cooed. I knew it, even if I couldn't hear it from where I sat.

"Damián!" Nancy snapped, and Mrs. Gómez called her out for it. I turned to Mrs. Gómez first, four desks in front of me. Then, I turned to Nancy, who was to my left, close to the window where the dove had visited. Then, I looked at my class and their eyes watched me. Were they waiting for my response?

"What?" I asked.

"Damián," Nancy said, wailing this time. "You're supposed to cry."

Why? I hadn't heard Mrs. Gómez. I turned to the window. The paloma was gone.

That was when it hit me. *My* Paloma was gone too.

My mother was dead.

8

FOR SOME REASON, I found myself a passenger inside an airplane. Xóchitl was nowhere in sight, just me and rows upon rows of empty seats. The last thing I remembered was that I had been driving to Chicago.

Outside my window, to my left, there was nothing but blue sky with specks of clouds over a vast ocean. The plane shook and, though I'd never flown before, I knew that it was turbulence, and I understood why people feared flying, why Sofía said she'd never fly.

This had to be a dream, of course. Right? Rarely did I question them and, if I did, I'd wake shortly, confused. But this time I didn't.

Someone touched my shoulder. A woman, unrecognizable at first, but soon her face cleared enough for me to know we'd met, though I couldn't quite remember where or when.

Another woman walked down the aisle between the seats, and soon, she and her enormous shadow disappeared into the back. That second figure had been tall. Skinny. Gawky. Grimy. Enough to send a shiver down my spine. If ever my interpretation of Death appeared before me, she would have been it.

The first woman sat next to me.

"Who are you?" I instinctively asked her in Spanish. "Where are we going?" In my mind, the words came out in English, but my tongue let them out in Spanish.

"What's happening?" I finally blurted out in English.

The woman spoke words that had no meaning. Dreams were messy, capable of changing people, places, memories, breaking them up like tiny puzzle pieces, before putting it all back together. The woman lifted her finger, in what I assumed was her way of telling me to wait. She pulled out a notebook and turned to a page bookmarked with something written in Spanish. It said something about not being a bird. She scribbled, her eyes darting to me, then to her page. When she finished writing, she ripped the paper and gave it to me. But the words also made no sense.

"What? What are you trying to tell me?"

The woman had a confused look on her face. She shushed me, then snatched her paper, crumpled it, and wrote something new. Something longer. She glowered at me like I did something wrong.

"Who are you? What am I doing here?"

My hand rested on her writing hand, but she slipped it away and pointed to someone standing between the rows.

I stood up from my seat to get a good look at the standing person, but the first woman pushed me down into my seat. "Hey!" Why had she pointed if she didn't want me to get a good look?

The standing woman turned to me and exclaimed, "¡Mi Damiancito!" She covered her mouth, like she was surprised to see me. She removed her hands from her mouth, which remained open, her arm extended to me. Nothing came out of her. She looked desperate, looked like a woman asking for help.

Paloma? I tried calling out to her, but my voice barely squeezed through. I stood up again and the woman forced me back down.

"God damn it. Stop!" I finally said out loud.

Paloma was gone. In her place, Sofía, a replica of the woman who'd tucked me in the night before her deportation, with her 80s pompadour and wearing a purple and black cardigan. Underneath it, the neck of a baby blue colored t-shirt. She resembled our mother so much. Perhaps I'd confused her a moment ago with Paloma. No. The other woman didn't have Sofía's sharp chin, furry eyebrows, and almond-shaped eyes. This had to be Sofía, and the other woman had to have been Paloma.

Turbulence shook the plane again and sent Sofía tumbling sideways.

"Sofía!" I called out, but she paid no attention to me. Instead, the other deathly woman's shadow loomed over my sister, and Sofía fell after another turbulent shake, disappearing into the shadows until I could no longer see her.

A loud flutter startled me, similar to when a car veers off the highway onto the pavement lines. The woman next to me tapped my leg, directing me to the window. The wing's flap quivered and smoke replaced the clouds. My heartbeat matched the plane's shaking as my fingers braced against the armrests. And because this dream felt so real, I wondered if people actually died in dreams. By now, I'd have woken up, but I remained there, trapped. Scared shitless as the plane went down.

The oxygen masks had not been released. I banged my fist at the masks' compartment. Punched and punched and punched. Nothing broke them out.

Looking around the cabin, I hoped to get one last look at Paloma or Sofía, but in their place stood a tall, muscular man with a black hat leaning slightly forward, covering his face. His presence sent shivers down my spine even more than the deathly woman.

"¿Apá?" I murmured when I recognized his parted-walrus mustache. He shot a look at me, then pushed himself forward toward the cockpit.

"Ignacio!" I shouted.

The woman touched my hand. "I'm sorry." Her words were clear this time.

The water grew closer. We braced for the impact, her hand tense over mine. I squeezed my eyes shut.

"SHH. SHH. SHH." XÓCHITL rubbed my chest after I'd jumped awake. "I'm sorry. We're safe."

With my seatbelt tightly wrapped around my left-hand fingers, my heart thumped against it. My other hand gripped the door's handle.

"There was a crash back there," Xóchitl continued. "I got scared, so I swerved and hit those lines on the side and hit a pothole."

"Are you okay?"

"Yes," she confirmed. Thankfully the car ran without an issue. Nothing flashed on our dashboard, either, to warn us of any damage to the car.

"You were talking in your sleep. Did you have a nightmare?"

"I'm good," I said, adjusting my seat as we approached a sign on the highway that said we'd be in Merrillville, Indiana, in a mile. About thirty minutes from her parents' house, and close to an hour to Ignacio's. But traffic would only get worse from here. Once we entered northwest Indiana, and the closer we drove to the Chicagoland area, people drove wilder than what we were accustomed to in Ohio. And Xóchitl hated driving through that, so I offered to take over. She refused, changing the subject immediately.

"Those were some good tacos, huh?" She patted my stomach.

"*So* good," I replied, letting out a chuckle.

Her grip tightened on the steering wheel as cars cut her off. They honked and flashed their headlights at us, and I wished Xóchitl would take the next exit so I could drive the rest of the way, but Xóchitl never gave in to other drivers' demands to hurry or move aside. She remained calm in the middle lane, never intimidated by them, her velocity matching the highway's limit.

The rest of the drive, I thought back to what I last told her about my past, before we ate and before I napped in the car. I had told her about Mrs. Gómez's news to the class that Paloma had died. Xóchitl considered Mrs. Gómez's public announcement inconsiderate. Unprofessional. I never considered it like that. To me, it was important for Mrs. Gómez that everyone know for sympathy's sake. Did she have children of her own? Perhaps not. Perhaps in her eyes, her students *were* her children and, like in a family, she needed to be honest and trusting. Maybe it wasn't her place to be so truthful right away, but she didn't do it out of malice or unprofessionalism. At least, I didn't attribute it to that.

What was Mrs. Gómez supposed to do? I wondered about that after my conversation with Xóchitl. Should she have sent me to the principal's office until Cecilia or Sofía arrived? *Did* she know Cecilia watched me when my mother or sister were not around?

That was the last thing we talked about before we stopped to eat. I omitted telling Xóchitl about Sofía's plan to fly to Mexico with me to bury Paloma and about her deportation that had changed those plans.

We arrived at Xóchitl's old home. Her mother, Doña Mari, a four-foot-nine woman with Betty Boop curls, was tending to her flowers outside the two-story yellow house. Once we exited the car, she hurried to kiss her daughter on the cheek, then hug and kiss me too.

"Olivia," Doña Mari said lovingly. She always referred to her daughter by her middle name. "¿Cómo les fue?"

"Good, Mami," Xóchitl answered in Spanish, because that's how Doña Mari spoke to us. Her father, though, spoke to Xóchitl and me in English and Spanish to Doña Mari. "Aren't you cold?" she asked after touching her mother's bare arm. According to my phone, it was a comfortable sixty degrees, but according to Xóchitl rubbing on her mother's skin, it was cold enough to wear at least a light long-sleeved shirt or sweater.

"Never mind that, mija."

"We had a pleasant drive, Doña Mari," I said. "Xóchitl learned a little about my childhood."

"Good. Tell us about it inside. Go on. Your father's waiting and there are enchiladas rojas waiting for you."

Xóchitl grabbed her large purse from the car while I pulled out a couple of our heavier bags. She said to leave the rest for later. She was hungry and so was I. Xóchitl hurried to her mother, their arms behind the other's backside. A picturesque image of a mother and her daughter, if there ever was one.

In the kitchen, Xóchitl's father, Señor Pepe, enjoyed his enchiladas while watching the late afternoon news on a tiny, boxed television. An old device that still used dials on the top and the bottom. He rapidly wiped his mouth when I walked in. He stood and shook my hand with his thick, calloused one, then went back to eating.

Señor Pepe had a large build that reminded me of Ignacio, except Pepe stood inches shorter than me. So, maybe a foot shorter than Ignacio. He had long whiskers that covered his mouth and I enjoyed seeing them on him, envied them, even, knowing that no matter how hard I tried, I'd never achieve that level of mustached-ness.

His voice was deep and gruff, thick like an echo, and he always struggled to breathe toward the end of his sentences. If there was anything that kept him young at heart, it was his love of Mexican wrestling. Plus, he had confessed to me that his childhood dream had been to become a wrestler. He'd trained for it in his younger years. Many times, I wondered if his breathing struggles were because of a luchador injury.

"Niño," he greeted me, as he'd referred to me from the time we'd met. Pepe stuffed more enchiladas into his mouth. Bits of soggy tortilla stuck to his mustache. "I'm sorry about your dad, niño. Mari said he's in the hospital in the city."

Apparently, they knew each other through their brief time working at the potato factory Pepe had been at for over 30 years. Ignacio's inability to hold a job meant he had worked all over the city, to the point where his chances of meeting Pepe, despite Chicago's considerable size, were quite high. According to Pepe's conversations with Xóchitl, Ignacio slipped up shortly after they started working together and admitted he used fake documents to get the job. Word spread to the company's owners. Pepe warned my father of his impending termination and of the owner's plans to report him to the authorities. He never saw Ignacio again.

"He is," I answered. "I'm heading out in a few minutes to see him. I'll let him know you send your regards. And I'm sorry he lied to you. My father tends to bend the truth sometimes."

"Don't do that. Don't defend him. He's a grown man. Yeah, he lied to get the job, but maybe his mistake was being too honest with me afterwards?"

It had been a stupid thing to admit and an even stupider situation to find himself in. He had plenty of opportunities to fix his immigration status. Not that I would've helped him, not after everything he put me through.

"He was lazy anyway," Pepe continued. "Probably would've been fired soon, even if his documents had been in order." Pepe roared with laughter and smacked his chest as he choked on his food. "Man, I never would've guessed that you two were related. I guess the apple *does* fall far from the tree with you, niño. Am I right? Thank God you're a good person, son. You're a good man to my Olivia and we appreciate that."

Doña Mari walked in with Xóchitl. She asked us to sit while she cleared the table, placing queso fresco and chiles en vinagre in front of us. "How many?" she asked me, pulling out two green plates.

"I got it, Doña Mari. Gracias."

I turned to Xóchitl, whose hands were gripping the back of a chair. She closed her eyes momentarily. She was tired. She'd been up much earlier than me. I pulled out what would have been my chair and asked her to sit, then served our food on Mari's green plates.

While we ate, Xóchitl and I told her parents about our lives in Ohio. About my interpreter job and the undocumented immigrants I helped get housing, financial aid, and educational options for their children.

Xóchitl spoke about her social media marketing job for start-up businesses, and with every word she spoke in excitement, Pepe's and Mari's eyes beamed with joy and adoration for their only child.

"We're very proud of you two," Doña Mari said. She also commented on how well I communicated in both languages.

"It was important for my mother and sister that I speak Spanish well," I confessed. "They'd correct me often, especially my mother."

Doña Mari's cell phone rang.

"Well, jovenes, y Don, I gotta go make more enchiladas." She picked up our dishes and placed them in the sink. Put her arms around her husband, who grabbed her hand and kissed it like a true gentleman. She blushed, and Xóchitl and I smiled at the display of affection even after close to fifty years of marriage. Doña Mari asked that he wash the dishes and Señor Pepe acknowledged her request.

Doña Mari grabbed an apron and her jacket with "Restaurante Doña Mari" printed in bold, yellow letters outlined in red. She was off to her small Mexican restaurant blocks away from her house. A small business that was the epitome of the American Dream, busy since the day it opened five years ago. Positioned just off the highway exit to her house, a billboard declared it a "must-visit restaurant just outside of the Chicagoland area," praised by a renowned traveler's website and magazine since its establishment.

I, too, announced that I would leave and expressed gratitude to Doña Mari and Pepe for their food and hospitality, as always.

Outside, as we pulled the rest of our bags from our trunk, Xóchitl asked if I was sure I wanted to see Ignacio. "Whatever you decide to do, I got you," she proclaimed.

"I know," I said, closing our trunk. Heading to the front of the house, she stopped me with an embrace and gazed into my eyes.

"Want me to go with you?"

"No. I got this. Promise."

"Sure? I'll pull the plug if you want me to." Her comment made me laugh so loud I snorted.

"Thanks, Love," I said, looking to make sure no one stared at us after she'd made me laugh. "I can handle it. *You* need to get some rest." We kissed, and I assured her I'd return that evening.

After we set the bags inside the house, and before leaving, Xóchitl reached inside her sweater pocket. She handed me my phone and said I'd left it on the table.

"Thanks." I slid it into my pocket. We kissed once more, and I headed out the door.

As I approached the hospital, deeper into the city, traffic worsened. It was ten times worse than when Xóchitl neared Merrillville. Drivers were so close to me, a rear-end crash was almost inevitable. I tried to remain calm, though. I was in no rush to see my father. I also couldn't risk an accident. The last thing I wanted was to end up stuck at the same hospital as Ignacio.

Instead, I spent the time planning and stressing about our re-encounter and recalling the day of my mother's funeral.

9

NOVEMBER 07, 1989

I GNACIO STOOD NEAR MY mother's coffin. His stance was proud, almost cocky. He smiled and tipped his hat at the ladies present. Like the other attendees, he wore what for him was typical attire: a buttoned-up black shirt only buttoned half-way to show off his bare chest, a black sports coat, dark slacks, his beloved black boots, and a black fedora.

I had once referred to him as the Man in Black, due to his preference for the color, but he didn't like that. He said I shouldn't compare him to Johnny Cash because he'd never listen to that kind of music, yet he loved listening to norteñas, rancheras, corridos, and Tejano music, which, to me, were kind of the same.

Jenni and I played Rock, Paper, Scissors, while observing my father near Paloma. Carlos interrupted our game.

"Do you know what happened to your mom?" he blurted, and I knew his annoying know-it-all persona would say something cynical.

"She died," I said dryly and went back to playing with Jenni.

"Is she going to heaven or hell?" he asked, because, aside from knowing it all, he was also a bit of a religious fanatic. "Because if she wasn't baptized, I don't think she'll get into heaven, even if she was nice." He hesitated as he said those last words, his eyes quickly dropping to the carpeted floor.

Jenni played rock and I played paper. I wanted to use my open hand to smack him for saying those careless words. He had insinuated

Paloma would go to hell... But if I hit him, I'd attract attention and Sofía would be mad at me, so, instead I mumbled, "*You're* going to hell."

Jenni giggled.

"Tía!" Carlos cried and took off, looking for Cecilia. I spotted her first. She gave me a look that said, *¿¡Qué están haciendo!?*

Then, I looked to Sofía, chatting with guests near our mother's coffin, a few feet away from Ignacio.

"Go with your mom, Jenni. I'm going to stand by Sofi."

When I approached Sofía, Ignacio extended his arm and demanded a hug, but I refused. His drunken behavior the night before Halloween still irked me.

SOFÍA AND I HAD been watching TV while Paloma and Ignacio were supposedly talking in her bedroom. It was a quarrel that turned into their typical "Why do you drink so much?" and "I won't kill anyone" exchanges. No matter where we moved to in the apartment, we could still hear them.

The door hadn't been completely closed, and through the opening I watched as Ignacio covered her mouth and told Paloma to quiet down. Sofía straightened, her hand on the armrest. She was ready to attack, surely, if Ignacio hurt our mother.

He made a last point that he had no drinking problem, opened the door, shut the bedroom light off on Paloma, and slammed the door closed. The door bounced back. Paloma sat in the dark, on the edge of the bed, crying silently. When she spotted me looking, she got up to shut the door.

As Ignacio walked out, the apartment door hit the wall hard enough to startle me. We could hear Ignacio's heavy footfalls as they thunked on each step out. Sofía murmured for me to stay there on the sofa, while she went to check on Paloma. Once she was in the room with our mother, I stood on the sofa to peek through the curtains behind me.

Ignacio was trying different keys on the car door, failing to get it open. After his third attempt, he looked around in frustration and caught me watching from the upstairs window. He waved sloppily, but lost his balance and had to lean on the car to stay upright. With a huff, he pushed himself off and walked away.

IGNACIO SNAPPED HIS FINGERS. He poked my shoulder. "Ey, I'm talking to you," he said, bringing me back from that memory.

Sofía pulled me in closer to her. "Leave him alone. He doesn't want to hug you."

Ignacio checked the room, locked eyes with Cecilia, who was watching while her thumb went from one bead of her rosary to the next. Ignacio humphed and headed to the back of the room.

"Are you okay?" Sofía asked.

I nodded.

"Did you say anything to Mamá?"

Was I supposed to say something to my mother? She was dead. She wouldn't respond. I studied my mother's body in the coffin. Her cheeks reminded me of the pit of a peach and the sight made me want to touch them. What would that feel like? Touching a dead body.

"Tell her you are going to be a good boy and that you're going to miss her, and not to worry because I'm going to take care of you." She paused. "Or say whatever is in your heart."

My mind blanked, so I turned to my father and asked if I could sit with him. Sofía's eyes turned to him. She inhaled, then exhaled hard.

"If you want to, but come back anytime. Don't let him make you feel like you have to keep him company. I'll be here by Mamá."

I smiled at her and she returned the smile.

Ignacio leaned forward in his chair, his gaze on the floor. He rubbed his hands. I approached him slowly, cautious to not startle him because he seemed to be deep in thought. When I stood before him, his eyes met mine.

"Why didn't you want to hug me?" he asked.

I shrugged at his question in a shy manner, ashamed I'd neglected my father in front of Sofía.

"I'm sorry you lost your mom, hijo, more than you can imagine." He tapped the chair next to him for me to join him. "Hey, would you like to live with me?"

"For real?" I excitedly asked, because it meant I'd *finally* get to know where he lived.

"Yes, but, shh, calm down. Nothing's certain yet."

Sofía continued chatting with guests. Their faces were familiar from Paloma and Sofía's job.

Finally, I thought happily. *Finally.*

But what about Sofía? My joy suddenly dimmed when I realized he wouldn't include her. Deep down, I knew there was a rift between them. If I went with Ignacio, would Sofía still take care of me?

I asked him about Sofía and his answer was noncommittal.

"Damián," he continued, "everyone should have parents. Just because your mother isn't here anymore doesn't mean you won't have any. I can be your parent."

"What about Sofía?" I asked again.

"Your sister's young. She wouldn't understand. *You* don't understand."

Understand what? The way I saw it, without Paloma, Sofía was the closest thing to a mother I had. Now I wasn't sure about going anywhere with him, let alone living with him. "I need to ask Sofi."

Ignacio grunted. "Está bien."

"Apá, where do you live?"

"I just bought a new house. It's a little far from here, close to downtown. Your mother didn't get to see it. You will, though. I promise."

"So, I can visit soon?"

He assured me that I could and a visit was good enough for me.

We sat silently, looking at my mother's casket until the silence turned awkward. There was nothing for me to talk to him about. My cartoons? School? He wouldn't understand and it wasn't like he was asking me about any of it. In all that time he hadn't been around, had we become strangers?

When the silence got too much, I told him I'd go back to Sofía.

"Go," he said, ruffling the back of my head.

MRS. GÓMEZ TAUGHT HER fifth-grade class while the fourth graders went over their assignments, and us third graders went over spelling test words. A woman's voice came out of the classroom's intercom speaker. "Mrs. Gómez, please come to the principal's office," the muffled voice said.

Minutes later, Mrs. Gómez returned, only peeking inside the room before asking me to walk with her.

As we neared the principal's office, Ignacio's voice drifted to me from inside the office. He was speaking in Spanish, saying something about Sofía. Unfortunately, our principal barely understood the language. There would usually be someone to translate for her, but not that day.

"Señora Gómez," Ignacio said when we entered. He pulled me close to him, digging his fingers into my shoulder. "Please tell the directora that Damián's sister got taken away." His voice had taken on an edge of desperation. My eyes grew as I tried to make sense of what he'd said. Who took her away? Where did she go? Did she do something wrong?

"Apá, where's Sofía?"

"Cállate," he gritted through his teeth.

"But... but she told me we were going to Mexico to bury mom." I had been looking forward to it. I was excited to finally meet Moisés, along with all the tíos, tías, primos, and primas. Mrs. Gómez knew this. My class knew this.

But my father shut me up again. He said we'd talk about it soon and instructed me to get my things. I didn't understand why.

Paloma's dead and now Sofía was... gone?

I was confused, frightened, like that day in the hospital. This was too much for me to make sense of in my eight-year-old brain.

I headed back to class, already lonely. No one was around, not a hall monitor or school guard to rush me. I was utterly alone in the hallway. This was the beginning of my solitude.

When I stepped back into my classroom, everyone's eyes fixed on me. "I'm going home," I reluctantly announced.

"Where are you going?" "What happened?" "Are you in trouble?" "Are you going to Mexico?" My classmates' questions came at me all at once.

"My dad's here. He said that my sister is gone, but I don't know where she is."

Nancy wailed. "Nooo, Damián. Why? Why are you leaving us?!"

Nancy, *La dramática*, Paloma had once called her.

Though I mostly disliked Nancy, I understood her worry. I shrugged at her, packed my bookbag, and answered any questions I had an answer to.

When our teacher returned, she stood by the door and signaled for me to go outside with her. Ignacio waited there. I waved at my classmates and followed her out the door with my backpack strapped to my right side.

She hugged me and said she'd see me on Monday. Then, she hugged me again, tighter and longer than the first time. My classmates peeked curiously through the door's vertical window.

Ignacio ripped me from her hold.

"We'll see, Maestra Gómez," he said.

"APÁ, WHERE'S SOFÍA?" I asked while he rushed us out of the school.

"Don't worry about it. I'll tell you later." Ignacio opened the front passenger door of his LeSabre. "Did you say goodbye to your friends?"

I hadn't realized I was supposed to. I still thought I'd see them on Monday. Ignacio buckled me in. "You're coming to live with me and your school's too far for me to bring you, so you'll have to go to school somewhere else."

But this was my school.

Mamá's dead. Sofía's gone and now he's going to take me away from my school and everyone in it.

My hands clasped together while I surveyed the school that held hundreds upon hundreds of children, from kindergarten to eighth grade. It was a marvelous building, with its mostly brown bricks. It had red edges, right under the ceiling and around each window and entrance. To me, it looked a bit like a castle.

"Ey, chamaco, everything will be fine. You'll make new friends," Ignacio assured me. "I'll come get your stuff at your old place later."

"Can I come with you?" I hadn't said bye to Jenni and wanted to see her. "Can Jenni visit?"

"Maybe. I'll talk to her mom."

IGNACIO CURSED THE HEAVY highway traffic and the drivers, mumbling bad words in English and Spanish every time he had to slow or stop. That was the nature of any big city, no matter the day or time. Always busy. Meanwhile, I occupied myself observing the people waiting in the middle of the highway for the train that was about to pass through. Folks in business suits, students carrying backpacks, and parents holding their children close. Some of them read, while others ate hurriedly.

We neared the famous Sears Tower, the tallest building in the world then. How spectacular it looked in front of me. I knew how breathtaking the city looked from above, people and cars looked like worker ants scurrying throughout. I knew this because I'd been there on multiple school field trips.

We passed Comiskey Park, home to the Chicago White Sox. "Apá, when are you taking me there?" He'd promised just before my birthday that he would take me there.

He smirked. "Hijo, I'm a Cubs fan."

He stuck his middle finger out facing the rearview mirror, which showed the stadium disappearing into the distance.

He'd lied to me. And so close to my birthday.

That was the day I became a Sox fan for life, a response to the disappointment I felt at his broken promise. That was the extent of my rebelliousness then, to root for the opposing baseball team.

Ignacio took the Chinatown exit.

Chinatown... Wow. I'd never walked amongst its residents, but had always wanted to. I'd hoped he'd stop before we made it to his place. I wanted to eat there and get lost in their world, in their language.

At the corner of Archer and Wentworth, I leaned out to take in the sounds. While we waited for the light to change, I opened the window to listen.

"¡Chingado, Damián! It's fucking cold outside."

He demanded I shut the window.

"Sorry," I mumbled as I cowered by my door, rolling the window up as he'd asked. I was abashed at how inconsiderate and absentminded I'd been, especially since the latter was the personal flaw of mine that had gotten Paloma hurt.

"It's cold, Damián, and I have the heat going."

He was right. The outside air whistled in, brushing my forehead. I hadn't closed the window completely, so I finished the job before he could chide me further.

Ignacio checked both sides of Wentworth. No cars approached, so he made a U-turn and a driver turning onto Archer blasted their horn.

"Remember I told you I just bought a house?" he asked, disregarding the driver and the almost-collision. "Well, I went the wrong way. Getting off the expressway to get there is confusing. Good thing we won't have to drive to my house from yours anymore."

Anymore?

"Want to listen to music?" He suggested, swerving on the road as he searched for a cassette, his eyes focused on the artists instead of the road. "Ramón Ayala! You like him, right?"

Sure. His music played on the radio often and I sang his songs, though I would have preferred Sofía's music, romantic artists like Los Temerarios, Los Bukis, and Los Yonic's.

"Dad, do you have—"

"You'll like this one, hijo. It's one of my favorites."

He popped the cassette in. *Dos Monedas* was the first song that played. He was right, I did like it. I'd heard it on the radio and sung the lyrics. But after Paloma had asked me to really listen, the song saddened me. It spoke about a drunk father who forced his son to ask for money to continue his vice. Before the song ends, the father wakes up and, upon opening his front door, finds the son dead in the cold, holding two coins in his hand. Dos monedas.

Norteñas like Ramón Ayala's continued playing in the car as we entered 26th Street past Western Avenue. Commonly known as *La Veintiséis*. Like Chinatown, I'd never been, only heard of it. This was undiscovered territory, at least for me, and it was very much alive. I took in as much as my eyes allowed.

The only other place I'd known to be so alive was downtown Chicago, but this was different. All the people that walked and drove on this street looked like Ignacio and me. There were people with baggy shirts and pants. They folded their fingers and signaled them at others. Music like what played in our car blasted out of other ones. Store signs promoted tacos, tortas, and pollos rostizados, and windows displayed Virgensitas de Guadalupe and Mexican flags.

A siren warned the drivers to move aside as the police cruiser weaved through the heavy two-lane road. Two lanes only, one lane to drive west, the other to drive east.

"You ever been here?" he asked. I didn't respond, only shook my head slightly. "It's a bit dangerous, so don't go out without my permission. You'll get hurt."

I continued staring at the immense new world outside the car, but listened intently as Ignacio warned me of the dangerous people that lived there, like the ones that had made those signs with their fingers.

"But this is as close as it gets to being in Mexico," he said. "I'm sorry you can't ever go there."

Wait.

"Why?"

Sofía had promised to take me, and now there had been two broken promises in a matter of minutes.

"Hijo, you're a mojado like me and like her."

We were wet? I didn't understand. I'd never heard that reference, except for when I bathed.

Ignacio explained that we were in the country without permission and said that if I'd have gone to Mexico with Sofía, I would have never been allowed to return. But why would I need permission? I thought he meant the type of permission I got when I asked Paloma and Sofía to go downstairs to play with Jenni.

"You woudn't be able to see your friends anymore."

So, I *could* still see Jenni and my friends if I stayed. That was alright with me.

He continued explaining, however best he could, that we'd arrived in the U.S. illegally with no papers. If we got caught by the police, we'd be in trouble and, he repeated, we'd never return.

That's what had happened to Sofía. The police had caught her.

We arrived at his house before I could ask anything else, not that I even knew what to ask. Everything came at me at once: getting pulled out of school, this new world, Sofía leaving because she got in trouble, but explanations would have to wait, for we had arrived.

"*That's* your house?" I asked. We had parked in front of an old, rundown place that had seemed blue from afar, but now looked more gray because of the chipping paint. Rusted nails stuck out of the wooden steps leading to the door. I thought the shattered window on the second floor was a giant spider web he'd not put away from Halloween. It was a highly noticeable shattered window.

"Don't be rude, Damián. Sure, it's a little ugly, but it's our house. Maybe we can fix it together, okay?"

"Okay," I whispered.

Upon entering the house, in the first room—the living room—a cigarette stench nauseated me. I asked him if he smoked while looking for cigarettes or an ashtray. Never had I known him to smoke, just drink.

"I don't, I promise. The previous owners did and the smell lingers still. But go on upstairs. I want you to see your room."

Every step creaked. In fact, the entire house creaked, no matter where our feet touched. But houses creak, anyway, according to cartoons and movies. There was even a loose board halfway up the stairs.

Upstairs, I found that my room would be half of the cold attic. To my left, there were boxes upon boxes stacked on top of each other. To my right, my bed with a three-drawer chest, a lamp on one side, on the other, a metal rack with wire hangers for my clothes. In the middle of the attic... nay—my room—hung a lightbulb that almost grazed my head as I walked up to the shattered window I'd seen from the outside.

At my old place, I shared a room with Paloma. Sofía had her own room and sometimes I'd sleep there too, but at Ignacio's, I finally had a bedroom of my own.

I hated the room.

My father, who had never made it upstairs with me, called for me to go back downstairs and see the rest of the place.

Downstairs, I peeked inside the bathroom in the middle of the house and when I flipped the light switch on, roaches scurried on the walls to hide.

"Dad, cucarachas," I stated.

"You had them at your place, right?"

That was true, but we kept the place clean. Paloma and Sofía were strict about that.

Ignacio waved for me to follow him into the kitchen, with its yellow walls and his fridge with unwrapped carnitas, an opened pack of tortillas, and a few beers. His bedroom was there, next to the kitchen. How tempting it must be to smell his cooked food right there, next to him.

God, why was my room upstairs? I hated the room even more.

An acoustic guitar hung on his bedroom's wall and above it, a pair of boxing gloves.

The last room was an enclosed porch with the stairs to the basement.

Ignacio turned the handle on the door that led to the backyard.

"This door will always stay unlocked in case we forget our keys. If you need to get in, there's a key to the kitchen hidden here." He grabbed one of many rocks from the kitchen window's ledge. He opened the bottom of the chosen one, revealing the hidden key.

"Oh," I mumbled at the coolest thing I'd seen at his house. "But what if someone breaks the window with the rock and gets inside?"

Ignacio looked puzzled. "You're right. That's why you're here. You're my brain," he claimed. Ignacio grabbed the rocks, threw the fake one by the basement stairs and the rest he threw all the way past the yard to the alley.

His yard was small, like at my old place. This one had a tall wooden fence surrounding the house instead of the shorter metal one I knew. His weirdly designed garage to the left of me was slightly open, showing only part of a covered car and tools near the tire.

The oddness of the garage was its lengthwise positioning. Instead of fitting one car or two cars from front to back, it only accommodated one car by its side. It reminded me of a storage shed, except bigger. And because the car had to be parked sideways, it would first have to enter the backyard, back up into the garage but park sideways. Like parking on a street.

It was such a peculiarity that I headed there, but Ignacio warned me to stop. "Don't go in there. I'm trying to fix that car and I don't want you to get hurt."

What could go wrong? I wondered. The car was covered. No oil spilled on the ground. The tools were visible.

"That's it," he said. "Nothing else to see here."

"Can I help you fix the car, dad?"

"Someday," he said, like he'd said about the house when we arrived. Someday.

For now, that car would have to wait.

10

NOVEMBER 02, 2022

*W*HAT IF I STOP *at his house first?* My father's house was only ten minutes from the hospital. Besides, he didn't know I'd be visiting him. No one had confirmed my visit, that I knew of. A minor detour wouldn't have mattered. But then, Xóchitl's words came back to me. *It's bad, Dami.*

"Fuck!" One hand gripped the steering wheel while the other struck it multiple times, with other *fucks* matching the hits.

I hated that seeing him felt like an obligation. Would I *really* regret not seeing my father, even if he did die?

Fuck. Ignacio's house would have to wait.

"Can I help you?" asked a tired-looking guard. People rushed in and out of the hospital. One person even came between us. No acknowledgment. No apology. Just turned sideways, walked in between us, bumped into me, and continued.

"Hey," I said, annoyed. "I'm here to see Ignacio Vásquez."

The guard went behind a plastic glass-covered counter and moved the computer mouse to wake it up, assisting the two other busy attendants. Luckily, no one else had stood in front of me. Still, I waved at the attendants and mouthed *sorry* at them for jumping the line. The guard handed me a clipboard to sign and asked for my ID. He grinned seeing the out-of-state ID.

"Ohio, huh? Where there's more than corn."

"That's Indiana," I said, matter-of-factly.

The guard laughed. "Shit, you're right. I ain't never been, you know."

"Ohio?" Surely, he'd been to Indiana. The state border was minutes away.

He moved my ID around, trying to make out the letters. It seemed the light above reflected too strongly, or the old guard was near blind. He typed my last name slowly on the computer, unrushed. Fortunately, my visit was not life-or-death. My eyes and his followed his index finger as he searched for each letter of my last name. V-A-S... "Neither," he said. "I stayed here my whole life." Q-U...

"Here? What part?"

"*Here*," he said mockingly, like I was an idiot for not realizing where this stranger had lived or traveled to. "The city. Actually, 83rd and Commercial. And this is as far north as I've been. Always work, then home. Work. Home. Work. Home."

I stood there pensively, wondering if this man had ever explored his city. It was his as much as it once was mine. From the moment I freed myself of Ignacio, I discovered Chicago and its hidden gems, going beyond the typical tourist spots. I had checked out the surgical museum and the Wizard of Oz Park. I'd drive for hours on the streets and get lost in the suburbs. I rode the buses and trains all day on my free days, and I loved every moment. Priceless memories.

"Anyway," he said. "Go down the hallway and take the elevator to the fifth floor." He handed me a guest sticker with my name and a room number sloppily written in black marker. The smell of the chemicals that made up the Sharpie wafted to my nose. I took the sticker off and shook it to clear some of its stench.

"Next," he called out to the people behind me.

The fifth floor was quiet, except for the buzzing of the lights above me and from the machines in the rooms. And the chattering of people somewhere I couldn't see. The floor was desolate mostly.

"Hello!" I said to no avail. I roamed the long hallway, peeking into the open rooms for any sign of Ignacio. When I finally found two ladies talking on their phones at a reception desk, they rudely pointed me away, suggesting I continue down the hallway. Did they even know where I was supposed to go? Couldn't I just wait? No, the older one insisted.

My sticker had fallen off me at some point. Or maybe I forgot to put it on and it slipped out of my fingers. I couldn't remember what happened to it, or what room number the guard had written. What I knew was that this was his floor, so I checked the charts outside patients' rooms. GARCIA, MURPHY, DOE. Strangers, probably. SMITH, LOPEZ, JACKSON. Around a new corner, there was another desk, but empty. *Keep checking until you find him, or someone shows up to help.* It didn't take long after to find his room.

I. VASQUEZ, his chart read.

The outlined body on the printed image showed the location of his stab wounds. Someone had written CIRRHOSIS / STAGE 4 on his chart. It made sense. Decades of alcohol abuse can do that to a person; did him in, for sure. He had probably been drinking before he got stabbed, it wouldn't surprise me.

Before I finished skimming his chart, a young nurse finally appeared. She took a few steps toward me after setting papers on that last desk. "Can I help you?" she shouted.

"I'm his son," I responded, giving her a thumbs up, and went inside.

Ignacio's room was just as quiet as outside. I figured he was asleep, so I carefully closed the door. But when it clicked, he awoke. He struggled to lift his head to check who stood by the door. Soon, he uttered, "¿Qué onda, mi mojadito?" Then proceeded to laugh.

"You still think that's funny?" I asked in Spanish.

A hard and dry cough followed Ignacio's laughter.

"Todavía no *pikinglish*, ¿Ignacio?" I mockingly asked, taking advantage of his weakened state, since this time he wouldn't be the imposing figure standing above me, warning me to not be a smartass or he'd slap it out of me. A man of the past.

Ignacio shrugged.

"¿Pa' qué? There's always someone to speak for me. Anyway, when did you get here? I was wondering if you'd come."

Man, he'd aged so much in the twenty years we'd been apart. His hair was now white, though his mustache remained black. His muscles had atrophied. Liver spots marked his temples. Veins bulged from his hands. It all seemed so unnatural for him. This was not the same man whose towering presence had frightened me all those years ago. This man was barely an echo of who he'd been.

What would happen if I pushed on his veins? Would he hurt? *Can I hurt you now, Ignacio?*

"You wanted to see me, right? What happened?" I asked.

"Pinches escuincles tried to rob me. I didn't want them to win, so I fought back."

"What made you think you could take them? Look at you. You're an old man now. You're not a fighter anymore. Were you drunk when they attacked?"

"I can defend myself. Not like you, miedoso. I could never get you to fight. Lucky you never got hurt where we lived."

Hmph. Lucky. Sure. "Would you have defended me, if I'd been in danger, Apá? Fought for me?"

"If I had to, yes. But you were smart about it, I suppose. You always helped others and they saw that. No wonder no one messed with you."

"Well, good thing I'm not like you, huh? I suppose I take after my mother more than you."

"You do, hijo."

I sat on an empty chair a few feet from his bed. The chair remained in its spot, I made sure of it, never moving it near him. "How are you feeling?" I asked.

"Me lleva la chingada, that's how. But that's what happens in the end. I lived. Loved. Did what I could with you. Y luego te lleva la chingada."

Want that in your eulogy? Live. Love. Do what you can. Then, you're screwed.

Ignacio asked if I'd been to his place. "Not yet," I told him. He confirmed the hidden key was still by the basement and said he'd moved stuff from the basement to the attic, since he figured I wouldn't return.

He figured right.

He turned to his side, facing me. "Güey, why *didn't* you ever come back? Didn't call? Write? You could've told me you were getting married."

My heart thumped fast, matching the sound of the machine he was hooked to. It could've been guilt or shame for not inviting him, or perhaps it was anger that began building up inside of me. "Does it matter? We celebrated nothing. My last birthday party was when my mother was still alive."

"Yes. I remember," he said, smiling. "But I treated you on your birthdays, no?"

"You gave me ten bucks to go out and get something to eat."

"You never said anything. When I asked, you'd say you didn't want a party. Why didn't you say something?"

"Of course I wanted a party. What kid doesn't want to be celebrated? Ignacio, do you even remember when my birthday is?"

Ignacio ignored the question.

"Look, I know I wasn't a good father, but I could've stood next to you when you got married. Who did you have? No one. You *have* no one."

Even in his worst state, he still managed to hurt me deeply, and that's when I understood it wasn't guilt or shame that were to blame for my increased heart rate; it was anger fueling me. Resentment. "I have Xóchitl."

"Ah, Pepe's daughter. Pinche Pepe. He told me *after* it happened." Ignacio wiped his eyes. "And then, when I landed here, who was I supposed to call? You changed your number. So, I had them call Pepe for one last favor."

Ignacio straightened himself up on the bed, groaning as he adjusted his body.

"I gave you a home, Damián. You had me when there was no one else."

A tear welled up in my eye. It ran down my cheek and I let it fall, saying nothing. If I did, I'd be admitting weakness to him, because, as he'd told me many times, *men don't cry.* But hadn't he shed a tear a moment ago when he wiped his eyes? I couldn't tell. It was dark enough to cry quietly in this room, without revealing ourselves.

My chest began to hurt because of my heavy breathing. Fortunately, Ignacio's machines masked my heaving.

And then, he said something that only enraged me more.

"I love you, hijo. Always have."

Damn it, Ignacio! Where had this fatherly love been? I needed it when I had no one. Now, in his worst moment, he suddenly had love for me.

"Damián, forgive me for never saying it to you, but you never said it to me either. Nunca."

Wait. Wha... What the fuck?

"Ignacio, was I *supposed* to say it to you? Do I owe you that? Do I owe you for giving me a place to stay and food to eat? Isn't that what a parent is supposed to do, provide for their child? And then you want me to say I... I..." The words struggled to come out of me. If I let them out, *if* I told him I loved him, I would be lying, even if they were empty words to express my rage. Even so, apparently, he had expected them from me first.

God knows I tried at that moment, but even attempting was painful. It hurt my stomach, my throat, my heart. So, instead, I smirked and in English I said, "Fuck you, old man."

Surely, he understood that, and if he didn't, I pretty much spelled it out for him the second time. "Fuck... you."

Saying that was like a relief that washed over the aches I'd just felt. It felt good. Never had I spoken to my father that way, for he instilled fear in me when I was kid, but now that I could, now that I had the upper hand, I said it. It needed to be said. And if I could have run to the rooftop of the hospital and shouted it over the city, I would have.

"I guess you *can* fight," Ignacio said.

The lights turned on.

"Mr. Vásquez, are you good?" the young nurse asked in Spanish. I wasn't sure if she meant Ignacio or me. Her eyes looked at Ignacio, then at me, then back to Ignacio.

I stood to leave, pushing the chair with my legs and tipping it backwards.

"I have to go, otherwise..." I held my tongue.

I grabbed the chart outside of his room, ripped the sheet with his report, and folded it. My hand shook as I wrote my name and phone number with the attached pen on the chart. I almost slammed the paper on the nurse's chest when she met me outside, but held back when I realized my feelings towards my father weren't her fault. Instead, I clipped the paper on the chart and walked out of the hospital without uttering another word.

IN THE CAR, THE events of the visit replayed in my mind. It was fresh. And raw. So raw that my body shook. One would likely mistake it for the winter's cold, but the temperature was nowhere near what it should have been.

It was painful, too, knowing he'd never asked about my life—our life, Xóchitl's and mine. No, he'd made this visit about him. About why we hadn't included him in our wedding. About how much I hadn't appreciated him as my father. He never even mentioned my mother. Clearly, she meant nothing to him.

At least we agreed on something, that I'm more like her than him.

My phone went off, notifying me of a text message. It was a brief message in Spanish asking to call back. A text from the phone number I thought blocked the night before. That follow-up would have to wait. Xóchitl was my priority. She'd called and texted more than once.

"I'm good," I assured Xóchitl over the phone. "My stay here may be longer than expected. I'll explain later. But I need to cool down first after seeing him. He's still a dick. Figured. That's why I didn't want to come."

There was a soft sigh from her end that sounded almost disappointed and I wasn't sure if that was directed at her or at me.

"Things needed to be said, anyway," I continued. "I'll keep you posted, Love. Promise to be careful."

Xóchitl said she loved me, too, and we ended our call.

Not ready to return to the hospital, I stayed put to consider finally making the drive to Ignacio's house. As I weighed that option, turning the car on to warm it up, the man from the radio show earlier came back on. A replayed interview. National corporate radio stations sometimes recycle their programs. This time, he was speaking about life and what happens after we die. The afterlife. What could he possibly know? I wondered. It's not like anyone has been to the afterlife and returned to talk about it.

Anyone who actually believed this person was a fool. Yet here I was, one of those fools, captivated by his words.

"It doesn't end here," the man told the radio host. "We have a purpose in this life, right? You, me, your listeners. Sometimes, though, people die early, and, if we're lucky, we're given a second chance at life."

"But what if you don't have a purpose? Or don't know what it is?" the host asked.

"Then Death, the Muerte, I like to call her, gives you a purpose. She forces you back."

"Were you forced back?" asked the host.

The man dodged the question. "The thing is, the Muerte can't interfere with human affairs. So, she has messengers. Now, if you ever encounter someone claiming to be a messenger, maybe you should believe them. There's a chance that the Muerte sent them back and gave them a purpose to return. To help people," he clarified.

This man was so confident in his discourse, but, as I'd told Xóchitl before, it was all malarkey. Still, I couldn't turn away.

Enough!

I switched stations to try to find something more enjoyable, but nothing pleased me. The Mexican radio stations I'd known were playing corridos bélicos instead of the banda I enjoyed. The hip hop stations were playing pop music instead. In the short time I'd been away in a new city, this one had changed, moved on without me. Or maybe it had done so long ago, after I'd stopped paying attention to it, once everything had started feeling pointless and repetitive.

With no decision made on what to do next, I turned the car off and figured a quick stroll would help clear my mind.

A car parked in front of me and it made me freeze. Rarely did I see ones like this anymore. It was an Oldsmobile Cutlass, like the one that hit Paloma, except this one was white and had a Virgen de Guadalupe painted on the hood. The dark-skinned virgin looked down on Juan Diego, roses painted at her feet.

The driver caught me staring. He walked up to my window and knocked on it, bringing me back to reality. I opened it and he asked if I liked his car.

"Yeah, it's cool," I said, and in an attempt not to come off as rude, I made small talk and asked him where he got it done. He said he knew a guy; everyone in Chicago knows a guy. This guy had a shop by 26th.

"I can hook you up," he said. "Just tell my boy I sent you."

I told him I knew who he was talking about, though, clearly, I had no clue. I also said I used to live that way.

"Cool! Let me get you his number. Tell him Nacho sent you."

If ever the universe sent a sign, it was this. This guy's name being Nacho, the street, the car... The message was clear enough, I had to visit Ignacio's old place.

"Don't worry, man. I got it. I know where it's at." I turned the car on and backed out.

"Bro, hold on. You don't even know his—"

"Thanks, man!" I yelled and took off.

11

THE DEAD LIVED ON this Day of the Dead while I slowly drove down Chicago's popular 26th Street. Ofrendas were displayed inside windows and in backyards. Calavera masks and skull-painted faces meandered the sidewalks; their hands balanced covered plates of food and white paper bags with what I assumed must've been pan dulce. I figured all of this was for people's dead relatives, as it is customary to leave a dead person's favorite foods on their altar.

What did I have for Paloma? Nothing, not even a piece of gum.

All this death roaming down this famous street on this festive day had a beauty to it, from the elegant paintings representing Death to the bright orange and yellow Cempasúchil flowers people crowned their Muerte's head with. The paintings depicted skeleton couples holding each other; in one, a woman with two faded roses over her hair bun wrapped her arms around her lover. He wore a black sombrero with tiny gold skulls at the edges.

A woman sat outside a store, eyes closed as someone painted her face white and her eyes black, adding a dot of white in each black void. The artist then painted a black line from her crimson lips to her hair, bearing bright red roses. A photographer approached the sitting woman, who posed for her photo, a sultry pose that showed part of her back and shoulder to the photographer. The woman raised her hand to her chin; someone had either painted or tattooed a skull on the back of her hand.

A few feet from her, people passed a tall and gawky-looking woman standing with her hands clasped. She wore a ragged and dirty robe.

Pedestrians dismissed the awful-looking woman, but she didn't dismiss them. She turned her head, surveying them all. It was like she was choosing a victim. The always heavy traffic down this street allowed me time to stare at her, mesmerized. The woman turned to me and I turned from her, frightened as a chill ran through me at the fact that she'd noticed me. My eyes slowly roamed back, but she was gone.

Could that have been Death, the Muerte the man on the radio had spoken about? Perhaps it had been one of her messengers, as that man had claimed.

At the corner tiendita near Ignacio's house, a small group of people gathered, holding lit candles and setting flowers and food on the ground, praying over the picture of a young man. He had likely died there, possibly shot because of the nefarious nature of the local gangs and their rivals, but that was only an assumption. Had I known this young man? Was he a brother, nephew, grandchild of someone I knew from my time living in the area? How sad, that lost connection. That detachment from a community I used to be a part of.

Fucking Ignacio let the house go to shit. It looked worse than how I'd remembered it from twenty years before. It had aged dreadfully, just like my father. The nails that had stuck out from my first day were still there, but were even more noticeable now. The cracks on my old room's shattered window on the second floor had grown. Whatever small patches of grass remained near the entrance had turned brown. I wondered what mess of a lawn must await me in the backyard.

This house that had once been blue had long since turned gray, and if it had ever been a living thing, it was now dead and in a post-mortem state.

When I'd arrived as a child, Ignacio had said we'd fix the place together. He was supposed to do the heavy lifting and leave the minor daily matters to me. I had done my part, but what had his lazy ass done? Nothing, clearly.

The weirdly designed garage in the back remained slightly open. Stuck. Frozen in time from even before I'd arrived. The covered car and the tools were in the same spot they had been in since my childhood. Time had given up on them, abandoned them, the way Ignacio's parents had left him.

Now that Ignacio wasn't around, I could finally put the things in that garage back in their rightful place, but where was their place? I never knew. A commotion inside the house summoned me instead. It was far. A crash against the window on the other side of the house.

As I walked to the fake rock with the hidden house key near the basement stairs, I waded my way through crushed beer cans and broken glass from liquor bottles. Obviously, Ignacio's alcoholism had worsened, which made sense considering the liver damage noted on his chart.

The kitchen was covered in layers of grease and grime. A slice of pizza sat on the coffee table in the living room and his dirty black socks with holes in different places lay on the floor, emanating a disgusting odor.

Long ago, I had lived here with him. I had done my part. Forced to keep the place clean, to scrub the kitchen and the bathroom. He had forced me to sweep, mop, and dust. I had wiped the windows and mirrors and kept our clothes and dishes clean.

Ignacio was the stepmother and stepsisters to my Cinderella, forcing his son to servitude while he did nothing, locking himself in his room most of the time.

In Cinderella's story, a fairy godmother saves her. There was no fairy godparent in this story.

Everyone should have parents. I can be your parent, he'd once told me. He didn't understand what being a parent meant. He had failed to nurture me, to teach me.

A parent doesn't ignore their child.

Perhaps it was a force of habit, or maybe it was something that had been imprinted in me from my childhood in this house, but I needed to tidy up. I checked under the sink for cleaning supplies, which he'd pushed to the back. While wiping and trashing garbage and piling his dirty socks to throw in the washer later, my mind wandered to my time under his care... his treatment under his rule. How he'd speak to me. The names he'd call me.

"I CAN'T EAT WITH this *mugrero* on this plate. Serve me on a new plate and wash this one," his thick voice demanded. "Pendejo," he'd say, "this shirt is stained. I can't wear this. Scrub it off." Or, "clean that mierda off the window. Now! I don't want to see it when I come back."

His go-to for my refusals to his demands were threats to La Migra. Kids had the Cucuy to scare them. I had La Migra, who'd take me away.

Many times, especially in my first days, he'd tower over me, holding a pan, broom, or newspaper, ready to strike. He wouldn't hit me, but of course I'd cower before him. Fear can be a powerful tool. It leaves no physical marks or clues on the body. Fear played a wonderful role for my father.

It hadn't taken me long after coming to live with him to learn my place in his world. Whatever fatherly love he'd shown me before Paloma's death and Sofía's deportation had been a ruse. He'd tricked me, tricked Paloma.

At age eight, I began my servitude at home, and by age nine, he'd promoted me, which meant, like most promotions, increased labor. In my case, that meant going out for groceries. The first time, he took a twenty from his wallet and almost pushed me out the door with no list or indication as to what to purchase.

"Güey, go to the kitchen and figure it out," he'd said. "I'm not here to give you all the answers. No one's going to. No one's done that for me."

I just had to return with a receipt. He wanted to make sure no one, including me, cheated him out of his money. No receipt? The Migra would come for me.

But it was dangerous. I remembered him mentioning that before.

"No seas cobarde," he'd said. "Nothing's going to happen. Just stay out of people's way."

So, I did. I learned to keep to myself.

When my ninth winter arrived, my father gave me a bonus for the cold weather: a dollar-twenty-five for bus fare. I couldn't risk becoming the kid from the Ramón Ayala song.

One day, many years later, after learning I wasn't undocumented, I asked Ignacio why he'd sent me out alone.

"No matter what, you'd always come back, no?" he'd answered. "You're from here. They'd just send you home. But if they caught me, I may not return. Who'd have taken care of you?"

Bullshit. He wouldn't lose me; I was like a prize... a title he'd won and couldn't afford be stripped from him.

A BUS STOPPED AT the corner, bringing me back to reality and forcing me to stop cleaning the window.

Turning around, my eyes fixed on the stairs and I wondered if I was ready to revisit my old room. Why wouldn't I be, though? I was already in the house.

My old room remained, for the most part, the same since I'd left. My bed, the old lamp on the short drawer, and the clothing rack by the shattered window were still in their place, just like the tools and car in the garage. Movie posters I had added over time were still taped to the walls, but boxes from the basement now occupied some of the void I'd left.

It was just past 5:30 p.m., and the sky had begun to blanket the street as the sun went down. That was the only beauty of this place, watching the sunset from that old, cracked window. I'd witnessed the day's end from there innumerable times, and this time I stood there once more to not miss it. At the very least, I wanted to take in the painted sky's dark blue as it melted into light blue, then to white, and to orange at the horizon.

In that semi-dark room with me, something roamed. Pulling down the string on the room's hanging light, I hoped to catch whatever it was. I heard a flutter near me, but didn't see anything. The light must have scared it, for it quieted down. I searched and searched, lifting my old sábana and the clothes I'd left on my bed that no longer fit me. It irked me not finding whatever was causing the flutter.

Annoyed, I moved everything: the bed, the drawer. I looked behind the boxes. Nothing. In my desperate search, a box tumbled down. Ignacio's old shirts spilled out.

The box piqued a new interest because now I wanted to find out what else my old man had boxed up. Placing the fallen box on my bed, I checked the contents inside it. Maybe something would come home with me after this trip.

The box contained more of his clothes: long-sleeved plaid shirts, jeans, and belts with GTO imprinted on the large buckles—GTO an aide-memoire of his home state of Guanajuato, a land half a century lost to him. Other boxes contained old VHS films starring Mexican legends like actors Mario and Fernando Almada and singer Vicente Fernández. *Real men*, according to Ignacio. Men who answered with their pistols and who had women clinging to them left and right.

There were also unfinished English-As-A-Second-Language books, books in Spanish, Playboy magazines, and vulgar sex comic books that had been sold at newspaper stands back in the day.

One box had my old schoolwork. I had never expected to find this. Schoolwork with As and Bs, tests with written notes praising my knowledge and attentiveness in class. Perhaps Ignacio had *some* love in his heart for me. Did his small heart still hold a place for me?

One long box at the bottom was heavier than I anticipated. I pulled it out along with some dust bunnies. Upon opening it, I was disappointed to find more clothes, but those didn't explain the weight. I pulled all his clothes out until I felt something thick. Four stacked briefcases.

They each required a four-digit code, which immediately made me suspicious. After all, there was no reason Ignacio should feel the need to lock things up in his own home. I took them out and placed them on my bed, searching through the mess I'd already made to try to find a clue as to what the codes might be, but I found nothing. So, it had to be done the long way: 0000, 0001, 0002.... When I reached 0728 on the first one, I grew tired. There had to be a better, faster way, even if that meant breaking them. They looked tough to break, but not impossible, and I would take the whole night to break them open if that's what it took.

What are you hiding, Nacho?

The four briefcases went downstairs with me. I set them on the living room coffee table and headed to the kitchen in search of anything that might help get them open. I returned with a flat screwdriver that I used to pry the first one open. The screwdriver slipped from my hands multiple times and sores began to form near my fingers. But eventually, it was a success. Summoning all my strength for one last attempt, I forcefully opened the first one.

This motherfucker.

There were letters inside, piles of them all addressed to me. They were from Sofía, all the way from Mexico.

With renewed energy, I fought to open the other three cases. My hands tingled and trembled, and I knew my body would hurt the next day, but it needed to be done. It must've taken me just over an hour to break them all open.

Each one held more letters. Plus, candies, comic books from Mexico, little trinkets Sofía or Moisés thought I'd like, perhaps. And then, after so much rummaging, I touched something hard. A movie. A home video... *the* homemade video. The one with Paloma's name written on the label. The one she'd told me to keep safe.

I took it out carefully, afraid that if I dropped it accidentally, it would shatter. Turning the video cassette every which way was like discovering it for the first time. I read her name, slowly, studied every curve and line the way it was written. I ran my thumb over the tiny bumps of the cassette, scratching every little bump, taking in the sound as my fingernail went through every indent.

Ignacio's selfishness had kept them from me. I could have seen her... them. Paloma. Sofía. Through her letters, I could have known Sofía and Moisés' life. Could have known my family.

My hatred for Ignacio grew, coursing through me like venom. Running through my veins, and in my heart, mind, and soul. True to God,

I wished him dead, wished he'd never been a part of my life, wished Sofía and Moisés' father had been mine too.

He'd already lied to me and put so much fear in me. He'd told me I was undocumented like him, threatened to call Immigration on me. I wondered what would have happened if he'd done so.

My fingers tapped on the movie as I considered my next step. Go back to the hospital and confront him about what I'd found, or stay and watch the movie. I could also call Xóchitl and explain my discovery.

No, stay, my heart suggested. Paloma was there after so long and I needed her. I needed my mother.

But I also needed a VCR to play the tape and Ignacio no longer had it by the TV, so I returned upstairs and continued searching the boxes, hoping to find it in one of the few unopened ones. I figured since Ignacio didn't like throwing things away—not that he was a hoarder, he just always worried that discarding things might somehow mean giving himself away to the feds or ICE—he might still have it.

Since there was nothing in my room, I headed for his room next, but found nothing.

In the basement, there was so much junk that finding the VCR felt like an endless quest as I rummaged through tools, nails, remotes, and my old toys. But thank God Ignacio kept things. Inside a taped Panasonic box, I spotted the VCR.

I pulled the tape off the box, dust flying all over my face. There it was. The 80s VCR that had played so many of my favorite movies that had taken me away from Ignacio the way he had taken me away from Pullman. These make-believe places and times were wonderful and magical, with exceptional characters. Films like *Back to the Future, Superman, Somewhere in Time, Pleasantville.*

Now, once again, it would play for me. Once again it would take me to another time.

With the VCR tucked under my arm, I sauntered back to the living room.

Once all was set, with the movie ready to play, I felt exhausted. It'd been a long-driven day, one of cleaning and running around.

You've made it this far. Don't let the moment pass. Push it in. She's waiting for you. They're *waiting for you. Push the movie in. Let it play.*

Was I ready for it, to see Paloma, Sofía, Jenni, Cecilia? All those people I grew up with could be there, stuck in time forever. Could I take seeing them again?

My finger held its position, trembling but ready to push the tape in. I felt my breathing increase, the beating of my heart, as I anticipated what awaited me.

Slam. The noise from upstairs returned. *Slam!* It was harder that second time.

SLAM!

That third one startled me. My finger pushed the movie in.

As I waited for the old machine to play the movie, I hopped off the floor to consider checking the noise upstairs, but after remembering to change the channel to watch the movie, and doing so, I relaxed on the floor. The old VCR shook and whirred until it finally remembered what it was meant to do.

There she was, on the TV screen. My mother, Paloma Flores.

"Damián, ven mijo," she instructed. "Sofi's waiting for you."

Stupid young Damián wouldn't hurry. Mamá waited for him. *If only I were there to push you to her.*

On the table next to where Paloma stood was a white-frosted cake for young Damián. Green lettering read *Feliz Cumpleaños Damián.*

Happy Birthday. To me.

The cake surely was too sweet. I imagined underneath all the white covering and the green dollops that edged it, the cake was chocolate (my favorite), with strawberries and red jelly in the middle (probably Sofía's choice). Too much sugar now would probably give me a headache.

My vision blurred and I figured it must be from the day's exhaustion, but I had to hold on. I thought back to those birthday parties, how I'd waited those mornings for Bozo the Clown to wish me a happy birthday on his TV show, just as he'd done to hundreds of children before.

"Hijo, hurry," my mother insisted, her voice shriller than I'd remembered. The camera panned through our living room, searching for young Damián who was playing with action figures with his friends.

You have no idea, none, of what you'll be missing soon. Listen to her, menso. Hug her, stupid.

But young Damián was in his own world, as always. He continued playing with his friends, looking at the camera at times and smiling before returning to play.

My eyes welled up watching what played on the TV. I tried to absorb it all, the way a child absorbs what they learn. My vision blurred and then the yawns began. A long stretch followed. It was one of those stretches that gives you vertigo, but heightens your senses after. I loved that feeling.

Where was Sofía in all of this? I hadn't seen her yet, just Paloma and their coworkers.

"Sofiiii," Paloma called with a smile. "¡Ya! Put that camera down."

She was the one recording! I'd been so consumed with missing Paloma, I'd dismissed my sister and what she'd done for us. What she'd done with this movie.

She was there the entire time. My sister, Sofía, a woman who'd lost so much of her childhood. A woman who could have chosen to stay safe in Mexico instead of risking her life crossing the border to help Paloma raise me.

There she was, my half-sister, recording these moments. Half a sister from our mother's side because I was the son of a son-of-a-bitch father.

Even in Mexico, after what had happened to our mother, she'd been there for me, writing to me umpteen times.

She'd only been present for half of my lifetime then, but even a single day with her was filled with love.

I'm sorry, Sofi. Yes, sorry for the selfish brat I'd been, often distracted and stuck in a world of my own.

Another yawn came, long and loud this time. I paused the movie briefly and Paloma's motionless eyes stared at me. They reminded me of the way eyes in photos always seem to follow us.

I leaned my body back on the floor, extending my arms behind me to support my weight, and when my arms shook, I pushed myself up, grabbed the remote from the floor, and sat on the couch. It was a terrible idea, for the couch was much more comfortable compared to the floor.

I leaned forward instead of sitting back, hoping that this way, I'd hold on longer before my tiredness made me give in. My chin rested on my hands.

I played the movie again. The camera turned in different directions, which made me realize how small our place had been, an apartment of maybe five to six hundred square feet. Back then, though, that was a big enough kingdom for young Damián.

Every passing second meant a second closer to sleep. My chin slipped from my hands a couple times, but each second brought me closer to oblivion. Accidentally dropping forward and onto the floor, I finally rested my head on the back of the couch and settled for listening to the movie instead of watching. Still, I tried to make sense of the scenes, eyes too heavy to keep open.

What time was it? It couldn't be *that* late. But when one is tired, what does it matter? One must rest. According to my phone, it was 7:28 p.m., not quite time for bed yet.

8:28 p.m. in Cincinnati.

Frustrated with my sudden sleepiness, I decided to take a five minute nap, except I wasn't a short-siesta kind of guy. I was a fall-asleep-and-wake-up-the-next-day kind of guy.

Paloma served our guests her pollo con mole. I wasn't watching it happen, but I knew what was going on. My ears told me. I felt the warmth of the kitchen, smelled her cooking, tasted it. It was so vivid in my tired mind that my mouth salivated and my stomach growled.

They laughed and ate. Children ran in my small kingdom.

Before giving in to sleep completely, I checked the TV and briefly watched as they danced to Los Temerarios' rhythmic cumbia that finally lulled me to sleep.

PART 2
PALOMA'S VISIT

12

T HE ROOM I WOKE up in was no longer Ignacio's or mine.

I scanned my new surroundings, rising from a bed that should've been too small for me. It was certainly not the same room I'd fallen asleep in, but it was as familiar as if it'd been pulled straight from a memory. The bed was in the same place as it'd always been, as was the closet and the chest of half-open drawers. It was my old room, the one in my childhood home. Hesitant and barefoot, I made my way into the hallway, where I was greeted by guests I had not seen in ages. My mother, who'd been dead for over three decades, appeared, as did my sister Sofía, who'd been gone from my life about as long.

The living room mirror confirmed my suspicions, as impossible as they were. I was inhabiting the body of my younger self, the boy I'd seen on Ignacio's TV. It must be a dream, I figured, because there was no other possible explanation. People didn't just get pulled back in time through the TV. There was no way for me to actually be here, celebrating my younger self's eighth birthday.

And yet... here I was and it felt as real as life had before I fell asleep. Even more so, maybe. If this *was* a dream, it was like no dream I'd had before. Even the doorframe my arms rested on felt real. To confirm the feeling, I pushed against it harder, rubbing my hands over the white wood. One of the tiny, sharp edge pieces sticking out pricked my hand, leaving a miniscule scratch mark. When I pressed on it, it stung and a small drop of blood bloomed where the splinter had gone in.

The floor clearly showed the indented groove of the connected tiles, but because I still needed confirmation of the reality of my situation, my toe rubbed between the connecting lines, and I could feel the indent between both.

The spicy aroma from the mole Paloma had made for my birthday hit me. My stomach growled. That felt real, too.

"What's going on?" My question was barely a whisper.

"What do you mean, 'what's going on'? It's your birthday, mijo," Paloma answered, before turning to everyone, "Ay, este niño. Give us a moment."

Paloma knelt in front of me, instructing me to put my shoes on and, lowering her voice, said, "Otherwise Sofi will get mad." She rubbed her thumb down my cheek, motioned her head to Sofía behind her, then winked. Her touch was cold, colder than I'd ever felt a person be.

"Why?" I asked her quietly, surveying the room.

"Because you'll get sick," Sofía responded, but from her tone, I knew she meant, 'Because I said so.'

"No." I leaned in closer to Paloma. "Why are you here? Why am *I* here?"

"It's your birthday, mi niño. They came to see you. Remember?"

Paloma smiled and somehow the warmth in her eyes made me certain that this was no dream, that I indeed was stuck in the past as my former self. Despite this new certainty growing inside me, I whispered a soft, "This—This birthday, it all happened over thirty years ago. How can this be?"

Paloma let out a tiny laugh, one that fit the situation. I was a child making up stories and her, a mother finding them delightful, but her eyes told a different story. She told me not to worry, but insisted we should talk in the bedroom. She had something to explain. Under normal circumstances, I would've thought she was going to scold me. She always had preferred to do that privately.

Paloma stood up and grabbed my shoes from the bedroom. She helped me put them on my small feet, as if I didn't know how to do it myself. Then, she pulled me by the hand and led me to my cake. There it was again, her cold touch.

"Ready?" she said to everyone, who then sang *Happy Birthday,* the children and a few guests in perfect English, with a little accented version from the non-English speakers. Then, the Spanish-speakers followed up with *Sapo verde eres tú*, a Hispanic version of the previous song.

When they finished singing, they chanted, "¡Mordida! ¡Mordida!" A hand pushed my face toward the cake. I slipped away just in time, but then a thought stopped me dead in my tracks. What if getting my face smashed into the cake worked the same way as splashing water on my face? Maybe it would help me wake up. So, I let the next person's hand push my face into the cake.

It was not like splashing water on my face. Instead, I felt embarrassed and wanted to cry when everyone broke out laughing and clapping at my frosting-smeared face. I still had no idea how I could be here with my dead mother and all these now-strangers and was no closer to figuring it out.

Sofía approached us with her camera to capture the moment. Paloma said we'd be back after she cleaned me up. She swiped two-fingers' worth of frosting and surprised Sofía by smearing it on her right cheek. We all chuckled.

Paloma hugged Sofía tightly and though she'd always been very affectionate, there was something more contained in that hug, something meaningful. There was a look on Paloma's face that told me she knew she could lose us at any moment and wanted to hold on as long and tight as she could.

She let Sofía go, gave her "o-kei" to all, and grabbed my hand. She led me to our bedroom and closed the door.

"Hijo, how long has it been?" she whispered with a smile, while I hopped back on the bed.

Confused, I asked, "Since I woke up?" But something about her tone told me she knew it had been much longer than that.

"No. How long? I... I..." Paloma paused. Kneeled in front of me. "The way you asked why you and I are here..." She paused again, this time letting out a breath. She looked away.

"Thirty years," I tested.

"¿¡Qué!?"

"Thirty-three, to be exact," I drawled. "I'm forty-one."

Did... did she know?

"Oh. You're almost my age." Paloma pinched her bottom lip as if analyzing our situation. "Dios, I've missed so much."

I wanted to ask my mother if I was dead, because she was, and perhaps this was one of those situations where one sees their loved ones moments before dying.

"Hijo, listen to me carefully. This morning, I... Look, this moment seems surreal, right? But this is truly happening, I think. Everyone, everything is real. Sofi is real. *I* am real. See?"

Paloma emphasized she was real, as if it was her who'd mysteriously traveled back in time and someone *needed* to believe her. But here we both were, possibly in the same boat. She placed my hands on her face.

"It *is* real," I said quietly, the way a child does in amazement. My fingers touched her face, followed by her hair.

"Paloma... um, Mamá, how did this transpire?" And as soon as that last word came out of my mouth, I realized how stupid it sounded. "...transpiró," I'd just said to her. But, perhaps, this was my way of proving to myself that I was truly a grown man.

She sat with me.

"I don't know. I woke up earlier in this bed, like you did a moment ago, with a terrible headache." Her fingers gently touched her right temple, a reminder of where her head had hit the pavement on the day of her accident. "Sofi called me, asked for my help to finish your cake. I remembered having already lived the day, which didn't help my confusion. You were in the kitchen with Sofi, figuring out her new camera and wouldn't stop talking about tonight's party. Same as the first time. Anyway, I returned to bed and laid down to make whatever sense of this I could. Eventually, I decided to play along. So, now, I'm just as puzzled as you are."

Paloma stared ahead while I pinched the skin on my hand. It hurt. I pulled the little hairs on my arm, then the ones on my head. Those hurt too. Nothing was taking me back.

Paloma asked what I was doing. I looked at her hair, but she shook her head as if saying, 'Don't you dare.' And with that, a tiny exhale came out of me. Then, unsure what came over me, other than it needed to be done because we were mother and child, I lunged at her for a hug, one just as tight as the one she'd given Sofía.

"I'm sorry, Mamá," I cried.

"Damián, ¿qué te pasa? You don't have to apologize for pulling your pelitos. I understand if you don't believe me."

"No, Mamá. I'm sorry. I'm sorry. I'm sorry," I continued, burrowing my head into her, using her shirt to wipe the tears and snot from my face.

Paloma pulled me away from her. She held me firmly, the way she used to when I needed a good regañada as a child. "Stop it, Damián. It's not your fault. ¿Entendiste?"

She knew. I didn't know what I would've done if she didn't believe me, so I was thankful I never had to find out. I was still in shock. What was I supposed to say to the living dead?

And that's why her touch had been so cold. She was dead and she knew it.

With my head resting on her legs, she hummed a song in English that she didn't know the words to, while drawing a circle on my hair with her finger, around and around my cowlick.

"Mamá, how do you know this song?"

"A man at work, fan of *los Bitles*, said he loves this song by *Yon Lenon*." I giggled at the way she pronounced John Lennon's name. "Said Yon Lenon wrote it for his son and tells the story of the love he has for his son and the joy the son gives him. He said I should sing it to you. So, I hum it for you, because I love you and you bring me joy. Mi *biuriful boy*. Mi niño bonito."

Such a sweet song. I liked it before, but now it had more meaning. Now, I loved it more than ever and promised myself that if I ever had a son, I would hum it and sing it for him too.

Did she also have a song for Sofía? For Moisés?

"Mamá, does Sofía know this is happening?"

"No. When I stepped out and into the kitchen, you—"

My head shot up. "Let's talk to her, then. You and me. I'm sure she'll understand if it's coming from the two of us."

"No, mijo. She wouldn't understand." Paloma sounded unsure. "It seems it's just you and me going through... this. I'm not sure how long this'll last, so let's make the best of it." She smiled, reached for tissues on the drawer in front of us, and wiped the frosting off my face. Her movements were hurried and rough enough to hurt, but I didn't mind.

"That movie Sofía is recording..." I stopped for a moment, knowing how crazy my next words would sound, but they were true. We were reliving the memory of what my sister had recorded. "...it made this possible."

Paloma said nothing, so I continued.

"I fell asleep watching it and woke up here."

"But," Paloma countered, "I woke up when she was figuring out how to work her camera."

I thought about that for a moment. Whatever or whoever was giving us this chance made it possible for her to come back before Sofía's recording, and for us to relive the recorded present. Could that mean we would be able to continue past Sofía's recordings?

It seemed it wasn't just a time-length issue. I didn't know the inner workings of magical time-travel or whatever this was. I would've assumed we were restricted to the areas that were directly present in Sofía's recording, but Paloma explained that she had sneaked outside already and taken a stroll around the block.

Now, supposing this was a time-travel situation, would it cause a butterfly effect if I tried to save her? All the knowledge of time-travel I possessed came from movies, and most of those made it pretty clear that changing the past never works out in your favor.

Test it. Tell her she's going to die.

As if she was reading my thoughts, Paloma said, "Hijo... I know."

"You know?" I asked, and she nodded. "What do you mean?"

My heart sank hearing her confirm it. "I know... I'm dead."

She knew.

Paloma remembered being in the hospital. Her memory was hazy, but she remembered the attending nurse. "Amaya," she said. "It was a lovely name."

The name rang a bell. Wasn't that also the name of the nurse that had called Xóchitl about Ignacio? Impossible. Paloma's and Ignacio's hospitals were twenty miles apart. Their stays decades apart.

"So, does this mean you're a ghost?" I asked her. "Is this God's doing? A god? Mamá, if you know you died, what did you see?"

Paloma didn't know. She couldn't remember how it happened or the pain she felt while she was dying. All she had was a faint memory of being suffocated and then nothing. She couldn't remember what happened after she died.

"It feels like only hours ago, I was at the hospital. But what I remember is you visiting me and bringing me that tape. Remember what I did?"

I shook my head.

"Prayed. Prayed to Diosito He'd let me see you again. I suppose prayers *do* get answered."

"Mamá, did you know you were going to die? You told me you would."

"No, Damián, I didn't. Sometimes we say these things when we're at our weakest."

Paloma composed herself and cleared her throat. "Now, what happened, happened. What matters at this moment is that we're together. I'm here with you and with Sofi."

Paloma smiled. Her grin looked forced. Then, she covered her face and wept, and not only did I not know why she was crying, I also didn't know what to do about it. It came so suddenly. So, I patted her back. That's all I could think of doing.

"I'm sorry, hijo," she said. "Moisés, forgive me. I didn't ask to see you."

That was one emotional pain I could never fully understand. A mother not seeing all her children. I'd needed my mother, but what about Sofía? Moisés? What made Sofía and me more special than Moisés? Why did we get to see her and not him? Me, particularly, it seemed.

An idea occurred to me. "Mamá, if we're stuck in this, it's like a second chance to do things differently. Maybe we can talk to him and convince him to come, no? Or go see him. We'd have to figure out a way and then I can finally meet him too."

"No," she hesitated. "It would take forever. I don't know how long we have or how far we can go out…Wait, you haven't met your brother?"

"I never got a chance to," I answered, feeling ashamed. "Sofía was supposed to take me to Mexico, but she left me."

"What do you mean?"

"Well, after you died, Ignacio…" I stopped. She didn't know of the rift between us. "My dad picked me up from school a few days after your funeral and—"

I stopped again because anger took over, it boiled in me as I thought of the miserable childhood that followed her death.

"Mamá, I hate him," I cried. "I'm sorry, but I do. You died, Sofía left me, and Ignacio took me in and everything changed." The blasting music on the other side of the door mixed with the sounds of the guests having a good time shielded the sounds of my crying.

"Oh, hijo, please don't cry. None of this was your fault. Maybe if your father's childhood would have been different, he would have raised you differently. After all, who we become later in life is a reflection of our past."

"What do you mean about his childhood?"

"Damián, do you remember that night you wanted all your Halloween candy? Ay Dios mio. Sofi was working and I was alone with you. You drove me crazy, so I gave in. What else could I do to calm you down but give you your candy? Well, after that, I stepped outside to calm myself and your father arrived minutes after. He was drunk and crying. I went to him, concerned, and you know what he did? He opened up to me, told me about his parents. It surprised me because he had never truly spoken about them until that day."

It dawned on me that we were alike that way, Ignacio and me. Like him, I rarely opened up about my childhood or my parents. Xóchitl knew so little because the shame and anger that ran through me always stopped me before I'd finish saying anything to my wife.

"His parents were nothing like mine, or the way I was as a mother to you or Sofi or Moisés. They were terrible people. We could argue that times were different then and parents raised their children differently, but it doesn't take away from the error of their ways. They would beat him for any mistake, no matter how small. His father burned and cut Nacho whenever he misbehaved."

Paloma showed me on her arms where she'd seen his marks.

"His mother hit him too, though not as hard as his father. She would slap him often, and when he needed her cariño, someone to hug him or console him, she'd push Nacho away, saying horrible things like, 'Why did God have to punish me with you? *Con lo que ni siquiera el Diablo quería.*'"

Wow. How horrible, for a mother to tell her child that not even the Devil wanted him.

"One day, when your father was around... your age," Paloma pointed at me, meaning like the child before her eyes, "his parents left him and never returned."

"Why, Mamá?"

"Who knows? He didn't. What's true is your father never saw them again."

I thought back to a high school friend who'd once told me he'd chosen to learn to play the tuba for his music class. When he revealed to his father the instrument he'd chosen, he was surprised to find out that it was the same instrument his father had chosen in high school.

It's inevitable, my friend had said to me. *We're destined to become our parents, to relive their experiences. It's a never-ending cycle.*

After Paloma's words about Ignacio, I understood what my friend meant. They made me realize why Ignacio treated me the way he did and it explained why I felt alone.

Except, I was not like him. I was nothing like my father. I had a childhood full of love, had Paloma and Sofía. I *have* Paloma and Xóchitl. I'm not alone.

You're wrong, my friend.

If we're destined to become our parents, then I'd choose Paloma, always. If Xóchitl and I ever have a child, I would not become my father. Our family would be one full of love, like what I had with Paloma and Sofía. Like what Xóchitl has with her parents.

Paloma embraced me tighter. "Hijo, decades of your life are lost to me and I hope you'll tell me *everything*. But even if you don't, I know, in the deepest part of my soul, that you're an outstanding man and of that I'm more than proud."

Someone knocked, then opened the door. It was Sofía, informing us it was time to open my gifts.

"Okei, mija," my mother said, then whispered to me, "We'll catch up soon. People want to see you. Jenni's here. Did you see her?"

Paloma helped me get down from the bed and led me to the door. "Go on, I need to change into a clean shirt."

Waiting for Paloma, I stood by the door like a scared little boy, despite the guests calling my name and Sofía signaling for me to follow her. Once Paloma returned, we sat near my gifts, and she whispered the names of the guests. Of course, I remembered some: Cecilia, Jenni, even Carlos.

"Mamá," I whispered back, "I'm going to forget most of these people."

She took me by the hand and walked with me to greet those I hadn't said hello to yet. Work friends, mostly, that I barely remembered. There must've been at least five Marías at my party.

"Hey, kiddo," said Janet, our old neighbor from across the street. She wore a Chicago Police Department jacket that her son Richie, a local cop, had gifted her.

How could I forget Janet? Despite the language barrier between my mother, sister, and her, she always helped us. If my English was no help, her Italian was enough for their Spanish. She explained things I couldn't, like bill charges. She'd ask her son Richie to drive us to important meetings and her kitchen was always open for us. Plus, she'd tell us when food pantries offered free food, or would have Richie bring canned goods for all of us. Janet even knew who in Texas could bring Sofía home safely after she crossed the border.

"Hello Jan, how've you been?"

"Oh my. Such a mature young man now. No more 'Hi, Gramma Jan'?"

Shit. I'd forgotten to act like a child. Thinking fast, I uttered, "Did you bring me anything, Gramma?"

"There's the Damián I know, always asking me for something." Janet reached into her purse and pulled out a five. "Here. Get yourself something to eat tomorrow at that place down the street."

Janet continued searching in her bag, mumbling that she had something else for me as she moved stuff around, and after digging through all her lady-purse belongings, she pulled out a tiny box with a blue striped ribbon wrapped around it.

I pulled off the ribbon and opened the box to find a polished Chicago Police Patrolman pin with the initials RV engraved at the bottom. It was a pin I remembered well. It had gotten me out of trouble once.

"I've noticed you playing with it every time you see it. Now, it's yours."

"Thank you, Gramma Jan," I said with a knot in my throat, knowing what it meant for her too.

"You're welcome, my dear." Janet pulled the pin out of the box and, with it, punctured the neck of my shirt. She asked me to not take it off, then planted a big, red kiss on my right cheek. With the back of my left hand, I rubbed it off. "*There's* the Damián I know."

The way she said it and the way she looked at me with a smile, made me wonder if she knew who I was deep down. If she knew young Damián was a façade.

Sofía called my name. She sat on the couch and I knew it was time to open my gifts, so I waved at Janet and went to my sister. Paloma and the others grabbed the cake to replace with more gifts. Bags and boxes and more bags and more boxes.

This was a birthday worth remembering and many times I had thought about it. But as time had gone by, the years and decades had passed and the memory had slowly vanished. Still, this birthday was stamped inside me, especially since it had been my last big one.

I wasn't sure where to begin. With the big ones? The bags? No, not the bags, I figured, because they probably had clothes in them and all kids know clothes are the boring gifts. No. The cooler gifts were in the big boxes and the oddly wrapped ones. Or the envelopes. Those probably had money and all kids love getting money.

Sofía gave me a look to hurry up, but how could I? I was savoring this moment. She reached for a box and handed it to me. Just as I was pulling the Batman paper off, someone pounded at our door. Paloma opened it and a bike wheel pushed itself in. Ignacio had arrived.

"¡Ya llegué, gente!" he shouted as he forced himself in, making Paloma tumble back a step. His right hand held the bike, while his left gripped an opened 24-pack. But case or no case in hand, everyone knew he'd started his drinking already. His tone and mannerisms were enough of a tell.

Our guests weren't innocent of drinking. Even Paloma had sipped from a beer earlier. She'd offered one to Sofía, but my sister was not a fan of that bitter taste and zorrillo smell. With Ignacio, it was different. His drunken presence bothered everyone, especially me. Some guests whispered, showing their discontent.

Paloma put her hand on his chest. "Nacho, not here," she pleaded. "Let's talk outside." And when Ignacio tried forcing himself further into our already-packed apartment, Paloma's voice warned, "No!"

Ignacio mumbled something before both my parents turned to me. With Paloma distracted, he took a step in, but she pushed back fast, shoving him backwards a step.

The music stopped. Time stood still as it switched to the next song, but not before we clearly heard her say, "You're too drunk."

My father's face turned to stone. Not even the next song's banging bass could mask his words when he let out, "¡Pinche Paloma! Vete a la—." He stopped before telling her where to go. All eyes were on him. He hurled the bicycle in. The doorframe blocked its pedal, so he kicked it. "*Váyanse* a la chingada," he told everyone before leaving.

My intrusive thoughts told me to run after him and push him down the stairs. Retribution for all the lies and the pain he had caused, for how he'd just treated Paloma, and for telling everyone to go to hell. But I'd waited too long to do anything. He was way ahead of me and people were standing in my way. I wondered if it would do me any good, though. It might bring me some satisfaction, perhaps, watching him tumble down, but would that change our future? *My* future after Paloma's death and Sofía's deportation?

It wouldn't have mattered. This eight-year-old boy was no match for the ever-imposing and currently inebriated Ignacio.

"¡Apá!" I cried after him, the way a sad little boy would chasing after his daddy. That wasn't me. That wasn't why I did it. I called out to him because once I got in front of him, I'd punch and curse him.

I stopped at the edge of the stairway, my foot hovering over the next step down. What lay ahead? I wondered. Could I go beyond, as Paloma claimed she had done?

Uncertainty came over me. I slid down the neighbor's door to the floor and put my head between my legs, rocking myself.

The door slammed downstairs and Ignacio's heavy steps shook the floor. When I looked up, Ignacio charged up toward me, so I burrowed my head back between my legs and rocked myself faster. My body curled in on itself and fell sideways, the way I'd seen armadillos do to protect themselves from danger.

An unexplainable push or pull forced me to open my eyes and suddenly, I was back to my old self on Ignacio's now-dampened couch.

Had I changed anything? Where was Paloma? Had I saved her? Had *she* saved herself?

The movie was still playing on the TV, showing young Damián opening the gifts that had been in front of me seconds ago.

Had I really been there, or had it all been a dream? Paloma didn't appear before me, didn't jump out from behind the wall, declaring, "Hola, hijo. Ya llegué." No. The place was as I'd left it, semi-clean. And Xóchitl had texted me.

A dream, perhaps.

The VCR whirred, a warning to stop the movie. I couldn't risk the old film getting stuck or broken, so I hurried to stop it. The sudden movement made me feel lightheaded.

I checked my phone again. Xóchitl's most recent text read, *Why aren't you answering me?*

I'm good, I replied. *Sorry. I'm at Ignacio's place. Was going through old stuff and fell asleep.*

She replied immediately. *Glad you're ok. My dad was going to send a search party for you. We called the hospital to see if you'd been back and they said no. They said no one's visited him since you left.*

Not surprised. He's a lonely old man. Don't think anyone's going to visit him... I saw her.

Who?

Paloma. And Sofia.

What do you mean?

There's a videocassette. Sofia filmed it when I was a kid and I lost it, but it was here the whole time. I watched it and I saw them.

Oh. Are you OK? Can I watch it? I won't if you say no.

Yes, but—

It was hard figuring out how to tell my wife I'd traveled back in time.

Her text came in before I tried to explain. *Are you coming back to my parents' soon?*

Not tonight. Sorry. I need to figure some stuff out first. I'll be OK here. Promise to tell you more. Get some rest soon. Love you xoxo

OK. Love you too XOLXOLXOL

That was Xóchitl's signature text at the end. Xs and Os with her last name initial after. *XOL*.

My stomach growled. I needed to get something to eat soon, but first, I let my head fall back, releasing my phone from my grip. My body and mind were exhausted.

What a bizarre and unreal Day of the Dead.

My phone vibrated and it was a text message in Spanish from the blocked number from the night before.

Hola, Mijo. It's your sister, Sofia. Call me.

13

SOFÍA

WHEN I WAS SEVEN years old, my brother Moisés Jr. was born, and I couldn't be happier to help Mamá take care of my hermanito. He was born on May 9th, 1973, one day before my birthday, May 10th—Día de las Madres... Mother's Day. So, technically, he was born when I was six years and three hundred sixty-four days old.

We loved Mamá and Papá. They were always kind to us. We got our regañadas de vez en cuando, like all children do. I hated those scoldings, so I promised myself early in life that I would behave and try hard in school. I loved studying and reading, and wanted to be a good role model for Moisés, who often mimicked what I did. He was a well-behaved niñito.

Papá worked most days, driving a cab around Moroleón, which concerned Mamá because the stress of it could affect his heart. He had a congenital heart disease. Then, for the last month of his life, Papá's health suddenly worsened and my heart broke for him and for our pequeña familia. His legs swelled. His shortness of breath increased. And in January 1979, at age thirty-two, our father, Moisés Alonso, died.

Mamá, also thirty-two at the time, lost the love of her life, a man she'd known since they were children. They'd been friends who grew up on opposite ends of the city. Their fathers had often met up to play cartas or dominoes at El Jardín and the two children would tag along and hang out.

My little brother and I were twelve and five when he died.

Days after his death, I learned that on that terrible day, while Mamá, my brother and I spent part of the day at the city's mercado buying groceries, Papá, who'd stayed home, fell coming down the two steps of our front patio. He choked on his saliva. According to the médicos, they assumed the numbness in his legs caused him to miss a step, causing his fall, which, in turn, caused his death.

Following his death, Mamá, Moisés, and I visited his tomb once a week. We prayed together and talked to him. Moisés and I would leave small gifts where he rested for eternity—toys, drawings, letters, candy.

Months after Papá's death, on Moisés' sixth birthday, we visited the city's mercado because Mamá offered to buy Moisés a toy, any toy. Moisés mentioned hoping to find a Mazinger Z figure, from a Japanese animé that had just arrived in Mexico. My brother loved the show, watching as many episodes as Mamá allowed him to. As we walked searching for Moisés' toy, saying our "buenos días" to each vendor, and the vendors returning the saludo, an ivory-skinned girl who looked my age, approached us and asked for something to eat.

"Want some money, chiquita?" Mamá asked as she searched for her wallet inside her purse.

"I have extra money, Mamá," I said. I'd just bought a bookmark that quoted *Jane Eyre* from a local bookseller and had plenty of money left over to buy the two of us something to eat. "Can I walk with her until she finds something?"

"Yes, but come back immediately," Mamá said to me.

The girl and I had gone off to find food and chatted as we waited. When I returned to Mamá, she was speaking to a man I immediately felt icky about. The moment I noticed his hand on top of Mamá's, I froze. Whatever he was speaking to Mamá about, I didn't care to find out. Mamá waved at me to hurry and the man squinted, frowning at me. Something in his eyes told me he didn't like me. Therefore, I, too, didn't like this man in black. I didn't trust him and a girl must trust her instincts.

"Hija," Mamá said. "This is Ignacio."

In the time I was gone, Ignacio had bought Moisés a Mazinger Z toy and had offered to treat us to some food. Turned out Mamá had forgotten her wallet at home, and that wallet had contained the money she'd set aside for Moisés' gift. If I hadn't met the girl or gone with her, I could've purchased my brother's toy, but Ignacio had happened to be there for the rescue.

FROM THAT MOMENT ONWARDS, Ignacio came into town more and more often, supposedly looking for work. His visits to our house started to become more frequent, every three or four days a week. Soon, his visits became daily and I didn't like seeing him in our home, sitting in Papá's chairs, drinking from his cups. In his attempts to connect with me, Ignacio joked and teased, and I smiled politely. With Moisés, it was a different story. He giggled at Ignacio's tickles and laughed earnestly at his stupid jokes.

Ignacio often griped about how tired he was after a hard day's work, yet I noticed no dirt or sweat on him. I also noticed how often he mentioned leaving jobs early because he hated them. Mamá didn't seem to mind and only shrugged at his comments.

The times he actually carried dirt on him, Ignacio tracked it into our house. He dirtied our dishes, never bothering to wash them or clean the mud left from his shoes, and Mamá cleaned after him. He ate our food without ever contributing anything.

And all he spoke about was boxing. He was obsessed with the Ferreri versus Zarate fight that had happened a few weeks before.

"Paul Ferreri never stood a chance against Carlos Zarate. Put Zarate in front of me *y me lo chingo*. I'll knock him out in seconds." Then, he would teach Moisés jabs, hooks, and undercuts.

Mamá wasn't fond of the violent sport or his choice of words.

"Ya, Nacho," she would say. "Don't give the boy any ideas."

Still, he continued teaching Moisés, who mimicked Ignacio's moves.

Those daily visits eventually turned to evening stays, with him sleeping with Mamá in what used to be hers and Papá's room. What right did Ignacio have to occupy Papá's place with her?

One day, I asked Ignacio why he spent so much time with us instead of at his home.

"Where do you live, Ignacio?" I asked him.

"Nearby, and call me Nacho, hija. Unless you want to call me something else. You're welcome to call me—"

"No!" I stopped him before he suggested I call him something he had no right to. "I asked where you live, Ignacio?"

"Uriangato," he replied, and promised to take us there one day, just not at that moment, because it wasn't safe.

"Why isn't it safe?"

Ignacio ignored my question, but I couldn't give up. I needed to know about his life there because he'd interrupted our lives enough. But Ignacio always kept his answers short.

"Your daughter asks too many questions," he'd discreetly told Mamá one day, but our place was small enough for me to hear many of their conversations, even from my brother's and my room upstairs. This time, I'd hidden under the kitchen window outside, listening.

"Sofía's not a gullible girl. She likes to question things," Mamá replied.

"She needs to mind her business," he followed. But no, I wouldn't mind my business. Ignacio had invaded our home. He'd invaded my family.

THE DAY FINALLY CAME when Ignacio agreed to take us to his house in Uriangato. It was his early Christmas gift to us, he claimed. Our first one without Papá. Mamá asked that it be the following Sunday since that was when Moisés and I had the most free time.

Ignacio's house was a small turquoise place with red metal bars on the windows and a red door. It had a black metal fence and a red gate that only spanned the front of the house, which made little sense to me. The other houses were far enough apart, unlike the connected houses where we lived. Ten of our houses could fit between Ignacio's house and the next one, so why put only part of a fence there?

"This is my home," he claimed. "The one I grew up in. The one my parents—" He stopped himself. His fingers slipped away from my mother's and he pulled out the keys to let us in.

The inside of his place was clean. *Too clean*, I suspected, considering Ignacio's indolent way at our place. I found it odd that there was a rag doll lying on his kitchen table.

"You have kids here?" I asked.

"Oh, no. Well, others were here a few days ago. They must've forgotten to take that with them."

"You have no photos," I murmured. It was as if he'd lied about the house being his and was only playing it off as his own. But he had a key, which was weird.

A small white dog with a mischievous grin was barking outside, interrupting my observations, and alerting everyone of his presence.

"You have a perrito?" My suspicions turned to excitement after seeing the dog. It scurried to the house's entrance, extended one of its little paws toward the house, then back out. In. Out. In. Out. Moisés and I giggled. The dog dropped to the ground and rolled itself into a ball.

"Mami, mira," I said. "It's like a little snowball."

"His name's Guasón, hija," Ignacio said.

Ugh. I hated when he called me "hija." His words were like nails scratching on a chalkboard and they made my smile disappear. I looked to Mamá, who gave Ignacio a scornful look, but he disregarded her.

"Like that clown in those superhero books you children like," he explained. "He's a little travieso."

Moisés asked Mamá to go outside to play with Guasón, but it was Ignacio who answered for her. "Go play outside, both of you. I'm going to talk to your mother for a moment."

"Not even a minute." Mamá said, unable to hold in her laughter, and it was Ignacio that time that gave her a scornful look. She tapped on his chest, then gestured with her head for us to step out.

Moisés and little Guasón couldn't get enough of each other, and I loved every moment of watching them play, laughing when my hermano ran one way, leaving a trail of dust behind, like in Looney Tunes. He was like the roadrunner, and the dog chased after him like the coyote, minus the accidents. When Moisés hid behind the house, Guasón's short tail wagged in anticipation of his return. "¡Cuidado!" I warned when Moisés, having not seen the playful dog, almost stepped on him, which happened more than once.

A woman and two children drew closer to us. Dirt and rocks crunched as she neared, yanking her children to hurry. Guasón ran away. "Who are you?" she asked, and though I feared her authoritative demeanor, I knew we'd trespassed on her home. That's when it hit me why Ignacio had left no trail of this other family inside the house.

"I'm Sofía. That's my hermano, Moisés. We're here with our mother and Ignacio."

"¡Hijo de puta! Why the fuck is he in there with her? Niños, stay here with this niña." The woman barged into the house and yelled for Ignacio.

Dios, I couldn't miss this, watching Ignacio be embarrassed and belittled by this woman, who'd just caught him *con las manos en la masa*, as they say. The children and I peeked through the semi-open red door. Ignacio stormed out of a room, tripping as he zipped up his pants. I managed a chuckle.

Mamá rushed out after and wouldn't look at the woman. "Discúlpeme, señora," she said, her tone shameful like mine was after one of Mamá's regañadas. Mamá gazed up at the door and when she saw us watching, said, "I... I didn't know he had a family." I wasn't sure if that was directed at us or the woman. Mamá grabbed Moisés and me by the wrists, avoiding eye contact with us or the people in the turquoise house behind.

On the bus back to Moroleón, I asked about the woman.

"I don't know, mija," Mamá said. Moisés sat on her lap, his head on her chest, napping. "I've never met her."

"Do you think that was his wife?"

"No sé. He said nothing about having a wife or kids. You know how he is. We ask him anything and he keeps his answers short or changes the subject."

I looked away from Mamá, feeling embarrassed for her, then angry that she'd involved herself with a married man, or that she hadn't answered my questions completely or confirmed my suspicions. Instead, I observed the people walking the streets, people going in and out of the clothing shops, who ate food by the carrito vendors. When I heard my mother sniffle, my anger turned to sorrow.

"He said he only had me," she said. "I believed him."

"You have me, Mamá. You'll always have me." My head rested on my mother's arm.

"I know, mi niña." Paloma put her arm around me and held us closer.

Mamá later confirmed that the woman was, in fact, Ignacio's wife. Apparently, the wife forced Ignacio to give her our phone number and called Mamá while Moisés and I were in school the next day, to warn her about Ignacio's ways. Her name was Teresa and the children were theirs. She'd had enough of Ignacio's unfaithfulness, for he'd been a man of affairs as far back as Teresa could remember. Between that and Ignacio contributing almost nothing to Teresa and their family, she had had enough. The fact that the children had witnessed the philanderer in their home with another woman was the final twist of the knife. Teresa later left for Mexico City with her children, never to see Ignacio again.

Despite Teresa's warnings, and much to my disappointment, Mamá continued her relationship with Ignacio.

She warned him to change his ways, and he did... temporarily. Ignacio had found steady work as a carnicero. He contributed more around the house, bought food for us and school essentials for Moisés and me. He became Mamá's handyman, fixing minor things around the house. In Mamá's eyes, I believed, she saw Ignacio as a role model for Moisés. She'd urge Ignacio and Moisés to spend time together.

But something deep inside of me, in my gut, in my soul, told me he hadn't truly changed. And a girl must trust her instincts, no? When Mamá asked him for favors, his complaining slowly increased, gradually turning into an outright refusal to help her. He gave us less and took more from us: less food, less fixing, less attention to Moisés. And though we believed he'd not cheated on Mamá since Teresa, he'd stare at other women, often following them for a better look, always excusing himself to find a bathroom, or buy something at a tiendita, or pick up something he'd find, but always going in whatever direction the women had gone.

NOVEMBER CAME AND IT would be our second Christmas without Papá. Ignacio had plans.

"Vamos, Paloma," he begged Mamá from the living room one morning before we left for school. "A compa I worked with said there's lots of work up north in Chicago." I'd been finishing my milk. Moisés gave no sign he'd heard, so I carefully glided my feet on our cold cement floor and peeked. Ignacio caught me eavesdropping. He stopped his pleading and told Mamá to think about it.

Promising myself not to say anything to Moisés until I had the facts, I couldn't concentrate in school. Walking home with Moisés after school, halfway down our block, I couldn't hold it in anymore. I told my brother what I'd heard. Mamá was leaving us.

"Why? Where's she going?"

"She's going up north. I heard Ignacio tell Mamá this morning that he wants her to go with him."

"Why is she leaving us?" Moisés asked with a trembling voice. He sat on the ground and I joined him.

"I don't know, but whatever happens, I'll take care of you," I assured my hermanito.

THE NEXT MONTH, I stopped going to school. Instead, I got work as a seamstress at a shop owned by a friend of Papá's. The friend hadn't seen me in a long time, so he believed me when I told him I was fifteen, which was the minimum age he required to work with him. I wasn't. I wouldn't be fifteen for another few months, but I needed the work to help mamá with expenses, since Ignacio gave her nothing. Plus, if she was leaving, I needed to take care of my brother somehow.

I never wanted to stop learning, though, so I saved some of my earnings for books. I loved Miguel de Cervantes, Jane Austen, Charlotte Brontë, Paulo Coelho, and Federico García Lorca.

With Christmas approaching, I was also setting more money aside to buy Mamá and Moisés gifts and that excited me. Though Mamá and Papá were not extravagant gift givers, for we were rather poor, they bought what they could for Navidad, Día de los Reyes, birthdays, and more. Last Christmas, our first one without Papá was not the same as before. Worse than not the same. So, I'd hoped to bring a little more joy to this one.

But my excitement vanished fast.

It turned out Mamá, now pregnant, had decided to go up north with Ignacio. She argued she could barely afford to take care of Moisés and me; that the little money she'd had after Papá's death was running low. She'd never worked, but a few months back, after realizing money was tight, she had begun earning money while Moisés and I were in school, doing minor cleaning jobs at stores and the mercado. But not even her earnings and my contributions were enough to cover our expenses.

"But Mami, what if I work—"

"Mija, you're already doing more than enough. If I go with Nacho, I'm sure we'll be better off. We can send you money. You can stop going to work and go back to school. He said there's plenty of work there, said he'll make sure we send you money."

"Mamá, why do you believe him? Ignacio barely holds on to his job now. He helps you less now, contributes almost nothing. Now he wants to take you away from us. What if you get lost over there? What if you can't cross? Or you get kidnapped? Killed? Mamá, we could lose you forever."

"Sofi, Nacho said it'll be—"

"And assuming you make it there safely, you don't know anyone. Everyone we know is here. What about Moisés?" My voice quivered. "Mamá, are you sure you want to do this?"

"Yes, mija, I trust Ignacio."

Her words meant nothing to me. "You've said that before. Why?"

"I... Because... He... He's been here, hija. Since your father died."

"Sí, Mamá, he's been here with you, but not *for* you. You're convenient for him. This place is convenient for him."

Refusing to hear my mother anymore, or continue to argue, I walked away.

In my room, I sat on the chair next to my bed, holding Gabriel García Márquez's *Cien años de soledad* to read, but the words on his pages made no sense to me. My mind was elsewhere, concerned for Mamá and our future. I lay on the bed and read the same passage over and over, something about death and separation, but as much as I wanted to understand it, I couldn't. My mind went back to my efforts to convince Mamá to stay. There would be no winning. Mamá would still shoot my words down; if not her, certainly Ignacio.

Why was she so set on Ignacio? Had Mamá considered taking us, her children, too? That's what we were, Moisés and I. We were her children. Me, not even a quinceañera. Had she thought me mature enough to raise myself and my little brother?

And what about our other family members? Our other aunts and uncles. Mamá's cousins. Papá's brothers. We hadn't even talked about them. Would they step up as the true padrinos and madrinas that some of them were to Moisés and me? Would they take us in, as they had promised Mamá and Papá, if something happened to them?

What about Mamá's sister in California? Tía Soledad. If Mamá and Ignacio were going to cross the border, had they considered going to her? San Clemente, California, seemed closer than Chicago. It would be less of a risk for Mamá.

Mamá entered my bedroom, interrupting my thoughts. Vicente Fernandez's *Ya me voy para siempre* played downstairs. When he sang never to return, those lyrics hit harder when I realized we could lose our mother forever if she embarked on this journey. I couldn't bear to have her see me cry, so I turned away from the door.

"Hija," Paloma calmly said.

"Call us and write to us. And don't forget us," I said through sobs. "But come back, please. I want to meet our new hermanito."

"I don't know how easy it'll be to return, but you'll meet him. I promise."

DECEMBER 12, 1980, WAS forever marked in my memory. The date because it's the day of Our Lady of Guadalupe, and the year because that's when Paloma left.

Arrangements had been made. One of Papá's brothers, Tío Beto, would care for Moisés and me. Our house would remain empty, though available for Moisés and me whenever we wanted to be there. Tío Beto would check on the place until we could fully occupy it on our own.

Moisés and I accompanied Mamá to our church by El Jardín to pray to the Virgencita Morena. Then, we ate and played *Escondidas*. Hide and Seek. Before the sun went down, we returned home. Ignacio and a stranger that would drive them to Mexico City were there waiting for Mamá.

"What's going to happen after Mexico City?" I asked her.

Mamá said she didn't know and the man said that someone else would take them to the border. "God be with them," the stranger said.

"What's God going to do?"

Mamá's hand clutched my shoulder. "Hija, we just prayed—"

I shrugged her off. "God didn't save Papá when he fell down the steps."

The man ignored me, jumping onto the truck's cargo bed and shoving the bags in the back. Mamá knelt in front of Moisés and me, hugged us, blessed us, and kissed us. Ignacio extended his arms at me. Was he really expecting me to hug him? I stepped back, holding Moisés close to me.

"Vámonos," Ignacio said coldly. Mamá followed Ignacio into the man's truck.

December 12, 1980, was forever marked in me. It was the day my mother left and I wouldn't see her again until four years later. For Moisés, it was the last day he saw Paloma alive.

14

DAMIÁN

NOVEMBER 03, 2022

S OFÍA'S VOICE HADN'T CHANGED. It was as if I'd last spoken to her days ago. At the same time, it was a stranger who spoke to me over the phone.

Listening to her story, learning about my family through her experiences, I let the tiny pieces of the concha I'd bought from the nearest panadería fall into my coffee; the sugar topping sweetened the drink's bitterness. Before our call, I'd made the trip out for sweet Mexican bread, after discovering Ignacio's stale pan dulce in an open bag near the kitchen sink.

After learning about my parents' move to the U.S., I asked about her deportation. Sofía explained that after arriving in Moroleón, she returned to work as a seamstress at her first job. Between what she saved from her earnings there and the money she'd saved at our old apartment—money Cecilia had sent her—Sofía opened a bookshop at El Jardín. *Librería PaloMo*, a portmanteau honoring our mother and her father. Despite the loves she'd lost—Mamá, her Papá, me—, her love of books remained.

And of current loves, Sofía spoke of her husband, Ángel, and their two children: a now seventeen-year-old son, Daniel, named after her father, and a thirteen-year-old daughter named Paloma.

"Daniel was Papá's middle name," she said. "Moisés Daniel."

I never knew that. Little Paloma's name, no explanation was necessary. I held no tear upon hearing her say that name.

"What about Moisés?" I asked.

"That man will never marry." She laughed, and I followed. "He's got his novias, though, ever the romantic."

God, I hoped he'd not taken after Ignacio, considering their history.

Moisés was a welder and Ángel worked for him. Sales, mostly. That's how Sofía and Ángel had met. Some twenty years back, she'd dropped off tools Moisés needed at his shop and Ángel received them.

"When are you coming back?" I cut Sofía off. Not that I wasn't interested in learning about Ángel or Moisés; I was, and was pretty sure there'd be plenty of phone calls to know more. No, what I wanted was to see her. My sister. The woman who should have taken over Paloma's role after her death. And my hope was she'd answer "soon," or "on the next flight" even.

"Sorry," she said, confirming the answer I'd suspected. "I can't. *We* can't yet. It hasn't been an easy process."

That I understood, from the countless immigrants I had helped. "Oh. Didn't know you've been trying?"

"We'd hoped to surprise you. We're still trying. There *is* a glimmer of hope, though. Last I spoke to our attorney, he said that it looks like we may finally get a tourist visa. And our plane ticket is ready, already paid for and everything." Sofía paused. "Ay Dios, I'm just a little nervous about flying again. Si Dios quiere, we'll see each other soon. How about you? When are you coming? It'll be easier for you."

"I don't know. I've never traveled more than the four hours it takes to get from Cincinnati to here. Plus, I don't know anyone there."

"You know me and there are so many tíos and primos that want to meet you. Moisés and I can take you to see Mamá. Everyone here is very nice. El Jardín is beautiful and Dani and Palomita know the best places to eat. You'll love it. We'll buy your tickets."

Panicking on the inside, I told Sofía I'd talk it over with Xóchitl.

Then I told Sofía about the movie. She gasped.

"You have it now? I—I thought we lost it forever. Where was it?"

"At Ignacio's house. I visited him at the hospital yesterday and after, I stopped here. Went through his old things and found it. Also, I found your letters." That last part, I whispered.

She whispered back, "my letters?" And I nodded to confirm, not that she could see me do it.

"I wrote to you, Damián, even after you were gone from our old place. Not knowing anything about you, I wrote to Cecilia. She wrote back saying you were living with your father, but she didn't know where he lived. So, I stopped writing."

How had Ignacio gotten a hold of those letters? Had he gone back to our place without my knowledge? Had he had our mail forwarded to us? How? I couldn't remember seeing those letters in our mailbox.

"Sofi, how did you find me?" I asked instead, knowing there'd be no immediate answer to the mystery of the letters appearing at Ignacio's.

"The kids helped me look for you on the internet. On social media. You're very difficult to find."

Yeah, I keep a low profile.

"Then, I found you in Ohio. I wasn't sure if that was you, but you look so much like your father, and when I saw Mamá in you, I figured it *was* you. When I read that you help people, I remembered how you loved helping others, and I *knew* it was you. I messaged you, but got no response. Afterwards, I found the company you work for and emailed them, but no one replied."

Except they *had* told me. They had forwarded Sofía's email to me, but upon reading her name, I thought it was some kind of sick joke. Or a scam. So, I deleted the email.

"Yesterday, I found Xóchitl. I recognized you in her photos. I messaged her, explained who I was and that I'd been trying to get a hold of you. She said she would tell you."

Xóchitl knew? Why hadn't she said anything?

"Xóchitl messaged me shortly after learning about your father being hospitalized. She said she didn't know what would happen if your father died and was afraid that you'd have no closure with him. Between us losing Mamá and you losing me, you'd have no other family besides her. Maybe it would have been best if she'd told you we'd been in contact, but Xóchitl thought it better if I alone reached out to you. With the sudden news of Ignacio's hospitalization and having to see him, my coincidental appearance could be the light to Ignacio's darkness. And believe me, talking to you fills a light in me, too, mijo. It fills my heart with joy. So, your wife pretended to not know. She preferred not to meddle, let you figure things out first. Xóchitl gave me your number, but said to text you first."

I said nothing for a few seconds that seemed eternal in order to process her explanation; Xóchitl's reasoning, according to Sofía. Once I felt ready, I moved on to talk about our mother. I asked if she'd seen Paloma. Hoped that in some way, Sofía had some kind of miraculous encounter with her, like I had. Sofía replied that she thought about her often, especially lately. I told her I'd been thinking about our mother too.

Wondering what to touch on next—because that's how it is, right? You have so many questions and so much to say, but in the moment, you forget it all—I played with my phone's app icons, opening them and then closing them. Killing time... and my phone battery.

"Sofi, I need to know something," I finally said. "What happened the day you left me?"

"Mijo, you don't know? It was your father. Ignacio's the reason they deported me."

My phone slipped out of my hand, but I reacted fast enough to catch it before it fell into the coffee the way the concha bits had. *Why, Ignacio?* How could things get worse with him?

"After your birthday party, your father visited more often, always insisting that you stay with him. A day. Two. A week, even. But Mamá and I refused, especially since his drinking had worsened. The day of Mamá's wake, Ignacio approached me and asked the same thing. He bullied me, threatening to do whatever it took to have you, but I stood strong against his threat. He insisted he was your father and I had Moisés. 'Why don't you bring him?' he asked, as if it was the easiest thing. 'I don't have anyone,' he claimed. I told your father that I'd promised Mamá that if anything ever happened to her—and, God, we never thought it would actually happen—I would take care of you, raise you.

"After burying Mamá here in Mexico, becoming your legal guardian was next on the list, but I hadn't gotten there yet because of what happened. So, I lied to your father. Told him I'd been speaking to a lawyer and I saw the surprise in his face. He said nothing. Then, you came over.

"A few days later, the raid happened while you were in school. My documents, the ones I was going to use to go to Mexico and come back, they were at the apartment. I had never needed them when I was at work. That day had been no different. I argued with them, told them you were alone, but they wouldn't listen. So, I gave them your father's phone number. I'm sorry, Damián."

Sofía paused. I heard her sniffling.

"I was so stupid," she continued, her tone now softer. "I couldn't think straight. God, why didn't I give them Ceci's number? Handing you to your father right away haunts me still. Forgive me, Dami."

Sofía needed no forgiveness on my part. And if she did, I'd forgive her a million times over. It wasn't her fault Paloma died, or the raid that happened. Or that in her despair, she had felt like there was no other choice but to give in to my father. Desperation can do that, force you to surrender.

And Cecilia, what would she have done? Would she have been any luckier against my father?

My heart broke for my sister and I could do nothing to hold her close, like she'd done for me when I was a child.

"Sofi," I said, thinking of Ignacio. "You said he was the reason you got deported. How do you know it was my father?"

"While in custody, they allowed me to dial someone, so I called him. After hearing my voice, the first thing he said was, 'I *told* you I'd do whatever it took to have him.'"

15

I GNACIO HAD CALLED THE raid.

Ignacio had taken Sofía away from me. Not only that, but he had separated other families, all because Sofía wouldn't give me up without a fight.

After our call, my mind wouldn't stop replaying my sister's words. I remained seated in the kitchen, staring blankly at the wall, still playing with my coffee that was now cold. With every swirl of my spoon in it, her words repeated. Like winding a music box.

Ignacio, how could you do that? To us? To them? I thought. *They were like you. Came here like you. Had homes and families, like you.*

Swirl. Swirl. Swirl.

My resentment only grew the more I thought about what she'd said and what he'd done to those people, all for his selfish reasons.

Swirl. Swirl. Swirl. Clink. Clink. Clink.

The more I swirled the spoon in the coffee, the more it hit the inside of the mug. The more the spoon hit, the more I hurt, and the more fury built up inside me.

That day, Ignacio hurriedly picked me up from school, ripping me away from my home and my friends. He also ripped Sofía from me. Because that's what he did: take, take, take, without giving anything back.

And what did he have to show for it all? Nothing. The old man ended up alone.

I had once been a joyous yet distraught child, but he took that too. He took my identity, the core of who I was. After he took me in, I kept to myself, mostly. I became reserved with most people.

I kept moving the spoon, no longer going in circles, just letting it hit the walls of the mug without paying attention to the spills I was making on the table. Instead, I thought about how I had shut Xóchitl out time and time again whenever she had asked about my past life. It wasn't fair, especially when she'd been so open about hers with me. Lovers do that, confide in each other. They trust each other. Perhaps I hadn't trusted her enough to fully confide in her, but she had trusted me and I had felt ashamed and pained when beginning to confess to her.

Who I became was all Ignacio's fault.

Without a second thought, I grabbed the coffee mug and hurled it across the kitchen. It smashed into pieces when it hit the patio door's glass. A new cracked window was born at Casa Ignacio.

Back in the living room, I dropped down onto the couch to relax a bit and considered going to Ignacio and confronting him about what I'd learned. I wanted to hear him confess the truth, see the guilt and shame in his eyes.

Why would he say nothing about it? Our relationship was already in shambles, it's not like one more stab in the back would've made much of a difference, and yet it did. Ignacio was a coward. He hadn't had the guts to admit to this, so it was odd that he would admit to something bigger. But I was done trying to understand him, for all I knew, the alcohol might've made him lose his mind. More leña al fuego.

Right there in front of me, the movie called to me. Figuratively, of course. My eyes drew back to the VCR that contained it, ready to play with the push of a button. Now, I longed to go back in time and find solace in my mother's smile and Sofía's eyes. Could it happen again?

Tick, tock, the clock above the TV went. Tick, tock, it went, urging me to decide. Tick, tock. Go or stay. Ignacio or Paloma.

Ignacio.

The movie would have to wait because I wanted him.

I grabbed a handful of Sofía's letters and placed my finger on the VCR's eject button. A loud thump came from upstairs, followed by a fluttering sound that drew me away before I could press the button. It was time to find out what pitter-pattered and thudded upstairs.

Heading up fast, I turned around the banister and something flew over me. Startled, I ducked and followed its flight path with my eyes. A white dove went straight for the shattered window, crashed into it, and fell to the floor. Hoping not to frighten it, I slid gently on the hardwood floor.

"How did you get in here?" I asked it, like it would respond. "Hang on." With my palms facing the bird, I curled my fingers as I approached, hoping to trap it.

But the bird wanted to escape and it wouldn't let me trap it so easily. When I was inches away, the bird picked itself up and flew away from me, to the stairs and back, then around the attic room. Finally, it landed and stayed on the bed frame.

The dove cooed as it watched me, which felt like an invitation to sit near it. Slowly, I stepped in that direction. With each creaking step, the bird's body twitched, but it didn't take off. Once I was close enough for the bird to jump on my shoulder or my leg, my body settled on the bed. The bird flapped its wings, but stayed, and I took that as a sign that it trusted me. It continued to coo, as if it was making conversation with me.

"You know, my mother's name was Paloma, like you. And she was lovely like you, too." I chuckled. "Wow, wouldn't it be something if that was you, Mamá?"

The dove tilted its head to the left. It replied with another coo.

"I know. I know. It's too much of a coincidence, but you and your buddies have been showing up a lot lately. I don't know. Maybe it's like Xóchitl said, something about spiritual love."

Coo.

"So, help me, palomita. Should I go see Ignacio? Or watch my movie?"

Crrr.

Hmm. That was different.

The palomita flapped its wings before jumping onto my leg. Its feet danced, tickling me, before taking off and flying towards the stairs, a few feathers leaving a trail in its wake. After the paloma turned back, it headed for the window again and crashed against it once more.

"I guess you want to get out of here," I said, opening the window. Without hesitation, the dove flew out. "Me too, palomita. I want to get out of here too."

Those few minutes with palomita made me reconsider staying for the movie, to see my Paloma, regardless of if it took me back to her or not.

Back in the kitchen, I made a new pot of coffee and poured myself another cup. Grabbing another concha, I went to sit on the couch again and hit Play on the VCR. It whirred harder than last time, which made me worry that it wouldn't work, but it was only a temporary setback. Seconds later, the movie played the next recorded scene.

In our old bedroom, a much calmer setting than the previous one, Paloma tied my shoes.

"You'll see Mrs. Gómez again," she said, combing through my hair with her fingers. "We like her, but make sure you listen to Mr. Adams."

It was my first day of third grade.

Immediately, my eyelids began to feel heavy again. It didn't take long for me to close them nor for the seconds to begin feeling like minutes. Once I opened them again, I chugged my coffee, hoping the caffeine and the drink's temperature would help keep me awake. Pausing the movie, I went for a second cup, before resuming.

"¿Listo, Damiancito?" Paloma whispered to young Damián. "Are you ready to go back?"

My head felt light. With my eyes closed, head resting on the back of the sofa, I mumbled a *yes*.

I felt a sort of pull and my head went spinning. The next time I opened my eyes, I was back in our old room.

ONCE AGAIN, MY BODY was that of my younger self. Vertigo set in, which I'd not felt the first time. It was a form of compression within me, like my mind and body needed time to adjust to their new weight and size. My vision was blurry again, but that I remembered from the first time.

Paloma now sat next to me, while Sofía was recording. In the video, Paloma had been tying my shoes and sure enough, she'd finished the job. My feet swung and the laces' loops with them.

"Are you ready?" Paloma asked again, jubilantly.

"What day is it?" I asked, recognizing the high-pitched voice that came out of me.

"Don't be silly, Damián. Grab your mochila," Sofía instructed, panning the camera to my readied backpack on the bed. "Hurry! It's time to go. Or you'll be late." She turned off the camera and walked out of the room.

"Mi niño. Welcome back," Paloma said.

"Hola, Mamita," I answered with a smile.

Mamita? I couldn't believe I'd just called her that. But it felt appropriate saying it as a child, even if she knew the truth. Plus, in her eyes, I was her little boy. Her niño. So, it made sense. "Mami, I wasn't sure if we would meet again. I was watching the movie and drank my coffee quickly, so I could stay awake and keep watching—"

"What? Don't you want to be here with us?"

"I do. But this whole thing, it's... irrational."

"Strange things happen all the time, mijo. I'm dead and yet, here we are. I know it's so nonchalant of me to say, but just hold on to... this moment, okei?" Paloma waved her hands around. "Now, are you ready?"

"I guess," I said in English and she gave me a confused look. Oh, yeah, she didn't understand English. Well, mostly. "So, I'll see my old school friends today?"

"If we can make it that far, I suppose. Let's see what happens. Hopefully, we can spend time together after school. In the meantime, tell me about Sofi. How is she?"

"I haven't seen my sister since you died," I said flatly.

"What do you mean? What happened to her?"

"They took her away from me."

"Who took her away?"

"La Migra. But it's Ignacio's fault. He made her go away."

Sofía yelled my name from the kitchen before coming in. With her camcorder in her left hand, she grabbed my backpack with the other and hurriedly walked back out.

"Let's go," Paloma said. "Your sister seems upset." She bumped her shoulder on mine, then grabbed my hand to help me down. Sofía's deportation story would have to wait. Hopefully, there would be enough time before the present pulled me out.

What a breath of fresh air it was outside, literally and figuratively. Despite the sunny Monday morning, we wore long sleeves to protect ourselves against Chicago's sudden bursts of cool air. My God, how long had it been since I'd set foot on my old street, Champlain Avenue?

Even though it'd been ages, I knew exactly how to get to school: we'd have to walk to 114th Street, make a left and go down two blocks to Forrestville, where we'd make a right and stay on the east side of the street for half a block. It was a five to ten minute walk, depending on our pace.

With her camcorder on her shoulder, Sofía walked backwards, recording me. Not being a parent myself, I wondered if I'd be just as eager to record every moment of my child's life the way my sister recorded this and all moments of my eight-year-old life.

"Careful," Paloma warned Sofía.

We took our time walking to the corner, which gave Jenni time to catch up to us. She was calling my name. Then, Cecilia reached us, a little out of breath from running after her daughter. Paloma kissed Cecilia on the cheek, which seemed to catch Cecilia off-guard, as they usually hugged. Paloma followed it with a hug for Jenni and asked them to walk with Sofía.

"Wachala," she said. It surprised me hearing her use a little Spanglish, considering how she and Sofía corrected my Spanish all the time. But I knew she asked them to go ahead so we could continue our chat.

As Paloma and I took our time getting to Forrestville, I told her what Sofía had told me over the phone. I had to make a long story short, had to give her the bullet points. There was no time to look at her reaction, though I took a glance and saw how focused she was on my words, rubbing her eyes discreetly, never attracting attention to us.

The girls were waiting when we arrived at Forrestville.

"We don't have all day, Comadre," Cecilia said jokingly.

"Don't worry about us," Paloma replied. "I'm relishing my time with my son." Wow, it sounded to me like a little bit of judgment on Paloma's part, even if no one seemed bothered by it. Paloma looked down at me and winked. "Go on, ladies. Dami and I will be fine."

As the three women continued on, Paloma asked, "Will you see Sofi soon?"

"I'm not sure," I confessed. Told her I'd not been to Mexico yet and that it scared me not knowing anyone but Sofía, who, I supposed, was like a stranger to me now.

"She never stopped searching for you, Damián. That must count for something. Besides, she loved you as her own. She told me many times and that love never goes away."

I shrugged at those last words.

"Sofía said that she may get a tourist visa soon, so there's hope," I said.

"Well, regardless of whether she gets it, go out there and see her. Get to know my land. Get to know our people."

"Okei," I promised her. Looking up, I winked at her.

"So, speaking of love, what about you? Anyone special in your life?"

Boy, was I excited to tell Paloma about Xóchitl, swaying my arms back and forth.

"Xóchitl and I have been married for a year. Right now, she's at her parent's house in Indiana, where I'm also supposed to be. Honestly, I couldn't have made this visit without her."

"Why?"

There were about nine buildings left before we'd arrive at school, so I used my time to tell her as much as possible. I told her about Ignacio in the hospital, our drive to Chicago, even briefly adding bits about how Ignacio had raised me, and my arrest at sixteen. Time seemed to slow down the more I confessed. I wondered if the movie's speed decreased as it played. It was an old movie, after all. The VCR was old, too. A path that usually got us to school in ten minutes, this time took easily double that time.

Upon arriving, Sofía had her camcorder pointed at Jenni, who confessed her excitement about starting kindergarten. She couldn't wait to meet her teacher and make new friends. Sofía assured Jenni that if she ever felt lonely, I'd check on her—I wasn't sure my sister understood the dynamics of American schools, or that we'd be in separate classrooms on different floors. She then pointed her camera at me and asked if I, too, was excited about the new school year.

"Síííí...," I said, rolling my eyes. Something inside me urged me to throw myself at her and hug my sister. As I held her tightly, I felt pained about what Ignacio had done to her, realizing this version of Sofía had not yet encountered the consequences of his horrid actions. Sofía had no idea what was to come in only a couple of months.

"I love you too, mijo. Now go tell Mamá you'll see her later. And listen to your teacher!"

Paloma knelt in front of me, blessed me with the sign of the cross, and kissed my head.

"Adios," I said to her.

"No!" she said with authority. There was a little rasp in her voice. "Don't say that." God, how stupid of me. "We'll see each other soon, Damián. ¿Va?"

Of course, I nodded. Not expecting it, she pulled me in for a hug, and I couldn't hold back my tears because I wasn't ready to let her go. There was still so much to say. Thirty years without her and I'd only had minutes to be with her, both this time and the last. I shouldn't have said goodbye to her seconds ago. Now I felt guilty.

The school bell rang. "Go on, mi chiquito. It's time." Paloma pulled me away from her, pushing me to go inside. Turning back before entering the school, Paloma and Sofía headed back home, Paloma then turning back to look at me.

Mrs. Gómez stood next to my teacher, Mr. Adams, in front of the school's main office. "Damián, come here, please," Mrs. Gómez said. *Oh no*. Was I in trouble already? My first day of the new school year hadn't even begun and I wasn't one to misbehave. Plus, this wasn't the day I'd transfer to her class. That'd be days later.

"Hey, buddy, good to see you again," Mr. Adams said. Mrs. Gómez said the same, asking how my summer went. I simply nodded. "Good," he said. "Well, before we go to class, there's someone here to see you. That's why Mrs. Gómez is here with me. In case she needs to translate."

My heart froze. "Who?"

Stepping into the office, alert as ever, I waved at my principal before my father's voice came from somewhere behind.

"Hola, Damián."

Ignacio was leaning on the wall, his left arm on the door frame. The dirt of his boot marked the wall. Standing tall, like a true narcissist. How did I miss him when I walked in?

"What are you doing here?" I asked in English. My eyes went wide in astonishment. I didn't remember him being at my school on my first day of third grade, so why was he here?

"Hijo, vine a—"

"No!"

I ran out of the office, shoving my teachers out of the way. I headed down the stairs toward the main door, hoping to catch up to Paloma or Sofía, or run into Cecilia, who'd gone inside with Jenni to her kindergarten classroom. I missed a step after what felt like a sudden shake and tumbled forward, hitting my head on the floor hard enough to knock me out cold.

WHEN I AWOKE, I was back on Ignacio's sofa, short of breath, gasping, and my heart pounding. My eyes examined the room. As I stood, vertigo forced me back down.

Once my surroundings started to make sense, the VCR made its whirring sound and shook. Could that have been the shaking that had made me fall?

Oh no, the movie. It continued playing, transitioning to the next scene. Panicked that it would get stuck or damaged, I rushed to stop it, ejected it, and waited, but nothing came out. The movie was stuck in the machine. Shit. Shit. Shit.

I slid my fingers in and scratched the movie up, hoping to jiggle it loose. It didn't work. My fist hit the damn machine. Still nothing.

A butter knife. Ignacio had used one once to release an old Mexican movie he'd asked me to rent, one of those movies where the women were topless and the jokes were dirty. Faster than I'd run out of that office, I ran to the kitchen for the first visible knife, and used that to get it out, unsure if what I did was correct or not. I didn't know what I would do if the movie got damaged.

Success! The movie came out, though not entirely. As I pulled it out, the tape stretched until I heard and felt a snap.

God, why? I was ready to grab the VCR and pull it off its cables and throw it against the wall, just like I'd done with that coffee mug.

Fuck! This was the one thing my mother had asked me to take care of and I had failed once again to do so.

Adding insult to injury, after breaking the film in two, I'd bumped into the table and spilled my second cup of coffee all over Sofia's letters. Grabbing my phone to avoid it getting damaged by the coffee, I went to the kitchen for paper towels.

Xochitl had texted me. I replied to all her messages letting her know all was well and that I'd be going to the hospital again soon. Afterwards, I looked online to see how to fix the movie.

A shop was open until 5 p.m. Thirty minutes away in the city of Blue Island. I'd have to hurry but needed to see Ignacio first. He was my priority.

Grabbing it all—the coffee-stained letters, the broken-film movie, even the VCR, just in case—I headed out.

BACK AT THE HOSPITAL, Ignacio was asleep, so I sat at the chair a few feet away from him, placing the letters on the floor. Then, I checked my phone for client emails, which had bombarded my inbox. Too many messages to go over. Something to work on at a different time. Instead, I checked the news.

Locally, about a mile away from the hospital, a convenience store clerk fatally shot a 16-year-old kid. According to the article, the boy attempted to rob the place, and while his gun was pointed at the clerk, another employee distracted the kid. The clerk shot the kid in the back.

This was a story that mirrored my life. I, too, had once been involved in a robbery. Like in the story, an unexpected employee had stopped me. Clearly, my fate had been different to this kid's. I had learned a new truth that day, it's when I learned Ignacio lied to me when he took me in. That's when I discovered I wasn't a mojado like him.

16

FALL 1995

S HORTLY AFTER STARTING HIGH school, I worked my first job at a small Mexican store, where I'd work after school until 9 p.m. On weekends, I'd be there from open to close. It was only during my brief breaks that I'd do my homework. Eventually, though, I started to feel like my job responsibilities outweighed my school ones, so I shifted my focus away from my homework. This overworked, undocumented (I thought), fourteen-year-old's grades drastically dropped before the end of my first high school semester.

But my work life was a relief from my home life, from Ignacio, who continuously threatened to send my ass to Mexico. He'd lock me in my room after stupid disagreements as if he thought I was dumb enough to run away. Frankly, with how dreadful living with him was, running away may not have been so terrible.

Since I started living under his roof, he'd forced my hand over the stove fire for burning his tortillas, pulled my hand for a few seconds into scalding water so I'd understand greasy dishes washed better at that temperature, and had thrown away excess food I'd made because 'I was getting fatter in my teen years and would be an embarrassment to look at'.

Then, after I started my first job, he continuously forgot about it. "¿Dónde andabas, güey?" he asked one evening, standing by the front door, holding a bottle of Old Fitzgerald bourbon. The image was reminiscent of El Borracho from the Lotería game.

"I was at work. You know this," I said, picking up the Old Style beer cans he'd left on the floor and adding them to the pile of others he'd not bothered to throw away.

"You live there now?" he said, glowering. "Because I gave you a home. Don't forget that, malagradecido."

"I told you I was working."

"Don't talk back to me, cabrón. I'll fucking slap you."

Of course I wouldn't. That was enough back-talk. Talking back to him meant he'd raise his heavy hand over my face as he'd done since I was a kid under his watch. Though he never struck, the thought of him hurting me was enough to scare me. When I got older and bigger, the physical threats lessened, at least when he was sober. Perhaps he realized that I'd caught on to his games. Drunk Ignacio, however, never learned anything. He was a different man, more stupidly valiant. And his drinking only got worse.

Drunk or sober, La Migra was a phone call away. *That* was the ace up his sleeve.

Before my first job, Ignacio had a string of jobs, each of which lasted him a few months at most. He worked in factories, construction, and restaurant kitchen jobs, never sticking around long. But my sudden employment changed things and opened a new door for Ignacio's opportunism. He took on a new role... as my banker.

"You can't put your money in the bank," he grumbled. "They'll ask you for your papers and you don't have any. I'll hold on to your money."

I was stupid enough to give him my cash pay every week, keeping only a few bucks, just in case. Besides, working at the tiendita bene-fitted us both, he convinced me. Groceries (and his alcohol) would be discounted.

IN MY JUNIOR YEAR of high school, I became friends with Pedro Alcaraz, a short-statured gangbanger wannabe who went by "Aguas" because he was the lookout guy for his boys. The nickname was his idea, and he wore it proudly, though I'd heard others call him Shorty, Oompa Loompa, Gomita, and Chato.

We'd taken an American Literature class, which for me, had been an elective, but for Pedro, had been a last chance requirement to increase his GPA. At the time, I was in the top 25% of my class. At the end of our first week, we received our first assignment: we had to read a book by an American author and discuss it in front of the class the following Wednesday. Pedro chose *The House on Mango Street* by Sandra Cisneros, a book I'd read in my freshman year of high school.

He amused me with his interpretation of the book. "Bro, this is an easy A," he whispered to me. "It's short, it's about Chicago, and there's something about mangoes, I think." He'd spoken to me like we'd known each other forever, but we were just two people sitting next to each other in class. Still, I smirked at his idiotic mangoes comment.

Wednesday came. The teacher called Pedro up to the front of the class. I'm not sure what was worse, his nonsensical interpretation of the book, or the fact that he froze in front of the class.

"Did you not read the book?" the teacher asked with a grave face.

Someone yelled, "Aguas!" then laughed, drawing other chuckles.

Pedro stared ahead at all of us, not in annoyance over whoever had laughed at him, but scared, swallowing hard, letting out 'umms' after 'uhhs.' He looked like he was sweating bullets. I had heard many things about him, about how he always talked back to teachers and clashed with authority, but it seemed people had exaggerated. At that moment, he didn't seem so tough. He couldn't even answer if he'd read the book or not.

"All right, guys, calm down," the teacher finally said to his class.

"Hurry up, Oompa," someone else said, not very loud, but enough for the class to snicker.

Poor Pedro. He was being laughed at, stuck, and needed some kind of help, and since I'd read the book before, I took pity on him and raised my hand. Before the teacher called on me, I said, "He's nervous. Can I go first?"

Pedro's face softened. What a relief for him, it seemed. He walked out of the classroom. Taking his place, I spoke about F. Scott Fitzgerald's *The Great Gatsby*, doing my best to explain the social class themes in the book and my admiration for the roaring 20s. With my job, I hadn't had time to read a new book and I'd also read this in freshman year. It also helped that I had loved the book then.

After class, Pedro was waiting for me by the door. "Dude, thanks for saving me," Pedro said.

"Don't worry about it," I said, hurrying to my locker, hoping to not be late to my Algebra II class, which was on the other end of the school and two floors up. "I'm sure you'll have to make it up."

Pedro followed me to class. "I can't. I don't have time—"

"Look, I've read it. Come to my job after school and I'll tell you about it. And bring something to take notes 'cause I'll be busy working." Once he confirmed, I ran to class.

He knew where I worked because he'd bought chips and soda pop there a few times. That afternoon, he came to the store as agreed, and after that, he stopped in almost daily. I'd help him with his homework and we'd chat and laugh. Even though we took different classes for the most part, we did take a few of the same classes, but at different times. Like physics, which Pedro thought was a gym class.

"That's Physical Education. Physics is a science class," I explained.

"Shit, I know that now. Why'd they let me take it? I got Fs in all my other science and math classes."

We laughed, but I wondered about that too.

All those times I helped him out, I never asked him for anything in return. It was nice having someone around and, because we'd become friends, this was my way of keeping him off the streets. I'd ask him to do assignments I made up based on his homework and he had to show me his work the next time we met at the store.

As it is with most businesses, December was hectic. It was on one of those busy December Saturdays, as endless customers came in for their lomo de cerdo for their pozole, masa for their tamales, cinnamon for their rompopes, and Bacardis and Coronas for their holiday party drinks, that Pedro asked the question that set the whole thing in motion.

He was sitting behind me, while I ran around helping the slurry of clients, but his eyes stayed glued to one spot, observing the cash that went in and out of the register.

When things finally calmed down, he asked, "Damián, you ever take any home with you?"

"What? The money? No." I scoffed because it was wrong. Unethical. And risky. Getting caught meant getting sent away.

He mumbled an "okay" and claimed he was joking, but after a few seconds of me organizing Marlboro and Pall Mall cigarettes in a compartment above my head, he said, "I mean, if you take some here and there, they won't even notice." I turned to Pedro and saw his eyes glued to one of the unopened Camel boxes. "Or take some of those. I'll sell them. We split the money." It surprised me that he hadn't asked to take a stack of scratch-offs.

"No," I said, in a way that showed I was done with the conversation.

"Cool," he said, letting the idea go, but only for a few days.

THE FRIDAY BEFORE OUR holiday break, Pedro interrupted my lunch. He slammed his backpack on the lunch table, carefully unzipping it and barely opening it so no one else could see what was in it. He turned it to me and asked me to look inside. There was a big knife in front of his books. It looked like a claw.

"That's a badass knife," I said, taking a bite of my milanesa torta. My teeth caught on a tendon or nerve. "Gimme. I gotta cut the nervio."

"Shut up. Listen. This is a Karambit. It's a combat knife. I stole it from my cousin 'cause I got an idea."

Pedro proposed we rob the store. Said he wouldn't use a gun in case he got caught. Instead, he would wrap the knife under his sleeve to make it look like a gun. I listened half-heartedly as he explained his plan. It was a dumb plan because, one, it was wrong, and two, it didn't matter if he had a gun or the knife. To be caught robbing a place was to be caught robbing a place.

"You're going to leave an hour early from work tonight. We meet in the alley behind the store, then we go in, disguised. You take the money from the register and that small safe below it, and I'll hold the store owner at gunpoint." He pointed his sleeved fist at me, as if he had a gun inside.

Pedro had accompanied me to the store so much he knew that at that last hour of the night, hardly any customers went in and few employees remained. He knew that on that night, only the owner and I stayed until close.

"Just tell him you gotta go home and finish your homework," said Pedro.

"Yeah, but what if a customer walks in? Or someone recognizes me?"

"Nothing is going to happen," Pedro assured. "We'll wear masks and gloves. It'll be fast and easy, and no one will get hurt. In and out, bro."

"I don't know, man," I said, hesitantly. "I've never stolen anything. Never threatened anyone. Shit, I've never been involved in a robbery or any of those fucked-up situations. Not as a victim and never as the perp."

The school bell rang and I still hadn't finished my torta.

"Look, you told me your asshole dad has been keeping your money, right? But I got you. We're in this together. We split the money. I promise. Just don't tell your dad where you got it from."

He'd remembered, knew what button to push. That was the little push that made me *consider* committing armed robbery, but only if we planned it correctly. And if Pedro kept his word on not hurting anyone.

A little extra money Ignacio would never know about. Just this time.

"I'll think about it," I said to Pedro unenthusiastically.

Pedro nodded. He smiled and with him, his eyes smiled too.

His plan stuck with me the rest of the day, distracting me from my semi-taught classes—teachers were clearly as ready to call it a day for their break as the students. I had hoped he would forget about it, but

Pedro met me by the tennis courts after school and went over the plan again while we headed to my job.

Realizing he was determined to do this and feeling pressured with no other option, I warned him, "We do this once, got it?"

"Yeah, yeah, yeah," Pedro said.

Not having committed the crime yet, I felt uneasy going in, like they'd know and all eyes would be on me like hawks. But I couldn't let Pedro see my nervousness, so I went over my plan—his plan—but I needed to say the words as if it were mine, to calm myself.

"I'll leave at 9:30. The owner should be okay with it since there are hardly any customers. He'll take the money from the registers at 9:50 to count for the day, and that's when we go in, once he opens the register. I'll block the door. You push him down to the floor. Push him away from the register because I'll need the space to take the money. And we get the fuck out through the back. We *don't* hurt him. Cool?"

"Cool," he said.

At 9:30, I clocked out, waved at the butcher—the carnicero—who needed a few more minutes to finish checking his meat delivery, and thanked the store owner for letting me leave early.

"Five more minutes," the butcher yelled out to our boss as I left the store.

Pedro waited for me at an alley a block from the store. Tupac's *California Love* thumped out of the Suburban he'd borrowed from one of his gang buddies.

Man, don't let the neighbors hear that. It might attract attention. They could see us. Recognize us. Me.

In the back seat, behind Pedro, was a black duffle bag with black gear: a sweater, sweatpants, latex gloves, winter gloves, and a ski mask.

Struggling to change, I muttered, "Who's the Man in Black now, Ignacio?" Then, a shiver ran down my back at the thought of him finding out about this.

Go in, get the money, get out. Go in, get the money, get out, I kept telling myself. It'd be easy. Just this once.

At 9:45, we got out of the Suburban and walked to the front of the store, watching from outside, waiting for 9:50, when the store owner would step out of his office. No activity in the store. As soon as the owner's shadow began emerging from his office, Pedro nudged me with his elbow to go in.

Pedro knew what he was doing. He went in fast, rushing to the owner and elbowing him in the face. He dropped to the floor immediately.

"Stay down, old man, or you're dead!" warned Pedro.

I, on the other hand, had never done this before, so I froze by the door, blank-minded despite having told myself what to do multiple times. Pedro, watching me stand like an idiot, yelled for my attention and to the register.

Pretending not to know how to open the cash register, I played with the keys until I hit the two keys that opened it whenever we needed to grab cash without ringing anyone out. I pulled cash out in bundles, though it would have been faster to take out the removable black compartment that held the cash and throw it in the duffle bag. But in the heat of the moment, my mind went all over the place.

Between the labored breathing and the moisture building in my hands I realized that for such a simple job, I'd signed up for too much. I had to hurry, otherwise I'd pass out from overheating and overbreathing. To help, I pulled half my mask off to breathe better, but had to be careful not to show the owner who was underneath the mask.

Something that should have taken seconds, took minutes, but when it was done, I shouted for us to leave. Pedro shouted back, "The safe, güey!"

"We didn't agree to that, Aguas. Let's go."

Shit! I had fucked up. The store owner knew Pedro by name and nickname. I hoped to God that no one had noticed my mistake.

Ignoring Pedro's request, I jumped over the swinging door next to the register, but my left foot caught and I dropped to the floor. Someone's feet approached fast. It was the carnicero with a meat tenderizer in hand, ready to attack. He swung at Pedro, who dodged the butcher and ran away, passing me to the front door I'd forgotten to lock. After getting up, I too ran in that direction, but the butcher's weapon struck near my spine. When I looked up from the floor in pain, the door closed. Pedro was gone. The carnicero pushed me down with his foot. Not that I'd have attempted to run anymore. Then, assuring I'd stay put, his heavy body sat on me. The butcher pulled off my mask.

"¡Pendejo!" he mocked. "And pinche Pedrillo's fast, no?" His hand dug into my right shoulder as he helped himself up and that pain from my spine traveled up to where he pushed on my shoulder.

"Stay down. You try anything stupid, I'll bash your head with this." I didn't have to look up to see the metal cleaver as he clapped it onto his palm. I was in too much pain to look up, to do anything.

A minute or two later, the police arrived. It was just one cop car whose headlights beamed into my eyes, blinding me. The cruiser's red and blue lights circled around the store.

The cop asked if there was anyone else. The butcher told him it was just me now, but described Pedro as well. The cop spoke through his shoulder mic. He didn't ask for backup, but told his comrades to be on the lookout for a young, short, Hispanic male.

"Pedro Alcaraz. Goes by Aguas," the cop said into his mic.

The cop handcuffed me. The butcher and the cop helped me up so they could take me away. I couldn't bring myself to look back, but I could feel the carnicero's and store owner's eyes locked on me.

17

ON THE WAY TO the police station, I kept my mouth shut. At a red light, in a part of town I didn't know, the cop adjusted his rearview mirror and took a long look at me.

"Hey, kid, lucky for you, no one got seriously hurt. Just you, and maybe your ego." *And the store owner.* Would he press charges? Against me? I hadn't touched him. "What's your name?" he asked.

"Damián," I answered with a quivering voice. Avoiding his gaze, I instead watched a man keep warm by a fire at the park yards away. Maybe, after jail, I could join him. Better that than the fate that awaited me with Ignacio.

"Damian," he followed, pronouncing my name in English. "I'm Richie. You from here?"

"A few blocks away."

"You got no ID on you." He sneered. "Smart, I guess. You got no idea how many idiots carry something that gives them away."

"I don't have one."

"Is that right? Why?" The light turned green. No cars approached. It was a tranquil night. Richie didn't move.

"I can't get one."

"Why?" he asked again.

"My dad says I'm not allowed to."

"Who's your dad?"

"Ignacio. Vásquez."

"Alright. We're getting somewhere. You've been in trouble like this before?"

"No."

"Why'd you do it, then?" he asked, to which I shrugged. "You work there, right? The butcher guy told me."

"I thought it'd be easy money."

My eyes watered. Snot dripped from my nose, but my cuffed hands couldn't do anything to clean it off. My arms instinctively moved up, but the tightened cuffs hurt my wrists. They were *tight* tight, sure to leave marks on me. Whimpering, I confessed, "I don't want to be sent to Mexico."

"You got no papers, huh?"

The green light turned yellow. Richie finally took off before it would change to red.

Once at the police station, Richie helped me out of the car. Something dropped, making a flat clinking sound on the pavement. Richie humphed.

"Where'd you come from?" Richie wondered. From my peripheral I watched him study what he'd picked up. He looked up at me, puzzled, and put the object inside his pocket.

Richie stared at me, sighed hard. Asked how old I was. "Sixteen," I answered. He paused for a moment, then asked again if I'd done anything like this before. "No, sir," I assured him.

Richie paused again.

"Turn around. Stand against the car." His keys jangled. "Don't do anything stupid, kid. And, *God*, I hope I'm not stupid for doing this."

What was he doing?

"Listen, it's been a long week and I've had a long day. It's late, I gotta do this shit again tomorrow and I don't want to deal with processing you and all that."

Apparently, the carnicero told Richie what few problems he knew I had at home and explained that Pedro had been a bad influence in my life these past few months. The carnicero would talk to the store owner, convince him not to press any charges, on me at least.

"Pray to God he keeps his word," said Richie. "Now, this is what you're going to do. You're going to walk in with me, and we're going to have a little chat. Most officers are gone for the day, and some are out on the streets. A few probably looking for your friend. It'll just be you, me, another cop, and the lady behind the glass window. So *don't* fuck up because, I promise, you'll end up in Cali."

Richie was not referring to the Golden State, but rather to Cook County Jail. Anyone who's from the city instantly knows it. This place, Hotel California, as it was called too, was notorious for locking up infamous criminals like John Wayne Gacy and the Chicago Seven, and I did *not* want to be a part of it.

"I don't understand. What's going on?"

"Merry Christmas, boy. Santa came early."

Befuddled, that's the only word I can think to use to describe what I felt at that very moment, because none of it made sense.

"Wait, won't you lose your job?"

"That's very noble of you, to be concerned about my job, but shut up and trust me."

Walking into the police station, with his hand glued to the gun on his belt and my nerves on high alert, Richie waved at a lady at the front counter and told her I was his nephew. Immediately, the lady rolled her eyes, as if she didn't buy into his bullshit.

"Want something to drink? Pop, water, coffee?" he asked as we walked into his office at the end of a hallway. I shook my head. He closed the door and pointed to a chair for me to sit, while he took a seat at the one behind his desk. He leaned back and left his mark on the wall, amongst many others.

"You grew up here?"

I told him I'd moved to Little Village when I was eight. Before that, I had lived in Pullman, I confessed.

"How long have you been..." Richie paused, tilted his head, his eyes closing slightly. "Wait, Pullman?" His body shifted forward. "Where in Pullman?"

"Near 115th," I intoned.

"Interesting," he said. He mentioned there was a woman he'd known who lived there. "On Champlain," he whispered.

That name. That street name. Champlain. It'd been years since I had last heard it, since moving to Ignacio's. God, my heart rejoiced, bringing a small smile to my face. How funny it'd have been if he was talking about...

"Janet," Richie said, and I burst out laughing.

"What the hell's so funny!?"

"I'm sorry. Didn't mean to be rude," I said, wiping my face after laughing so hard. "There was an old woman. She used to live on my street, across from me. Her name was Janet."

Richie slammed his hand on his desk, killing my joyous mood. He placed his nameplate in front of me. He then reached into his pocket and slammed his hand again, holding something under it.

His hand lifted and a pin appeared, with RV initials imprinted. Richard Verardi, his name plate said. RV, those were his initials on the pin Janet had gifted me on my eighth birthday.

"That woman, she was my mother, Janet Verardi." He took the pin back. "This pin fell out when you got out of the car. You had it, right? Where'd you get it?"

I told him it was a gift from his mother. He checked the pin, twisted it between his thumb and index finger, by the needle.

"All this time, kid. Here I wondered what happened to this, and a few years ago my mother said she'd given it to you for your birthday. Said how much you admired it."

See, Richie, I wasn't lying.

He fixed his gaze on me. "Hey, I'm sorry about your mother. I remember her well. Paloma, right?"

Yes, you never forget women like my mother and Janet. "I'm sorry about Janet. I remember her too. I used to call her 'Grandma.' She told me to not take the pin off and I haven't, not since then. It's fallen off a few times, but fortunately, it's never been lost."

We sat in his quiet office without saying a word. It was *too* quiet, enough that we could hear every tick of his watch. I didn't know the time but figured it was probably somewhere around 11 p.m. All I wanted was to go home, even if I dreaded being near my father. There was always the homeless man at the park.

"Hey, listen. Remember when I asked you if you had papers, and you said you didn't want to be sent to Mexico?" Richie asked, and I nodded. "That's... not happening."

I had figured that by now, at least until the store owner pressed charges. But that would be future Damián's problem. When he asked if I knew why, I shook my head. "Damian, you... you were born here."

What? No. Ignacio said... Time stood still. I felt it in my face, frozen in shock at Richie's words. The room suddenly went from warm to hot to... to... What the hell? Yes, from warm to hell because that's how I'd felt being under Ignacio's care, like I was in hell. So, I knew it well.

My fingers fastened themselves around the chair's arms, waiting for this cop to explain himself.

"Kid, I took your mom to the hospital before she gave birth to you. My ma asked me to because, for some reason, your dad couldn't go. I would've brought her home too, when they discharged her, but your dad took care of that. Still, I was there to take her home, made sure your parents made it home safely with you. So, kiddo, you were born here. You're a U.S. citizen."

The more Richie spoke, the tighter my grip on his chair was. My mind tried processing it all, acknowledging and deciphering every sentence, and though I understood what he was saying, at the same time, it was like he was speaking a different language. If this was true, why had Ignacio lied to me?

"I'm sorry you had to find out like this," Richie said, his tone truly asking for forgiveness.

Richie asked if everything was okay at home, if I was going to school. I couldn't bring myself to say anything, so I simply nodded. Food on the table? Yes. I would've made a joke that I was getting fat, like Ignacio had expressed, but the anger inside me was building. I hated that I had let my father body-shame me. He had done so much bad already.

Then, he asked if my father abused me. Did he hit me? Touch me? I looked at him, puzzled.

"No," I said.

"You sure?"

"Yes. Yes, I'm sure. I'm good, I promise. He's just a dick." I wanted to keep going and tell Richie of the times Ignacio had threatened to send me to Mexico, of the times he'd placed my hand over the fire on the stove, or the times he'd locked me in my room for stupid shit, or that I'd been his personal servant since I was eight. I wanted to tell him that he'd sent me out as a child even on the coldest of days to buy food for us, or that he'd been keeping my earnings these past couple of years. But I said nothing because Ignacio never hit me.

"Well, I can't do anything if there's no danger, but maybe I can help you. Keep you out of trouble like what you did today, because they sure as hell won't take you back at that store. So, here's what we're going to do. You're going to work for me. Well," he clarified. "I want to offer you a job."

No way. No way this cop, this man I'd known for minutes, an hour or two tops, was willing to lend me a hand. He'd already risked losing his job by letting me go. Now he was asking me to work for him. So, I asked him, "Why?"

"Well, lucky for you, Damian, we have history. My mother, God rest her soul, and your family, your neighbor, that whole neighborhood, there's a special place in my heart for them."

Richie explained that the station got many Spanish speakers, who barely spoke English, and lots of words and phrases got lost in translation. Therefore, he was offering me my first interpreter job. "After school, be my translator. Give me a call and I'll pick you up, take you home."

There would be conditions, though. He would pay me cash. Not a problem since I'd become accustomed to that at the store. It wouldn't be much, but he would compensate me for my time. Also, I'd need to stay on track with my schoolwork. Keep my grades up. Never miss classes. Unbeknownst to me, Richie had set me up on a path to help immigrants in the future.

Richie extended his hand and I stared at it dumbly.

"Well? You want the job or not?"

Of course I did. We shook hands.

IT WAS CLOSE TO midnight when Richie dropped me off at home. Ignacio peeked through the curtain, watching me step out of the cop's car. He opened the door and waved at Richie from afar while he waited for me.

"¡Ey! ¿Qué hiciste?" Ignacio slammed the door closed and rested his back on it to support himself. He was drunk. The place smelled like it. His breath smelled like it. Los Cadetes de Linares played on the stereo next to the TV. He loved that accordion sound. What better music to get drunk to?

Ignoring him, I began going up the stairs to my room, but he caught up to me fast. A couple of steps up, he pulled me down by my shirt. My still tender back ached worse after my body slammed on the floor. I grunted and wondered how soon I'd heal.

"Hijo de la chingada, I'm talking to you. What happened?" Ignacio's foot dug into my chest. A glimmer of joy shone in his eyes as he stood over me, as if he knew he could hurt me even while inebriated.

"Go to hell, Ignacio." Even in pain, it felt good saying that to my father. "You don't want to know. Trust me. You *don't* want to know what I just found out." I pushed myself up with my elbows, but Ignacio's foot pushed me back down. Close to me, by the couch, an opened twenty-four case of Old Style was on the floor. Some of those beer cans were crushed next to half a bottle of Cazadores on the table, others were on the floor.

"Don't call me Ignacio. I'm your father. That means you respect me, ¿¡oíste?!" His foot drilled deeper into my chest. Rage took over his face. His eyes bulged out and his nostrils puffed, but it didn't take long for his demeanor to change.

"What did you do?" he wailed, finally taking his foot off of me and heading to the couch. "What did you do?" Every word was emphasized. Ignacio leaned forward. His hands covered most of his face, as if what I'd discovered worried him. "What did you tell them?"

"I know, viejo, I know what you did." I said, crawling slowly to the door while groaning in pain. My heart was pumping so hard it might as well have burst out of me. His mouth was agape on his shocked face.

"I'm not a mojado, like you said. That cop, Richard, knew my mother. He'd taken her to the hospital before she gave birth to me because you couldn't be there for her. He then followed you home with us because he wanted to make sure we'd be safe. I know now, Ignacio. Why? Why did you lie to me?"

Ignacio's thin lips turned into a smirk. "So, you made a new friend to tell on me, huh?"

"Ignacio, stop ignoring the question."

"What's your plan, eh? What's going on in that stupid little head?" Ignacio's words came out like a true drunk, because, as they say, drunks always tell the truth.

"To start," I answered, "I won't be your slave anymore. And you'll no longer keep my money. From now on, when I come home, you don't tell me what to do. Keep out of my way and soon, I promise you I'll be out of yours."

I wasn't sure if there was any ounce of sobriety left in him, if he even had the capacity to understand me right then.

"You finally have the *huevos* to speak your mind, Damián, but you're scared. I know. I can see it in your face. *Hear* it," Ignacio hissed. "But guess what? You've got nothing on me."

Ignacio paused. "Okay, hijo." Him calling me that felt like the biggest hypocrisy. "I'll leave you alone, but..." Ignacio slammed his palm on the table and shouted for me to look at him. I jumped a little at the sound and at the firm demand in his voice. "But when you need me, don't come crawling to me—"

"Nacho! Why did you lie to me?" I cried out.

Ignacio grimaced before letting his head fall against the couch. He closed his eyes. Seconds later, he was out. His snores filled the room like the aroma of beer and tequila, and I never got my answer.

We rarely spoke after that. Ignacio went back to working full time, this time in construction. He finally took care of groceries for the two of us and paid the house bills, all with his money. He even paid someone once a month to clean the house. Someone like him, with no papers, so he could underpay them. I still took care of the place, though. Old habits die hard.

I asked him for very little unless absolutely necessary, like school signatures. Other things, such as school supplies, Richie helped with most of the time. I felt more comfortable asking him for them than I did Ignacio. In a way, Richie had become a better father-figure to me than my actual father. I'd pay him back, I always promised, but Richie refused my money.

Years later, Richie confessed that he'd wanted a family, but his wife divorced him shortly after marrying him. She had wanted someone who would arrive safely at home every night, someone who wouldn't let their job consume their life. Richie admitted that I was like a son he'd never had.

After the store robbery, Pedro stopped speaking to me despite me never ratting him out. It was my old boss who, a few days after the incident, reported him as a suspect in the robbery. Just Pedro. Just the same as I hadn't ratted Pedro out, he didn't name me and neither did my old boss.

Ironically, Pedro bought the store many years later. A devil on the inside, he only hired undocumented people and paid them miserably. He added payday loans and charged customers ridiculously high fees. Twenty-five dollars up-front for every hundred borrowed for two weeks. Need five-hundred bucks? Better be ready to pay $125 before getting that loan. Plus, fifty percent interest per week on the balance owed if not paid within those two weeks. Miraculously, his math skills improved drastically from the minute he bought the store.

Then, there was the fact that he was selling alcohol and cigarettes to minors at higher-than-should-be-legal prices. He didn't get caught until he sold a case of Remy to a kid with no driver's license. Cops pulled the kid over. One officer searched the car and found the case with the store's address on a label.

MONTHS AFTER LEAVING IGNACIO'S house, I visited him one day because my first landlord was close to evicting me from my first apartment. No longer working or keeping in touch with Richie, I worked for measly tips at a restaurant, plus less than the state's minimum wage.

"Here's your money," Ignacio said, handing me two hundred dollars. "That's all I have left from when you were a kid." He pulled out of his wallet an additional fifteen hundred dollars, then walked away.

"I'll pay you back, viejo," I yelled as he dragged his feet to his bedroom.

"You know where the key is, if you need to come here," my father said, slamming his bedroom door. I wouldn't see him again for twenty years.

18

I OWED MY FATHER nothing. Not even this visit. He'd taken so much from me. No amount of money could ever make up for all he'd done and taken. Twenty years before, I'd told him I'd pay him the extra money he'd given me, but now I owed him nothing.

"Güey, you're back." Ignacio's hoarse voice broke that remembrance. His beady eyes stared right through me. He'd adjusted his body to his side to look at me, but having been so deep in my thoughts, I hadn't noticed him do so.

His thin arm, skeletal almost, pointed at me. He opened his hand as if expecting me to grab it, but I wouldn't do that. Instead, I pushed my chair back.

"Did you go to the old place?" he asked.

How would Ignacio, in his fragile state, handle me spewing what I'd discovered there? The letters. The movie. That I knew Sofía was gone from my life because of him. Could my confessions kill him?

"I did, Ignacio," I said.

"Good."

"And I found out some things."

He turned from me. His body faced up again. "The letters?"

"Yes." I grabbed some from the floor and threw them at him. My hand reached for the movie, but there was nothing. Great! I'd left it behind.

"I'm sorry, Damián. Your sister—"

"Sofía."

"—Sofía sent them to your old place. More and more arrived. I didn't know what to do with them, so I hid them from you."

"¿Qué te pasa, Nacho? Why didn't you just give them to me? We could have kept in touch. I'd have known what her life was like, what my family's life was like. Even if I never went because you said—"

Ignacio interrupted me. "After you last stopped by, days later, I figured you wouldn't come home. I had a crisis. My past... *our* past was tormenting me. But I couldn't find the strength to tell you. So, I boxed them up and put them in your old room, hoping to go over them one day."

"You were going to read them and not say anything?"

"Maybe get rid of them—"

"Rid of them?" I interrupted that time.

"Burn them, I guess. Then, I piled other boxes over them and, eventually, I forgot about them."

"You *forgot* about them? And it never occurred to you, at any moment in your miserable life, to... I don't know... write back and let her know I was with you?"

"I'm sorry."

God, I wished he'd stop saying he was sorry.

"You know, I talked to her. To Sofía."

"You did? How is she?"

"Shut up. You don't get to ask that. You don't get to know about her life or mine." At that moment, I hoped that, once the words came out of me and he found out what I'd learned through her, he'd writhe in pain and just die.

And just as I'd witnessed my mother do on her hospital bed, hours before her death, Ignacio covered his head. This time, however, I didn't dare move. Instead, I kept talking.

"She told me, Ignacio, that you're the reason she's in Mexico. Sofía promised our mother to raise me if anything ever happened to her, but you didn't care.

"Why did you want me so much? Why was I so important to you? Was it because you couldn't hold on to your parents, to your wife and other kids? Was it because Sofía didn't love you that you wanted to prove someone would? Did you want someone, some*thing, any-thing,* to hold on to, to call yours?

"Ignacio, you held me hostage. I did everything for you and you did nothing. You lied to me, you snake. And then you made me fear you, fear getting caught. I was too scared to do anything because I was terrified I'd lose everything I knew, even you."

I got up from my chair, slowly inching toward him.

"When I finally got caught, a stranger unraveled your lies for me. Ignacio, I could have had a life full of love, but you gave me one full of misery."

His monitors went crazy the more I approached him, only stopping once I was standing over my father.

"Why was I so important to you, old man?"

He gasped for breath and I watched, emotionless. It made me think of Atropos, one of the three fates in Greek mythology, who would cut the thread of one's life. If I were Atropos, I'd have cut his thread long ago.

"Mine," he gurgled, his eyes glassy and looking up the way I imagined people did moments before they were gone.

I kept going, that intrusive thought burst out of me declaring, "Die, viejo, just die—"

"Sir!" A woman's voice came from the door, her silhouette blocking the light outside Ignacio's room. After clearing my throat and composing myself, I brushed past her.

The woman, the same nurse from the day before, went inside, and seconds later, stepped out of the room. Turning to her, the nurse held Sofía's letters and my phone.

"Is he dead?" I asked. Looking into her crystal blue eyes made my tensed body relax. She had a mesmerizing gaze, such peace in her eyes. They looked like they could calm any storm.

"No, he's not," she said in a soft accent. "I stabilized him. He'll rest now."

"Then leave these letters for him. Hopefully, they'll remind him of his sins." I turned from her. That peace she'd given me had vanished. "Call me when he's dead."

19

I'D LEFT THE MOVIE in the car's backseat next to Ignacio's VCR. From the hospital, I headed to the video store thirty minutes away to get it fixed.

"My pleasure working on this. It's been a slow day," Jimmy, the old man behind the counter, said with a smile, though his sigh told me something else. He explained he'd probably close his business soon after many, *many* years there. He was a child when his father opened the store back in the 50s. "I was probably five years old," the old man recalled. Now, it was a miracle he had been able to keep the store open this long.

"He started it selling Zenith televisions. We later sold and fixed VCRs, then added DVD players and plasma TVs."

"Do they still make plasmas?" I asked him, making small talk.

"No," he said. His steady hand carefully cut the damaged film at an angle. He was calm while performing his art, the way a surgeon would be at an operation table. Funny, in a way, Jimmy was saving Paloma and Sofía's life for me.

"LCDs came after and now there's smart TVs. It's too much. There's no need for old folks like me."

He did his job with such ease, I couldn't avert my eyes as he ran a razor across the white label with Paloma's name and split the cassette in two.

This poor guy, such a nice and sweet old man, was about to lose his family's business. Did he have family? Wife? Kids? Or just him?

I should've asked him. I liked Jim so much I wanted to feel more sympathy for him. But I didn't ask, not sure why.

After putting the cassette tape back together, he offered to convert the movie to digital at no cost, because I'd "been a pleasure to have around. No one sticks around anymore. Everyone's too busy. They leave their things, even if I take minutes or an hour or two to fix. I call them when it's ready, but I don't see them for days. Sometimes, I never see them at all." He pointed to a pile of VCRs and DVD players that were stacked on top of each other. Dusty flat screens with receipts taped on the front stood on the floor.

"Maybe you'll see me again," I said, offering an empty promise.

"Well, if you have time, my wife and I would love to have you over. She's a superb cook, and it's usually the two of us only at the house behind this building. Our son is busy with his wife and his kids down in Oklahoma. We hardly see them."

"I'd love that," I said with a smile. "I'll let my wife know."

I didn't know how much worse could I feel, especially knowing that once I completed this transaction, I would probably never see him again. Yet he offered to convert the movie to digital, so perhaps we'd take him up on that.

"Your VCR?" Jimmy said as I pulled my wallet out of my back pocket to pay him.

"How long will it take to fix?"

He checked the clock. It was almost closing time. He took a dusty VCR from the many he'd pointed at before. "If you need it, here. You can borrow this one. Sounds like you really want to watch your movie. I'll call you tomorrow and let you know how long it'll take me to fix. Enjoy your movie." The old man extended his wrinkled arm for a handshake.

OUTSIDE IGNACIO'S HOUSE, WITH the car's ignition turned off, just me and a beef sandwich on my VW's passenger seat, I stared at nothing, wondering if that VCR would work the same way Ignacio's had. Perhaps it was the movie that made the magic happen, or a combination of the two.

My phone rang. It was an unknown number, meaning it would go to voicemail. Once the voicemail notification came in, I checked it.

"He's good. Calm and sleeping," the nurse's recording said. An hour or two ago, I'd wished my father dead, so hearing those words, a relief came over me knowing I hadn't killed Ignacio.

I deleted that message immediately after listening to it. Any others would have to wait, even Xóchitl's. She'd been in contact with Sofía behind my back and that secret had still hurt, it was a still-tender emotional cut and I couldn't risk her words opening the wound up, not when that could make me say things I might regret later.

Finishing the last bites of my sandwich, my attention was on the spot by the corner tiendita, where the people had been praying. Had we known each other? Such a shame having lived so close to each other, yet being strangers. Had Ignacio ever said anything to our neighbors about us? About me? Living at Ignacio's, I always missed that neighborly connection my previous family and I had had with the Pullman residents.

A gust of wind shook my car and, along with it, the picture the people had left. The shattered glass reminded me of the shattered window just above me. Checking my old bedroom window, I noticed something was bumping into it. The dove. Or a different one. Who knew? Perhaps there were others that also lived here. After all, I'd already released one.

It didn't matter. Seeing it excited me. I hoped it was a sign from my mother up above. Wiping my greasy hands from the sandwich, I grabbed the restored VHS tape with the borrowed VCR and went back inside Ignacio's house.

This paloma couldn't contain itself, flying desperately from one end of the room to the other, then back, and still crashing against the window. After hitting the glass surprisingly hard without breaking it, the bird picked itself off the floor and continued. Crashed, then up again. Crash. Fly. The last crash was but an inch or two off the glass and against the wall. This time, the bird dropped and didn't move.

"No, palomita," I gasped. "Are you dead?"

When it didn't move, I found myself wanting to cry for it. "Why did you have to come back?" The bird finally tilted its head up, but remained there. Thank God it wasn't dead.

Kneeling in front of it, my fingers gently slid the bird into my palm. The dove's eye moved up and down as if it were studying me, and yet it remained still and silent.

"Are you okay? Didn't hurt yourself too bad, did you?"

The bird finally replied with the familiar *coo*, then lifted its wing, shaking it a little.

"Stay here," I instructed, placing the bird on my comforter, then bundling the fluffy bed cover around the bird and taking it all downstairs, careful the way a new parent carries their newborn. On the sofa, I nestled it on the right side of the three-seater. The middle part would be for me. Making a quick run to the kitchen, I opened a porch window and left the kitchen door ajar, in case it wanted to leave.

Feeling cold, I grabbed Ignacio's long black coat that hung from his bedroom door and used it to blanket myself. I didn't want to bother the bird with my bedding.

I returned to my avian friend, who seemed in better spirits. Palomita pranced on the bedsheet. Before my butt hit the sofa, the bird flew to the TV. Then, to the coffee table. Delighted to see it be the lively bird it should be, I asked it, "Hey, want to watch this movie with me? Meet my Paloma?"

Palomita cooed. *Was that a yes?*

As I popped the movie in the borrowed VCR and waited for it to begin, the dove's tiny feet scurried on the table, its wings flapping. I could feel it behind me because of the bit of air that hit the nape of my neck. When I picked myself up to go back to the sofa, the bird flew back to its spot next to me, nestling in.

"If I fall asleep, *please* don't peck at my eyes, okay?" I requested. Palomita replied with a *crr*.

As my body rested, I felt the shift one feels when drifting off to sleep after a long, hard day. I gave in to the movie, my mind playing the trick-or-treating scene that was playing on the TV. I knew exactly what I'd be reliving in 1989.

THE ARRIVAL BACK IN time was wrong, though. I was not out trick-or-treating at nighttime with my friends, but sitting in the kitchen next to my mother. It was daytime.

"Mi niño, you're not well," Paloma said with such concern as she twirled my hair. I wasn't sure if it was the time-traveling, or the fact that eight-year-old Damián had been feeling this way before my arrival, but nausea turned my stomach.

My body straightened. "What day is it?" With blurred vision, I looked to my mother and then to the wall calendar on my left.

"It's... after Halloween," she said in a dismal tone, stirring her coffee.

"After Halloween?!" I shouted, trying to make sense of the November and December strip on the calendar.

"Así es," she confirmed.

"Mamá, why would you do this to me?" I asked, accusing her of meeting on the day of her accident instead of Halloween. My stomach grumbled because of all the candy young Damián had devoured the night before. Stubborn little Damián.

My vision cleared, focusing on the wall calendar to show a drawn image of a charro holding a woman's hand. The woman sat on a balcony. *Is he serenading her? What's he singing?* The bottom strip did not have any marked or crossed off dates. There never were. Sofía preferred things in their best conditions, even if we'd get rid of them later, like that wall calendar. Knowing what lay ahead for this trip, oh how I wanted to rip that calendar apart. Damn Sofía's rules.

But if Paloma didn't choose this date, why were we here?

"Mamá, I don't remember Sofía recording this day."

"You're right," Paloma shrugged. "But remember, we're not boxed into her recordings. It's possible—"

"No! She... she... recorded on Halloween." I refused to believe we'd gone that far ahead. There was no way I could bear watching her go through her accident again. Unless... unless we changed the day's events. We could change our route, maybe even stay in, changing the day's actions.

"Now that we know what's coming," she said, staring at nothing, "you'll see that it wasn't your fault. Maybe you'll find the answers you're looking for."

Answers to what? I already knew some careless asshole hit her and took off. Probably some easily distracted jerk, like me. What would it matter knowing who hit her after so many years? That fool was probably already long gone. Perhaps even dead.

My body hurt. Bile pooled on the sides of my mouth, the discomfort only growing the more the stressing images of that day ran through my head. I squeezed my eyes shut, hoping for some miracle to take us instead to what played on the TV moments ago, but that only brought my frustrated tears out. They splashed on the table and bounced onto my hand. A knot formed in my throat.

"Damián, do you want to leave me?" Paloma sounded frightened. Why would she ask me that? "You close your eyes when you want to leave me."

Her words hurt me. It had pained me, not having a mother like others still do. Now that I had her, no, I didn't want to leave her. Her shoulders shook gently, like she was scared. She must've known, somehow, that when we weren't together, there was a void. A solitude, I imagined. Nowhere to go until we meet again, or until she finally moved on to whatever came after. Maybe she was right about not knowing what happened in between, but I suspected she had an inkling.

I swallowed the pool of bile in my mouth, bothering me as it went down my tightened throat. "Mamá, I don't leave because I don't want to be with you. It's when Ignacio appears that I go back. He's the reason I'm gone from you."

It dawned on me then that he might show up and rip me away from her again. Although, in this case, maybe he'd be a necessary saving grace before her accident.

I wondered out loud if he'd show up.

"I don't remember him in these moments before. I'm sorry," she cried. "Maybe this is all my fault."

Perhaps it was. On the one hand, Paloma had stated that she had wished for this, for us to see each other again. On the other, I'd longed for my mother. But who would've expected it to be this way? Not me, certainly not by reliving one of the worst moments of her brief life.

Minutes ago, I'd blamed her for our meeting on this day, and if it couldn't have been the recorded Halloween event, I certainly would've preferred the day before, when we had hurriedly searched our Family Dollar for my costume. Or the day after Halloween, when my classmates and I had shared our collected candies. But, though we ended up reliving this wretched day, I should have been more appreciative. Should have thanked her instead of blaming her for our time together.

"No, Mami, it's not your fault either. I'm lucky to spend time with you."

Paloma placed her icy hand on top of mine, reminding me she was really dead. Suddenly, the red of her painted nails shone intensely. Other colors around me became brighter: the aqua from her blouse and the way her green and yellow earrings sparkled when the outside light hit them. The blues, yellows, and purples perfectly dressed the Maria dolls she'd brought with her from Mexico. They sat idly in the middle of the kitchen table. Even the purple and pink colors that made up the tortillero had suddenly grown more intense. Yet, Paloma seemed unbothered by the bursts of colors. She barely seemed to notice the change, except for the red in her nails, which she picked at.

And just like that sudden burst of color had appeared like a beautiful peacock showing off its feathers, a smokiness wafted in. The chorizo she'd cooked in the morning—well, the Paloma of the past—was now cold, but it still made my stomach growl. I needed to eat, even if my nausea remained and I had technically just eaten a beef sandwich outside Ignacio's before arriving.

"Are you still a little comelón?" Paloma asked. I hardly refused anyone's invitations if there was food involved. Paloma giggled, saying she imagined how llenito I looked as an adult, to which I explained I'd been considered obese by my doctor, at two hundred fifty pounds. It was because of Xóchitl's motivation to eat healthier that I dropped to one-ninety.

"What else did I miss in your life, mijo?"

I began to cry.

"Mamá, there was no one there for me at any of my graduations. And at our wedding... well... you should have been there. Ignacio wasn't. I didn't want him there, but you should have been there."

Paloma wiped my tears with her thumb. Her hand moved to the back of my head, humming John Lennon's *Beautiful Boy* before saying, "Tell me about her. Xóchitl."

"Mamá, she's amazing. Funny. What I did to get a woman like her, I'll never know." We smiled and mine was one of those sheepish ones. I told her how we met at the movies. Xóchitl had sat in front of me and her big, curly hair had blocked some of the screen. After a few minutes, seeing that no one accompanied her, I asked to sit next to her, and she gladly obliged.

We chatted during the screening about things that had nothing to do with the ninja movie on the big screen. People shushed us on multiple occasions and employees walked in to check the theater. After the movie, we made fun of the ridiculousness of what we'd watched. She talked about her favorite way to eat tamales. "Guajolotes," Xóchitl called them. We met for a date at a place near downtown Chicago that made them, just the way she liked them. There, she confessed her love of gingerbread men, and I confessed my love for eighties Mexican music, which I played on the jukebox, singing the lyrics to Luis Miguel and Juan Gabriel songs.

"And, well, now we're married and living four hours away in Ohio," I said to Paloma. "There, I help undocumented people, like I used to translate for you."

"See, we were right to correct you. *Entendites,*" she mocked.

I rolled my eyes. "Sí, mami."

Also, I explained Xóchitl's social media job and, when Paloma gave me a puzzled look, I explained the internet as best I could. I talked about how much the world had advanced in the thirty-plus years she'd been gone.

"Like *Los Supersónicos?*"

"Yes, Mamá, like *Los Jetsons*," I emphasized.

My stomach called out again. Paloma stood and grabbed a couple of plates. My head hit the table as I told her I didn't want any.

"Hijo, you have to eat. It's either this or we go out like we did on this day, but I know you don't want to go out there, right?"

Of course I didn't, but I also didn't want to eat. Sometimes, you just don't want to eat when you're hungry. We could do it peacefully in the kitchen, but that wouldn't change the present. After all, she hadn't shown up after our previous encounters. Nothing had changed the outcome. At least right now she was safe. As long as we stayed in this kitchen, reliving this second, she wouldn't get hurt, I believed. If we went out there, it could happen. That car would come for her.

"Well, how about this?" Paloma suggested, putting the lid on the pan with the eggs and chorizo. "Let's go out there. Change our route from last time. Let's revisit our old neighborhood and see where the moment takes us."

Her feet glided to me and she tugged at my arm, pretending to pull me with all her strength, playfully lifting me up by my armpits. She made me giggle, though on the inside the laughter felt fake.

Outside, that sparkle in her earrings was gone. Clouds had gathered and the wind had picked up, reminding me of the true chilly temperature November should be. The street was just as somber as it had been that fateful day.

Paloma headed towards the McDonald's, but I nudged her to go in the opposite direction, the way that led to my school. For a brief moment I felt like the child I once was with her, me walking in front of my mother, jumping over cracks, and letting my fingers run over the buildings' rough concrete. The tiny bumps slightly hurt me, but never marked my soft skin red or cut me. At the corner of Forrestville and 114th, we stopped.

Paloma wrapped her arm around me as I took in my old streets. There were some parked cars and one or two that were still on the road, approaching. Down the street to 115ᵗʰ, a busier street, I could see that cars and trucks were back-to-back in both directions.

A woman across the street walked with her toddler in hand. We waved at them. She picked up her child, pointing at us and they both waved.

"Damián, ¿y mis nietos?"

"No," I whispered flatly, my mood doing a one-eighty.

"Don't you want children?"

How could I tell my mother that I wanted none? I refused to be a father when I'd had no one to model myself after. Certainly not Ignacio.

"Well, what about Xóchitl? Does she want any?"

"She does, but every time we... uh..." My face turned red at the thought of talking to my mother about my intimate life with my wife. I snickered the way a fifth grader would when looking at the human body in a textbook during sex ed class.

"But Mamá," I said, trying to avoid the sex talk with Paloma, "I don't want to be my father. I can't have a child resent me the way I resent Ignacio. If anything, I have you to look up to, but I've barely known you."

Paloma sat on the front steps of the first house on the corner, tapping the concrete, inviting me to join her.

"Hijo, even the ones you admire have their faults. I'm not innocent. I made mistakes, too. I tried my best to be an exemplary mother to you, Sofía, and Moisés. All of you turned out to be wonderful people, better than I expected, but that doesn't negate the fact that I left Sofía and Moisés when they were children. What kind of mother leaves the children she loves? Sofía... my Sofi became the better version of me and, in the end, that's what we want as parents, for our children to do better... be better than us. She cared for Moisés head-on, did the same with you. You say your father ruined your childhood—and I'm not saying he didn't— but...well, I did that to Sofía. I hope she forgives me."

"But you're nothing like Ignacio and I'm not as wonderful as you think. I could have gotten my old boss killed."

"What do you mean?"

Shit. I hadn't told her about the robbery.

I confessed.

"Ay, hijo," Paloma said, and I couldn't tell if her face and tone were of disappointment, concern, or shock. "Gracias a Dios no one died and Richie came back into your life. I'm sure he was the beacon you needed at that time, not that your life's path wouldn't have been a righteous one."

That beacon had been long gone.

There was still a darkness inside of me, a need to hurt Ignacio, especially now that he was in his weakest state. That darkness was urging me to use it to my advantage because, although I hadn't killed him on his hospital bed, I had watched him almost die and did nothing to help. If he had died then, wouldn't I have been just as guilty as if I'd physically killed him?

"Last time I saw him, I wanted him dead," I said.

"Oh," she breathed. "Is that what you really want?"

Yes, I wanted to say, but was unable to look at my mother from the shame I felt admitting that desire.

"You're angry, mi niño. I understand that, but don't let that grudge take over. Maybe instead of wishing him dead, what you need is to let him go."

"How do I do that?"

"Forget him. Let him be. Whatever happens to Nacho, that's not on you. Close his chapter in your life forever."

Those last words Xóchitl had said to me before. "But what if I have to see him again?"

"Then see him. Finish whatever business you have with your father and then let him go. He brought you misery. You don't need to fix anything with him. That's not your responsibility. You don't need to forgive him just because he's your father. Just let him go."

Paloma was right. I considered what she'd just said as we stayed silent for a moment. Until then, Ignacio had never said sorry for the emotional turmoil he'd caused me. All this time, I had been waiting for him to say it, but the damage had already been done. There was no point in agonizing over him saying "sorry," when I knew that even if he did, I wouldn't forgive him. So yes, I just needed to let him go.

Clouds still gathered. The sky was now mostly gray. Fearing our time was coming to an end, I stood and pulled my mother up to continue our journey down our tranquil neighborhood.

"Mamá," I said, holding my mother's hand, skipping the lines and cracks of the sidewalk, like I used to when I was a playful child. "Why did Ignacio want me so much? I asked him and he didn't tell me."

Paloma cleared her throat. "After Moisés died, my children needed their father, so when your father and I met, he admitted to wanting to be that paternal figure for them. Sofi wouldn't accept him, though. She distrusted Ignacio."

"But Ignacio was married and had children," I said, remembering my conversation with Sofía.

"Right. Your father wasn't around for his family much, he later confessed. Before us, he'd lied to them about looking for work, when he was actually just training to become a professional boxer. But lies eventually unravel. Well, he had a shot in Uriangato against someone local, like him, and word spread to his wife. The night of his big match, Nacho's opponent knocked him out immediately and his dream of becoming a boxer died. His wife, after finding out he'd lied instead of taking care of his family, distanced herself and their children from him. Nacho tried mending his relationship with his wife by looking for work in Moroleón. But soon, he found other young men who dreamt of becoming boxers and, for a moment, his hope returned. You probably already know this, but if there was something else that defined your father, it was being a womanizer. So, despite trying to repair his relationship with his wife, he also slept with other women."

"Including you?"

Paloma snatched her hand away from mine and, if she would've slapped me then for my harsh words, I would've deserved it. Her scornful look was enough. *How dare you!* it said to me.

"I'm sorry, Mamá."

"Look, when we met, I didn't know he was married or had children, or of his promiscuity. I never questioned him. It wasn't until the day his wife found us in their home that I knew. Sofi was right not to trust him."

Paloma continued with the same story Sofía had told me over the phone, about Ignacio's proposal to move to Chicago, and how Teresa had taken his children away after discovering Paloma at their house in Uriangato. Paloma claimed Teresa did it out of spite, but, honestly, their children may have been better off without their alcoholic father. The way I saw it, Teresa was protecting her children.

"What happened to his wife and children?"

"Who knows? Last I heard, Teresa looked for your father after he and I moved here, wanting a divorce. The evening she stopped at our house to confront him, Moisés said nothing, so she left. Other than the time she caught your father and me at her home, she and I never spoke or met."

We were so immersed in her conversation that I hadn't noticed the building we were nearing. My body froze in its place, feet away from the fast-food restaurant's entrance.

Paloma pulled on my arm for me to continue. I hesitated and she told me to look at her. "It's going to be okay, hijo. Remember, every cloud has a silver lining."

What *good* could come from this? She and I knew what came after that visit. Paloma pulled on me again. I let out a tiny exhale, a non-verbal agreement that, though I didn't want to go inside, I'd do so for her.

Ordering our food was still my job, since Paloma still spoke no English, even in the afterlife, or whatever this was. For me, I got my usual from back then: a kid's meal with a cheeseburger. For Paloma, a número uno.

Unlike last time, I chose to keep my mother company while we waited for our food, standing over a speaker that played some sort of elevator music. Once our food was ready, we made our way to the tables closest to that empty play area and Paloma continued talking about her move to Chicago. Eyes peeled, I checked around for the little girl I'd met that day. Had she already left? Considering the alternate route we took and the additional time it took to get here, I figured she was long gone.

"Soon after we moved here, your father returned to his old ways. He lounged instead of looking for work or helping me at home. And when he did find job opportunities, he would have excuses for avoiding work: forgotten documents, missed interviews, termination. Eventually, that hope for a better life with him vanished.

"Before you turned four, I needed help planning your birthday party. His response was, 'Men don't plan parties. That's not my responsibility.' He made me so angry. When we argued about it, he stormed out of our little apartment and didn't come home for days. When he did, out of nowhere, it was to tell me he'd found a place to live. Just for him. He was going to leave me and, to further hurt me, he demanded you go live with him. He threatened to send me back home. When I said no, he thrust his hand over my mouth to shut me up."

Paloma breathed hard. "But we still celebrated your birthday. Just you and me. Remember?"

Her smile was sad as she watched me swirl a French fry in the mound of ketchup I had poured on my burger's wrapper. No, I couldn't remember. It'd been so long ago. Paloma gasped for air as she covered her mouth. She looked like she was about to cry, but she didn't, booping my nose instead. I gave her the widest grin, like Lewis Carroll's Cheshire cat to Alice.

"After your father left, I told our neighbor Janet about my struggles and she suggested Sofi cross over to help me. Moi was thirteen. Though it pained me to leave him in Mexico and have her travel alone, I figured with her help we could raise you together and send Moisés more money until he could eventually come too.

"So, the day of the candy incident, after your father confessed the truth about his childhood, he finished by threatening to do whatever it took to have you."

Words said to Sofía during her detention, Mamá. In the end, Ignacio had succeeded. He had won. He'd even taken Sofi away from me.

The soggy fry continued swimming around in the ketchup. I let it go and played with my burger. Paloma should've told me to stop playing with my food, but said nothing, maybe because she knew I truly wasn't a child. The supposedly melty cheese was now as dry as the meat and bread, and a dead piece of it clung to the burger's side. The single pickle slice in the burger irritated me.

Irate customers were complaining to the kid behind the front counter, who wore a fatigued look on his face. Though he offered no apology, he bravely faced them off as they complained about the breakfast cut-off and how they only had so many minutes left on their lunch break. It was not his fault. I sympathized with the kid.

Paloma was still talking, but I'd stopped paying attention, instead focusing on the kid. When she uttered, "tu papá", my sympathy turned sour. Despite Ignacio being on his deathbed, and what Paloma had said about his earlier years, I refused to feel bad for him.

Paloma stopped talking and played with her napkin, turning it into a flower. I'd never known of this origami talent she had.

Out of the corner of my eye, I spotted a familiar face. My attention turned toward the worker again, but this time, it was the smiling girl approaching me from that direction who drew my eyes. It was her, the girl I'd been searching for, the one I'd met in the play area thirty years ago.

"Dami!" Xóchitl said excitedly.

The moon girl from Indiana had arrived.

20

"**O**LI!" HER FATHER CALLED. "Don't be long. We're leaving soon."

The moon girl, as I'd called her, was my girl, my wife, my Xóchitl. We'd met over thirty years ago.

The girl turned at her father's request, giving me only seconds to whisper who she was to my mother, to which Paloma asked, "How?"

The girl turned back to me and smiled again.

"I'm going to find out," I said, and waved at the girl to follow me to the other side of the play area.

"It's you, right?" I asked her. "Oli, you're my..."

Before uttering her name, she confirmed it. "Yes, Dami, it's me."

In the decades between meeting her for a few minutes and seeing her again at the movies, fragments of that little girl had stuck with me, the way the tips of her frizzled hair expanded to touch the slide she had come out of, the way she had shocked me afterwards, and the way her bronzed skin had glistened before me. She'd had enough of an impact on me to be kept in a special place in my mind, and later, in my heart. She'd cemented herself in me in those few minutes, despite the day's tragic outcome, even if for little Xóchitl, it had been just a day like any other weekday.

Xóchitl checked to make sure she was completely out of her father's view before pulling me in for a hug. "Can't let him see me hug a strange boy," she joked. We giggled in sync as our foreheads touched.

Funny how the day we'd met, her name had been lost to me. But it was so unique, matching the woman I married. God knows I tried remembering it, and her father and his mustache. He'd sported his signature whiskers then, just as he did in our present time, though this younger version of Señor Pepe's mustache was less gray and a smidgen shorter.

I pulled away but didn't part from her hold. "How are you here?"

Xóchitl had called me multiple times, she explained. Then, she tried the Saint Anthony's Hospital closest to Ignacio's house. When the hospital confirmed Ignacio's stay, she drove her father's yellow Dodge Neon there, hoping to find me.

"I was a little nervous seeing him and I would've confronted him for you, but he was sleeping. Then, I saw letters on his table addressed to you, so I went to the closest address. Our car was there. I knew you had to be inside the house."

Xóchitl had knocked on the door while I was sleeping. After heading to the back of the house and seeing the kitchen door open for the little dove, she'd let herself in and found me on the sofa.

"And the bird?" I asked.

"What bird?"

"A dove was sitting on the couch with me."

She confirmed she'd seen one by the garage but had paid no attention to it.

"No wonder I saw little feathers on the sábana next to you," Xóchitl claimed. "Anyway, I sat next to you to watch what you'd left playing and then I woke up like this in my dad's car. We were on our way here."

So, the movie had the power to pull anyone watching it... No, that couldn't be right. What if Ignacio had watched it? The magic felt personal. Maybe it would only let those close to me come back this way. If Ignacio ever found his way back here, he could fuck everything up for everyone, more than he already did.

Another odd thing about Xóchitl showing up now was that Paloma and I had delayed our walk, so she technically arrived after the time she had actually arrived back in 1989. Time must not matter in these time-traveling magical experiences.

I told Xóchitl that I would explain what little I knew at a different time. First, she needed to tell me what images were playing on the screen when she sat down next to me.

"You were trick or treating. Is that today? Halloween?"

"No, it's two days after," I confirmed, checking on my mother to make sure she was okay waiting. Her neck craned when I peeked. Señor Pepe was still waiting for their food.

"What did you guys *order*?" I joked. Xóchitl shrugged, wide-eyed and thin-lipped. "Xóchi, do you remember this day?"

Xóchitl shook her head, and I explained why Paloma had brought me to the restaurant, that while Paloma waited for our food, just as her father was doing at that moment, Xóchitl and I had met where we stood. "Before you left, you told me you were heading home to Indiana—"

Xóchitl gasped. "I remember now. My dad had taken me out of school to go to his job."

"Yes! You said that," I said, relieved that she was beginning to understand. Pulling my girl to where she could see Paloma, I said, "Now, see that woman? That's her, my mother."

"What?" she whispered, mouth agape, as she gazed at Paloma.

"Love, that's Paloma. We're reliving the day before she died, the day she was hit. She wished to see her children again, and somehow, through the home movie I found at Ignacio's, I've been traveling back in time to see her. But only she and I know what is happening. And, well, now you know too. Everyone else is living normally, as they did in 1989."

"What about my dad? I... I..."

"I know. You were scared, right? He probably thought you were being your playful self in the car."

"Yes. He tried calming me down and said we were almost there. He meant here, tried to get me excited with a new toy."

Xóchitl paused, as if trying to finally make sense of what was happening. "Oh my," she whispered. "Dami, so what... what's it been like being here with her?"

"It's been... eye-opening. Do you want to meet her?"

Of course she did, she nodded, turning to Paloma. Before introducing them, she needed to clear something up for me.

"Love, why were you in touch with Sofía without my knowledge?" Xóchitl turned to me quickly with a worried look on her face. She squeezed my hand tightly.

"I'm sorry," she said. "Your sister's message came to me shortly before news of your father's stabbing. Everything happened so fast and I figured that if it was all too much for me, it would be so much worse for you."

Xóchitl should have still said something.

"Sofía will still be around," Xóchitl continued, "but your father... How much longer will he be around? You're holding on to so much anger towards him and, between handling your sister or your father, I thought it best you see your father soon. Get some answers. Find peace. Heal here and here." She pointed to my heart, then to my head. "I'm sorry. I was going to tell you about Sofía, I just wasn't sure how soon to tell you."

She was probably right. It was too much to take in at once and that was *before* these visits with Paloma. Still, she should have said something.

"Fine, I get it," I said. "But you have to tell me these things. Whatever the challenge, we'll deal with it together. In good times and bad, in happiness and in sadness. Okay?"

Xóchitl nodded.

"Thank you," I said. "Now, let me introduce you to my mother, Paloma."

My heart hammered as we approached Paloma, harder and faster with every inch we neared. Nervous as hell, I experienced a sense of elation simultaneously.

"Mamá, this is Xóchitl. Xóchitl Olivia Luna."

Paloma's face lit up along with her bright smile. Her arm rubbed Xóchitl's arm. She ran her fingers through Xóchitl's frizzy hair. Her fingers gently caressed Xóchitl's cheek.

"Hola, hija," Paloma greeted her. "Damián's told me so much about you. Estás preciosa." Paloma looked at me approvingly, then said to Xóchitl, "Hermosa, like a flower. No wonder your parents named you Xóchitl. Did you know your name is the Náhuatl word for flower?

Sofía told me. She'd learned it for a class history project on surnames. Well, through her research, she'd feed me bits of trivia, and yours she happened upon."

Xóchitl shed big, bulbous tears that, after running down her cheek, free-fell onto the restaurant's dirty floor. Paloma grabbed a napkin and cleaned the tears.

"Pequeña, please don't cry. You're going to make *me* cry."

I was crying, too. Paloma used the wet napkin on me. She asked Xóchitl for a hug, and when Xóchitl nodded, Paloma fully embraced her like Xóchitl was one of her own. She kissed her cheek. Pulling away from Xóchitl, my mother said softly, "My heart is overjoyed. There couldn't be anyone better for my Damián."

Xóchitl lunged at my mother for another hug, their last one. "I'm sorry for what happened," Xóchitl cried.

"Mijo, are you ready?" Paloma said as she ran the back of her fingers on Xóchitl's cheek again. With a crack in my voice, I said I was ready.

As if on cue, Señor Pepe approached us, calling for his daughter to leave. "Hola, niño," he said to me. Surprised at how he directed himself to me, I said nothing. Just waved. How did he know to call me that?

"Let's *go*, señorita," he urged his daughter. Hadn't he noticed his daughter bawling moments ago? Was that a guy thing, being blind to our loved one's feelings? Pepe thanked Paloma. He lifted his arm at Xóchitl, suggesting she take the two bags of food. The other arm held the drinks.

"Con gusto," Paloma replied, smiling at Pepe and waving at them as they left the restaurant.

Once they were out of sight, I explained Ignacio and Pepe's history while Paloma packed our food. I told her how Pepe helped Ignacio get a job with him and that Ignacio lost the job because he'd opened his mouth about not having papers.

Paloma grabbed my hand to leave, but I pressed it down, realizing what would happen next. I couldn't go through it again. Why wasn't Ignacio showing up like he always did? If he did, he would be saving us from that tragedy. Maybe there'd be an inkling of forgiveness for him from me.

If ever there was a moment to rip us apart, now's that time, Ignacio.

He was nowhere in sight. We had no choice but to continue. My hand loosened.

Sauntering through the parking lot, scared, concerned, and no longer feeling like the child I once was, different theories played in my head in regards to what I could do to change what would happen in a matter of minutes. It was just a matter of time and this movie's magical experience played it terribly when it came to time. Could crossing the street earlier or letting Paloma walk ahead of me change things? Would that be enough to save her from the monster behind the wheel?

Paloma extended her free hand for me to grab on to her, urging me to hurry. She had my unopened toy in the same hand she was using to carry our food, but this time, I wouldn't fall prey to my desires or inattentiveness. This time, there would be no urge to play with the toy and I wouldn't let myself be distracted by the dove that would surely appear soon.

The coast was clear. Still on high alert, I ran to my mother, who waited at the end of the parking lot. Next to her, I motioned for her to stop and check before crossing as I watched the cars driving through the busy 115th street. Our little residential one-way remained tranquil. No cars from 115th drove crazily in the wrong direction. What worried me most were any cars that would speed from 114th towards us. My hand clasping hers, we continued to our place.

A couple of buildings from ours, we crossed safely to our side of the street. Curious, I released my mother's hand and stepped down from the curb, standing between two parked cars, checking for that brown Cutlass. One car approached, but it wasn't a brown car and it was a block away.

Paloma ripped the plastic bag with my toy in it. As soon as the toy airplane was free from its casing, it slipped from her fingers. One wing got damaged after hitting the pavement, reminding me of the time it landed in the puddle and of the damaged wing in my dream before arriving to Hammond. Paloma tinkered with it, trying to straighten the loose wing that held itself still, but that limped down.

"Damián!" a voice called behind me. Xóchitl waited across the street. Paloma hadn't noticed her calling me, so she was still messing with the toy. Excited, I ran to my wife, but stopped midway on the street when I heard Paloma yell.

"¡Hijo!"

Before she could grab me, Paloma tripped. She pushed me forward and I landed on all fours in the same spot I'd landed in when her accident had happened before. Xóchitl was no longer there. Instead, a white dove flew away. To my left, the toy airplane lay in a puddle, wing broken.

Tires screeched on the pavement. Before I could fully turn around to check, it hit my mother and her body hit the ground. I recognized both horrible sounds. Knowing how Paloma's story ended, I didn't go to check on her. Instead, I chased after the culprits in the car. Forcing myself up, my hand slammed at the passenger's window, where a woman turned away from me.

"God damn it!" I shouted.

The driver, though, hadn't turned from me in time. I knew him, I'd been waiting for him.

Ignacio.

"God DAMN it!" I cried, kicking the door. When I tried opening it, in a frenzy, Ignacio reached over the woman and abruptly opened it, sending me to the ground. The car backed away.

"Ignacio!" I shouted after the brown Cutlass that was driving east toward the next street, Langley Avenue. Neighbors came out of their buildings. Their muffled words filled the air.

"Ignacio!" I yelled again, anger boiling inside me.

"Ignacio," my small voice called out a last time before falling to the ground again, defeated.

21

I GNACIO KILLED PALOMA AND, needless to say, I was livid upon my return to the present.

Ignacio killed Paloma.

Well, he hit her, and the next day she died because of it. Therefore, it was his fault. If he had just stayed alert, Paloma would still be alive and Sofía may still be here.

Was I wrong to only blame him? There was someone else in the car with him, a cowardly woman hiding behind Ignacio. I had no clue who she was. It wouldn't have surprised me if it was some random woman he picked up while drunk after meeting Paloma on the night of the candy incident. What I knew for sure was that he hadn't cared about the consequences of his addictions, or how he'd impacted others' lives because of his selfishness.

Another one of Ignacio's lies had been exposed.

Kicking the sofa and throwing the coffee table toward the slim hall, I yelled out my frustration before dropping to my knees, the way I'd done moments ago as a child on my old street. "Fuck you, Ignacio. Fuck you and your stupid couch. And your goddamn coffee table. And your... Fuck you, Ignacio."

"Damián!" Xóchitl's voice came from the kitchen. "Babe, you have to see this." She paused, watching me on the floor in front of the TV. On the screen, the scenes of that old Halloween were still playing.

It was him, I wanted to say, but no words left my mouth.

Xóchitl walked past the thrown table and joined me. She placed her head against my arm. Her arm rubbed my back up and down. "Want me to stop the movie?" I nodded at her question. Xóchitl kissed the top of my head and, on her knees, reached the VCR to stop the movie. "Dami, there's something you have to see, when you're ready."

"It was him," I could finally say. Turning to her, I dolefully asked, "What is it?"

"A white dove. After I woke up, I threw the garbage outside, by the alley. I sensed something behind me. When I turned around, the dove was above the garage, flapping its wings. It looked at me, as if inviting me closer. I walked past it to come back inside, but the bird called out and flapped its wings faster."

My God, she *had* been there with me. Little Xóchitl had said she'd seen the bird outside by the garage. With a sad smile, I stood and helped her up so we could figure out next what the palomita wanted.

The white bird was still on top of the garage. Once we stood in front of it, the bird came down by our feet, waddling near the covered car. It cooed.

"Is it telling us to check inside?" I wondered out loud.

"Do you think..." Xóchitl grabbed my hand and I feared she suspected the same thing I did. I hoped she wouldn't say it. "Dami, think that's the brown car that hit her?"

She started for the garage, but I stopped her.

"Xóchi, before we go in there, you... How did you find..." Would she think me crazy for flat-out asking if she'd been with me minutes ago? As children? I was unable to think of the right words to say, but thankfully, she knew what I wanted to ask her.

"It's okay. I was there with you," she confirmed. "I told you, I found your father and the letters and drove here. You were sleeping and then I watched the movie next to you, and... Dami, what was that? I was there with you. And your mom? Oh my God, I met her."

Xóchitl turned and faced me. She wrapped her arms around my neck, and my arms went around her waist. She placed her head on my chest.

"She felt so cold," Xóchitl said through sniffles. "I'm so sorry for your loss. I know I've said it before, but I can't imagine how you felt all those years without her or your sister. I'm so sorry."

Just like she'd done to me moments ago inside the house, I rubbed her back and kissed the top of her head. Xóchitl wiped her face on my shirt. She looked up at me, her wet and red eyes stared into mine. Our souls were one. We were meant to be together.

"I told you I knew your mother through you and I was right. Paloma's exactly who I imagined. Thank you." We went in for a kiss, in sync, me feeling her sweet lips on mine, passionate like it was when we first fell in love. Our lips parted and I let her head rest on me while I stared at the damn garage, taking in our moment together and, at the same time, eager for an answer to our suspicions.

Palomita cooed. Xóchitl replied, "All right, enough lovey-dovey," and snickered as she pulled away from me, tapping my chest.

Deep breath... and let it go.

We lifted the garage door by the middle handle, but the heavy door was stuck and barely budged. It had perhaps settled after decades of no use. We tried again, this time placing our hands under the garage door.

"One, two, three," I counted, and, using all our strength, we succeeded in lifting it. The heavy door groaned along with us. The tools that had been on the ground since before I'd moved in, were still there. I kicked them out of the way, finally out of place. Xóchitl and I pulled the cover off of the car. The startled dove flew away.

There it was, the brown Oldsmobile Cutlass, the one Ignacio had once seen in a TV commercial when I was a child living with Paloma and Sofía. Never had he mentioned another car like he had that one. The car that hit my mother was right there in front of us, *had been there* all those years.

I walked around it to the passenger side, hoping to find anything that would prove Ignacio's culpability. There was a scrubbed dent. Could that have been Paloma's blood he cleaned off? My thumb rubbed over the spot and the almost invisible rust scratched my finger. "The whole time I was here, I never dared to come in."

Xóchitl kept quiet. She didn't move, except for her eyes that followed my movements.

"The day I arrived, after Ignacio showed me around, I saw this covered car. He warned me to stay away. I remember seeing, clear as day, tire tracks that came in from there..." I walked to her and pointed at the alley, then the middle of the yard, then to the car's parked spot. "To here."

"Why didn't you ever just look?"

My fingers tapped the top of the car. "Ignacio warned me every time he caught me nearing the garage. He was a big man and scared me. I thought he'd hurt me, but he never did."

Except he had. I thought back to the night of the robbery, to how he'd thrown me to the floor and dug his foot into me. "If only I had been braver, I could have put him away. Reported him to the cops. To Richie," I muttered at the end.

"So, what are you going to do?" Xóchitl asked.

"I don't know," I deadpanned.

Would the police even care to process Ignacio if he was dying?

The day's light began to disappear. Through the warm November evening climate, a quick burst of wind hit us. "Let's go back inside," I said, and together we went back in, leaving the car exposed.

Silently we drank a café with canela that Xóchitl prepared and had it with bread from my earlier run to the panadería. I considered showing her my room, the only other place in the house she'd not seen (except for the basement), but truthfully, didn't have it in me. The bad experiences in Ignacio's house outweighed the good, so I let the idea go, unless she asked to see it.

My wife caressed my arm, wondering how long I'd stay at the house. I told her I was ready to leave. Finishing our merienda, I picked up our cups, washed them, and Xóchitl followed me to the living room. I grabbed the movie; she gathered the remaining letters, and I requested she leave the sofa and table alone. No need to put them back in their spots. Ignacio's winter coat came with me and we exited through the front. To say good riddance to Ignacio's house, I considered throwing the rock with the hidden key to the alley, but I didn't want to see the uncovered Cutlass. It would hurt me, so I didn't go back there.

We agreed to meet at her parent's house in Hammond. The letters went into my backseat. She got in her father's yellow Neon and drove behind me. Though she had her GPS to guide her home, I checked on her through my rearview mirror. At the stop sign a block from 26th Street, a dove flew up behind us, then past us.

BEFORE JUMPING ON I-55 North, we stopped for gas at a station in a Jewel-Osco supermarket parking lot. Waiting for her car to fill up, a fender bender took my attention away from Xóchitl. It triggered memories of Ignacio hitting Paloma and something told me I should go see him before going to Xóchitl's parents.

One last visit to confront him about what he did.

I told Xóchitl what I'd do next. Not averting her eyes from the individuals who argued over who was at fault, she asked why. Paloma had said to end whatever business I had with Ignacio and I wasn't done. He still needed to confess what had happened that day. I needed him to say it. Xóchitl offered to accompany me.

"I need to do this on my own. Please," I begged. Surely, she'd understand.

"Okay, do what you need to. My phone will be on in case you need me. You let me know and I'll go there right away for you. I'll make sure it looks like an accident." She signaled "accident" with her fingers and winked, to which I let out a raucous laugh.

"What the fuck are you laughing at?" one crasher yelled, then lowered his voice. "Mind your fucking business!" And maybe we shouldn't have done it, putting ourselves at risk, but we laughed harder.

With her gas tank full, we pecked on the lips and I tapped the top of her car for her to go ahead, then went inside the supermarket.

"MR. VÁSQUEZ!" IGNACIO'S NURSE jumped from her chair. "I wasn't expecting you yet."

"Well, first, forgive me for my attitude earlier." I pulled out a greeting card bought at the supermarket. THANK YOU FOR ALL YOU DO, it read on the front, with different colored letters that went from pink to purple to blue to green to yellow. The last three words were the same shade of pine green. I also gave her a three-pack of Ferrero Rocher chocolates.

"Thank you and there's no need to apologize." She placed the gifts next to her computer. When the guilt didn't fade from my face, she told me she understood how stressful these situations can be, especially when dealing with someone like Ignacio. "I expect these behaviors." She offered to walk me to Ignacio's room. When her badge hit the corner of her desk, it detached from her and fell to the floor. Upon picking it up for her, I recognized the name.

"Amaya? You were the one who called my wife a couple of days ago?"

"Yes, sir. It's part of my job. I'm also... a messenger, of sorts. Been one for a few years now."

"Oh. Like an angel?" I asked.

Amaya looked away, as if trying to find the right words.

"I guess you could say that. Sometimes people need help ending their journeys in this world before moving on to the next one, and that's where I come in."

"Like a...?"

"...death doula," she finished my thought.

"It's very complicated to explain now," Amaya said in a monotone, her eyes staring directly at my father's room, as if he was her mission before his death.

"Amaya, how long have you worked here?" I asked the intriguing nurse. She seemed young, younger than me even.

"A few years already," she answered simply.

There was something familiar about Amaya. I just couldn't put my finger on what it was. I'd have to figure her out later. Amaya opened Ignacio's door and held it for me, inviting me in. I stood, frozen, not because I'd be seeing my father at any second, but because I was unable to stop gazing into Amaya's crystal blue eyes.

"My story's one for later. Now, you came to see your father, right?"

"Right," I said. "Is there anything I should know?"

"Your father should be letting go soon. Will you?"

What did she mean by that? Of course I was ready to let go of him.

"Young man, he's barely holding on. Amazing how long he's lived, considering the damage he's done to himself. Well, consequences of his actions," she said matter-of-factly with a cold stare in his direction. Consequences of his drinking, indeed.

Ignacio's chart hanging outside his room said nothing else to me other than what I'd already seen on my first visit. Whatever else was written there, I couldn't make sense of it. I wasn't sure why I was checking it again. Nothing there was of importance anymore, especially not after she'd basically confirmed he was on the brink of death.

"Go in, Mr. Vásquez. Do what you must." She pushed me in; fed me to the monster felt more like it. Meanwhile, she headed back to her workstation. Within seconds, Amaya was talking to another patient or guest.

Ignacio rested peacefully, a perk he didn't deserve. Why wasn't he writhing in pain?

"I hope you burn down there," I mumbled while each of my steps lightly touched each tile of the floor. The closer I got to him, the more enraged I felt thinking back to his last truth. Yet, despite wanting him hurt and having confessed it to Paloma, there wasn't enough malice in me to do anything. I'd probably forever cower before my father, even after his death.

The chair creaked as I lowered myself on to it, readying to text Xóchitl. "Hijo," Ignacio whispered. My eyes met his before I could hit the Send button. Instead, phone set aside, I waited for his next words. "Did you go back to our house?" he strained to say.

"No."

"You didn't?"

"I did, but it's not *our* house."

"I'm leaving it to you. It's all paid, hijo."

"Don't call me that." It burned me inside whenever he called me that.

Ignacio repeated it. "Hijo—"

"Stop! ¡Ya no me digas así, Ignacio!" God, how I wanted to pull the pillow from under his head and put it over his face, suffocate him, so long as he stopped calling me that. I shook my head. I didn't want that malice in me to grow. I wasn't Ignacio, there was no way I'd go down that path. I refused to become the devil he was, like his father before him.

Ignacio turned from me. His beady eyes looked tired as he gazed at the ceiling. "Damián, is there anything you need to say to me before I go?"

What was he expecting, for me to say I knew what he did to Paloma and Sofía? Did he think that after all the apologies he'd said, I'd forgive him? Did he want me to thank him for the extra money he'd given me, or for the gifted house?

"Ignacio, you ripped my childhood away, lied to me, and sent Sofía away. ¿Qué quieres de mí, Ignacio? You said you loved me. Did you mean that? Or did you feel obligated to say it? Are you waiting for me to say that back to you? Because I assure you that's *not* what I want to say."

"Well, what is it you want to say?"

"Goddamn it, old man. I feared you. *You* made me fear you. You hurt me. Hurt Paloma and Sofía and all those people that loved you. And people you didn't know that didn't deserve to be sent back because my mother and sister refused to give me to you. How dare you? If only... Fuck. If only I would have had just a touch of courage in me, I'd have paid attention to what you did, and you would've rotted in jail, died there instead of here."

My father smirked, as if he was proud he'd gotten away with all his sins. He turned to me, pointed to a tray with a jug of water. "Damián, I'm thirsty." I had no sympathy for him, so I pulled the tray away.

Ignacio closed his eyes. "Hmph! Está bien. So, you're mad at me because I lied to you about not being a mojado like me and made your sister go away. That bitch didn't deserve you."

I jumped up from the chair. Stood straight up. Tall. I imitated his stance as he'd done countless times to intimidate me. Ignacio opened his eyes. They were red and glassy, smiling at me. The light from the lamp outside reflected in his stare. They glowed the way a demon's eyes would glow.

"Don't worry. You'll see her soon," he calmly said, so nonchalant, like he'd held my sister hostage and would soon release her.

With his long black coat on me, slowly, I inched closer to him in the room's darkness. Ignacio widened his eyes. The pace of his breathing increased.

"Ignacio. I *know* what you did."

The machine sounds grew as his desperation grew. Either they would give in and die, or he would.

"Say it, Ignacio."

He covered his mouth.

"Say it!"

Ignacio shook his head.

"You killed her, Ignacio. You killed my mother."

Ignacio gasped. His eyes jerked in every direction. He continued to shake his head. Why was he denying it?

"But you weren't in the—"

"I saw my mother and watched it happen. The car you wanted, it was in the garage the whole time. That's why you never let me go there."

I cleared my broken voice, so he'd hear my every word.

My body cast a shadow over him. Grabbing his weakened body, mostly deadweight by now, I pulled him to my face. His body limped toward his bed. My tears rained onto him. My mouth met his ears and, with the most intense growl I'd ever given, whispered, "I hope to God you go to hell for what you did to her. To us. Fuck... you!"

His machines fired rapidly and, if that called Amaya in along with security to take me out, I wouldn't care. His body shook and I hoped it was in fear, like I'd shaken against him. Ignacio placed his hand on my cheek. He caressed it. As he opened his mouth to let out whatever spewed bullshit, my words came out first.

"BURN IN HELL! I'M DONE WITH YOU!"

I let his body drop, but my grip held onto my father, bringing me down with him. His body hit the mattress, and my head followed on his chest.

"I'm done with you," I cried. "I'm fucking done with you!"

My fist hammered his side, drilling deeper with each hit, the way I recalled him doing with his foot on my chest all those years before.

"I'm done with you!" I exclaimed, ready to land a last strike on his ribcage, ready to break his bones, ready to break him. But I stopped, realizing how fragile my old man was.

I'm not Ignacio.

His body stopped shaking. He calmed. His breathing was heavy. Knowing he had minutes left to live, I let him go and turned around to leave him so he would die alone, like he deserved.

When I was steps from the door, his machines started going crazy, beeping louder and harder. Ignacio uttered his last, sad "Hijo," and though I wanted to turn to see him one last time, not out of love, but to watch him take his last breaths, I didn't.

"I'm sorry for what I did to you, Paloma," he cried. Turning back just enough to catch the faintest glimpse, I felt him writhing before whimpering, "Perdóna—." I opened the door and stepped out, letting it close before he could finish asking for forgiveness.

WITH MY EYES CLOSED and no more tears left to shed because of him, I listened at the door, but heard nothing from inside his room. Not even the electrocardiogram machine; there was no flatlining sound like in Hollywood movies. What I did hear were footsteps approaching. I opened my eyes to find Amaya before me. She placed her hands on my arms and rubbed them up and down, sighing.

"Amaya," I said, coldly. "That's it. He's—"

Amaya shushed me and walked with me to the elevator. Nurses and patients continued about their business as if nothing had occurred. Some people waved at Amaya. She waved back. "Go on. I'll take care of him and call you if we need anything from you. Go home, Mr. Vásquez." She pushed the button to go down and left me standing there, alone.

People soon joined me, waiting to go down too. When the elevator doors opened, I let them in and let it close; I'd take the next one.

ANOTHER WHITE DOVE SHOWED up in the darkness outside, while I was letting the parking lot lights guide me to the car. Had it followed me all the way from Ignacio's? My tired body crouched down on the cold ground next to the bird.

"Are we not done yet?"

The dove responded with its familiar coo.

"I *still* don't know if you're her. Did my mother send you, palomita?" A sudden realization came to me, to which I let out a loud gasp. "Did *Amaya* put you up to this?"

Palomita tilted its head the way animals do when we talk to them, as if trying to decipher our language. It inched closer. I placed my index finger near its feet, hoping it would jump on, but the palomita flew away.

Rude.

With a loud grunt, I picked myself back up to find my car.

Inside the warm Jetta, I pulled out my phone and checked up on Xóchitl. The drafted text remained unsent and she had confirmed that she made it safely to her parents.

He's gone, I replied after deleting the draft.

Xóchitl immediately responded. *I'm sorry, my love. Are you OK?*

Yes, I texted. She offered to drive to the hospital, but I told her not to worry, that I'd be with her soon. We ended our chat with our always *I love you*s and her with her signature *xolxolxol*.

Finally, some peace. Silence kept me company and sometimes that's all we need by our side, nothing but silence. But my mind soon reverted to Ignacio. It seemed like I still had unfinished business with him. What should be done with his body? With his house? Car? Belongings? Other than Paloma's death, I'd never experienced one so close to me, so I didn't know who would be in touch and how we'd handle things.

To take my mind off Ignacio, even if just for a moment, because a peaceful mind was now out of the question, I reached for the letters Xóchitl had placed in the back seat. In every letter Sofía had written that she missed me. Some told of Moisés' life. Most said she'd pray for our mother and me. But in one, she mentioned the movie and included the titles of each event recorded: my eighth-birthday party; back to school; Halloween with Jenni and Carlos; and Paloma's Mexican funeral.

"¿Velorio de Mamá en México?" I questioned as I read the last part. A shiver ran down my spine. Why would she record that? Not that it was uncommon. Clients had told me about it from back home. Still, this was my first time having a recording of it in my hands. It was odd and morbid and it piqued my interest. What would happen if I watched it? Could I go back for that last part? I wasn't there for her funeral, but if there was something I learned from this magical experience, it was that Paloma and I hadn't been boxed in to the movie's recordings. At the very least, if no more magical time-traveling happened, I'd finally know a little more about my family and their land, even if I learned it while watching from Ignacio's couch.

With the letter stuffed in the coat pocket, I texted Xóchitl to tell her I had one more thing to handle at Ignacio's. Ignition on, I went to Ignacio's for one more watch.

22

I T WORKED. I WAS Damiancito again, I knew it from the now-familiar nausea in my gut after going from one place to the other.

Before opening my eyes, I breathed in the new air because I knew I wasn't in Chicago this time. Plus, it felt warm but comfortable, a climate unlike Chicago or Cincinnati.

Mexico was loud too, except for the house in front of me. Someone drove nearby. I could feel their loudspeaker most on my left ear, telling me they were on a perpendicular street.

Ready to fully take it all in, I opened my eyes and as the blurriness adjusted, I surveyed the long, narrow street with connected houses. People walked and watched from the slim sidewalks, and between, the stoned road allowed one car at a time in both directions. I could never. Probably would scratch every single parked car or scooter, and there were many scooters. But the people that lived here drove through with expertise.

Two houses down, close to where I'd heard the loudspeaker, was a tiendita. Children came out with refresco and sabritas, while the adults carried black plastic bags. With my eyes cleared, I read the sign above the next tiendita: PAPELERÍA VALLEJO.

Someone placed their hand on my shoulder, startling me. "Hola, Damián," Paloma said. The sun was too bright, so I shielded my eyes to get a good look at her. She wore a purple long-sleeved shirt with white in the middle and a purple ribbon tied around her neck. The same one she wore while resting in her coffin at the funeral home in Chicago.

"Mamá, ¿cómo?" I still wondered, even if the answer would be the same as it had been before. Paloma crouched next to me and pointed to the house in front of us, saying she wanted me to meet someone.

"It was her, that's how," she said.

Whoever she pointed to was impossible to see because of the brightness outside. In fact, everything inside the house was dark, barely lit.

"Sofía," I exclaimed at the only recognizable person. Stepping forward, Paloma stopped me. She asked me to wait and watch all the people gathered around Sofía, paying their respects. Paloma named the people there, but I didn't care to know them yet. I shook my mother's hand off my shoulder and went in, weaving through the crowd, though no one minded me.

"Sofía," I called again, but like all the others, my sister ignored me. With her gaze down, she acknowledged the guests' words of consolation, nodding as they went on.

"Mamá, why won't she answer?" I asked, but my mother had remained several steps behind. "Sofía!" No one flinched at my loudness. It was like I was dead to the world. This was a first in this experience.

"I told you to wait," Paloma said, finally catching up with me. "I tried to warn you that no one will see us, Damián." Paloma looked around. I looked too. "She's gone. Let me see if I can find her." My mother asked me to wait and relish this unique moment, visiting finally. It was a chance I had never gotten, despite Sofía's promise after our mother's death.

My pulsating heart thumped in my ears. I stopped to calm myself. Once ready, I walked to Sofía, who whispered in Spanish through sobs, "Dios mío, help him find peace and answers." She held the recorded movie Paloma and I were in.

"Mamá," I said upon Paloma's return, "I still don't understand. I wasn't with Sofía when this happened like all the other times. She recorded this after her deportation." Plus, she held the movie instead of recording the moment.

"Like I said before, mi niño, I wake up before you arrive and I'm gone after. That's all I know for sure. Nothing in between."

Paloma continued her search for the unnamed individual. While waiting, people passed around and through me. Their bodies whooshed right through mine in a blur as if I wasn't really there. I felt their heat. Some were extremely hot. Others were cold, but never as cold as my dead mother. Their scents were different, too. Some were pleasant, like flowers and cool water. Others, unpleasant, like sweat and cumin. Chile was a big one. The familiar vinegary scent and taste made me sneeze. No one said "salud".

Standing so close to Paloma's casket felt a little more haunting than it did back in 1989 at the funeral home in Chicago. Unreal, perhaps. But this whole thing was exactly that—unreal. Perhaps it was because her ghost-self was also here, alongside me now. I wondered what went through her head watching her other body in front of her eyes. My head rested on her side, pondering if all the tíos, tías, primos and primas there believed Paloma was with them in spirit, because she was. I could confirm it, if ever asked.

A teenage boy, slim with patches of hair on his face but a fully formed goatee, joined Sofía. His head leaned on her left side and Sofía moved her arm behind him to embrace the young man.

"Ay, mi Moisés," Paloma cried, as if he'd been the one who died. Paloma made her way to him, making me temporarily lose my balance. I didn't know ghosts could lose their balance. Paloma kissed his head and, unbelievably, Moisés scratched the spot her lips touched. He then followed with a thin-lipped smile, one that resembled our mother's.

Sofía whispered to Moisés. They excused themselves and went up the stairs on the side of the house. Paloma nodded for me to follow them while she'd remain near her body. If I were in Paloma's shoes, I could not be around my dead body.

The room they entered was a bedroom with a bureau near the entrance. This had to be Sofía's room, based on the lipsticks, mascaras, and hairbrushes on the furniture, plus her clothes that lay on the bed on the opposite wall. Moisés passed through a tiny middle space. At the end was a bathroom to the left and another bedroom next to it. The Bruce Lee and Sylvester Stallone movie posters taped on the wall told me that was likely Moisés' space. The only thing that gave their bedrooms privacy was a dividing curtain hanging by a rope.

The bathroom's large blue metal door creaked when Sofía closed it. It was so loud, I wondered if the guests downstairs had heard it. The neighbor's dog probably did; it barked after the door's impact.

Moisés walked through me. He reached under Sofía's bed, pulling out a camcorder, different from what she had in Chicago. After opening the compartment the cassette would go in, he shouted to let Sofía know the movie wasn't inside it, to which she yelled back that she'd left it downstairs. He closed it and sat, waiting for her. The letter with the movie titles that I had read in my car was sitting on a small table near my brother. I leaned in to read it just as Sofía passed through me and grabbed it. Together, they walked out, camcorder included. Seconds later, I followed.

"Mami, will you tell me who these people are?" I asked Paloma, but because our time was near ending, she suspected, she asked to stroll her old streets instead. Soon they would carry her body to the church. Just outside the door with me, an inch from stepping out, Paloma turned back to Sofía. My sister placed her hands on our mother's casket and gazed at the spot where we stood, as if she understood that our mother was leaving. Sofía placed her index and middle fingers on her lips, raised them, and whispered, "Hasta pronto, Mamá."

"Hasta pronto, hija," Paloma replied.

Men I'd never met and probably would never meet, closed Paloma's casket. They began to make their way toward us. A hearse waited. Paloma explained that they'd be heading to a nearby church, where they would hold a mass for her. Afterwards, they would lay her body to rest at a cemetery minutes away from the church.

"Let's go to the Jardín," Paloma suggested. "The church is there, and you'll love the area. It's a community plaza unlike the ones we had back home."

We walked down her old Calle Centenario. These blocks seemed never-ending, compared to those I knew in Chicago and Cincinnati. Each Mexican block seemed like five of mine, so making it through four of hers felt eternal to my little legs and feet. What made up for the tiresome journey, aside from the splendor of this Mexican city I'd not visited, were the street vendors that filled the garden. There was a life I'd not known here; perhaps a little like Little Village from when I was a child. These vendors sold burgers and tacos and cheap toys that replicated characters I'd grown to love. Superman—no—Strong Man. Spider-Man, sure, but with antennae on his head. Across the park, stores and restaurants kept busy behind arched portals. Most impressive of all was the colossal church.

"El Templo del señor de esquipulitas," Paloma said.

In the center of the garden, where we stood, children played around a white kiosk. A photographer, visibly annoyed at the children interrupting his photo session, directed a young quinceañera wearing a sizable purple dress. She looked like a true princesa in her gown.

Paloma took my attention from the photographer.

"Do one thing for me, Damián," she asked. "Come back and visit. Get to know your brother Moisés, our family, and their children. And bring them this movie. They should see me like you did."

"Like I did?"

Paloma snickered. "Well, probably not the same way, but they should watch it."

Agreed. They should. My family had as much of a right to watch this movie as me. It was theirs, just as it was mine. Once Jimmy digitized it, Sofía and Moisés would certainly receive their copies.

We watched from one of the kiosk benches as people paraded following Paloma's hearse to the church. Birds began to gather before us until there were so many, they muted everyone at the park. White doves slowly took their place. My mother put her hand on the ground—perhaps I should have done that to the palomita at the hospital parking lot, because one of them accepted her invitation. She caressed the pretty white bird with the gentlest touch. The bird cooed at her caresses.

"Remember, Damián, when palomas visit, I will be with you. My spirit and my love will never leave you." Paloma lifted her hand and the bird flew away.

"Sí, mami," I acknowledged. My head rested on her side. Paloma wrapped her arm around me, and as she twirled my hair, she hummed the only song she knew in English. Though still with a heavy accent, the lyrics were much clearer now as she chanted John Lennon's *Beautiful Boy*. Then, she kissed the top of my head.

"Adiós, mi Dami." In one of our visits, she'd told me not to say it to her. But I couldn't deny her saying it to me. It was time.

"Adiós, Mami," I said. As she rested my body on the bench by slowly removing herself from me, I closed my eyes, but soon checked on her as she made her way to the church.

Paloma was gone and nothing would stop me from letting my sadness out. Never had I cried for anyone as much and there was no one there to console me that time. No Paloma. No Sofía. No Xóchitl.

Invisible to the world, a ghost amongst these people from the past, I curled into myself. A pool of tears formed on the ground under me, a ripple forming with each drop.

Everything hurt. My eyes, my chest, my arms, and legs. I was ready to return, but nothing sent me back. Just like at the restaurant, I hoped for Ignacio. At least he'd haunt me back to my reality, but even he was gone now and I did not know how to return. My only hope was to tighten my eyes shut and focus on Xóchitl, on our home, our life.

Nothing.

I was trapped in a past I'd never known.

Someone sat beside me, near where Paloma had sat. Probably a random Guanajuatense, I assumed. Except this woman knew me and I jolted from my spot when she said, "Hello, Mr. Vásquez."

23

AMAYA

I N 1978, I MET the first girl that captured my heart. It was her kindness that drew me in, a small act, but one that stuck with me until the end of my days.

I was twelve years old and skinny, almost sickly looking, though I was healthy enough. Hungry one day, I went to the mercado in Moroleón to ask for food. It wasn't the first time I'd begged for food there. The girl's mother offered me money, but the girl offered to come with me and buy me food with her own money instead, so her mother could buy her hermanito a birthday gift. We roamed the mercado together, looking for some food.

"¿Cómo te llamas?" the girl asked me.

"Amaya Salomé Quintero Vargas. ¿Y tú?"

"Sofía Alonso," she said in a guarded, cautious manner. She didn't seem like the type to trust people easily.

Sofía stopped us. She scanned me up and down, ignoring the people that passed by and bumped into us. "Why are you alone and why did you ask for food?"

"My family's home and money is tight."

My casita was about ten minutes from the mercado. Papá's fall after a roofing job left him paralyzed. Tetraplegia, the doctor called it, after Papá lost all movement. I hated hearing him always complain of intense pain on his back. There was nothing we could do to ease it.

My sweet mother took care of us all, tending to my father and stretching herself thin to meet our needs. But her skills were not the kind this society deemed useful and she had never learned to use sewing machines. Sewing by hand, it turns out, takes so much effort and time and doesn't pay enough. Needless to say, money and food were scarce for all of us: my parents, my two brothers, my three sisters, and me.

The morning I met Sofía, I'd had half a bolillo with milk for breakfast, and the other half I saved to eat later in the day. Except, my insufferable hunger was too much and I couldn't take food away from my sisters and brothers for my personal needs, so I snuck out of the house to beg for food.

Sofía's mouth dropped upon hearing my situation. "Oh no," she said. "We've had difficult times ourselves, especially since my father passed, but we haven't had to beg for food. I'm sorry you have to."

Sofía searched through her purse. "Well, I can't help with much, but can I at least treat you to a torta and an agua?"

"Yes." I smiled at my new friend. Most other people would have dismissed my begging. I was used to it. If they gave me anything, it was usually moneditas. Leftover change. Nothing grand. If they already knew me, they might offer me a little bit more money. If they knew me personally, they'd tell my parents, and my parents would punish me.

"Amaya, let's be clear," Mamá had once said. "We're not beggars. We have a home. We are healthy and have food." Not much food, sure. And as far as being healthy, well, I supposed we were fortunate, except for Papá.

This girl, however, had offered more without any hesitation.

Sofía grabbed my hand and a warm tingle ran up my arm. The hairs on my arm raised. We hurriedly went to a torta stand she knew. The woman running the stand recognized me and forced a smile. She had scolded me the first time I had asked her for food, but over time, her heart lightened. Now, she would always give me a little extra for the money I'd collected to pay her.

"Hola, Chula, ¿qué te doy?" the tortera asked Sofía.

Sofía nudged me to order. Though the woman and I were no strangers, a shyness came over me and I whispered in Sofía's ear.

"She wants una torta de jamón y un agua de limón, por favor."

While we waited for our order, seated at the torteras stools drinking our aguas, Sofía commented on how pale I was and how blue my eyes were. She claimed never to have seen anyone with eyes so blue. "Como el mar," she said. My face flushed and I could feel the heat radiating from it, but I was elated knowing that my eyes resembled the sea.

"I'm adopted," I joked.

"Really?"

"No," I laughed, and explained that I looked like my mother when she was a child. My father, brothers, and sisters were also light-skinned, though a shade darker than me. Mamá had told me my father's ancestors were Portuguese and hers, Spanish. She explained that that was why our skin was lighter than everyone else's.

Sofía talked about books she loved and what boys she liked. Boys, to me, were of no importance, at least not in the way they were for her. She pointed at some who passed by, but I didn't care about them. I said nothing, staring instead at her brown eyes. Being with her, it was easy to forget anyone else around us existed. I was enamored with how the outside light hit her eyes, the glow giving them a honey color that matched her skin.

The tortera finished dressing our tortas, adding chiles, avocado slices, and a dollop of crema she spread on the top bread. Sofía reached into her purse, pulling out the bills and coins she'd need to pay, but insisting I keep the rest. Something fell out of her bag. It was a bookmark. Before I could bend to pick it up for her, Sofía said, "That's all I have. It's not much, but it'll be enough for something to eat here for the next couple of days. Take it. All of it."

A smile was all I could muster as a thank you. Sofía reached for me. Her soft fingers tickled the top of my hand. She turned my palm face-up, placed her money on top, and closed my hand over it.

"Wouldn't you rather buy your brother something?" I asked, remembering Sofía's words to her mother.

"He'll be fine. I have more money at home and can come back later to buy him something." Her hand cupped mine. Without thinking, my other hand covered hers, then I embraced her.

"Gracias, Sofi," I murmured.

The tortera bounced the bags of food on the tabletop. "Hija, for you, your mami and Moisés." She handed Sofía a hefty bag, smiled the loveliest smile at my new friend, and handed me my torta and drink.

After thanking the tortera, Sofía turned to me. She assured me we'd see each other again and said she'd treat me to something else next time. Then, she rushed back to her mother and brother.

Jolly as could be because of the kindness this girl I'd randomly encountered had shown me, I strolled past the different vendors and their food, jewelry, clothes, and toys, making my way to the food court. On my way there, I remembered Sofía's bookmark and hustled back to the tortera. No one had picked it up. It was still there on the ground. I picked it up and slipped it inside the plastic bag with my food as I searched for her. My friend didn't show up again, no matter how loud or how many times I called her name. My exhausting search ended when I reached the food court.

Peeling back the aluminum and wax paper that covered my torta, I pulled out the bookmark that quoted *Jane Eyre* by Charlotte Brontë: "I am no bird; and no net ensnares me: I am a free human being with an independent will."

"One day, when we see each other again, you can explain this to me," I said to myself. But my friend Sofía never returned to the mercado for me.

PAPÁ DIED WHEN I was 19. Renal failure, the doctor said. It all happened so fast in those last days of January 1985, after his sudden symptoms: uncontrollably itchy skin, swollen feet, problems sleeping, mental sharpness deterioration. The biggest indicator of his health declining was how little he urinated. When Mamá noticed it'd been days of no pee, she grew concerned. But, again, it all happened so fast.

After his passing, I promised myself to learn all I could about renal failure. One day, I'd save someone else's life in honor of Papá. I convinced my brother Martín, the oldest, at twenty-three, to emigrate to the U.S. with me. I told him Mamá's sister, Tía Meche, could take us in. Meche had had many conversations with us about feeling lonely after her children had left for school far away. Her husband, Tío Porfirio, had to work from sunrise to sunset to pay for their education, a luxury we'd never be able to afford. She was lonely and lived near a school that offered affordable classes, so of course, she jumped at the opportunity to take us in.

Two months later, Martín and I risked our lives for the so-called 'American Dream'. We traveled with strangers, many of whom couldn't keep up and were left behind, some to die, as the more experienced travelers had told us. Martín was almost one of them. He came close to drowning while crossing the Río Grande. The water pushed us apart and, in his exhausted desperation, Martín lost control of his swimming. Fortunately, two men, who had said to have crossed multiple times, grabbed his arms and helped him finish the swim.

In this perilous venture, we hid from Federales. Martín and I argued. He fought men who stole our food to feed their children, even when all we had was split evenly amongst us travelers. The pressures of the distressing journey made monsters of all of us.

During one of our more relaxed moments at a safe house, while Martín rested to recuperate from a stomach bug caused by the dirty river water he'd swallowed, I asked the remaining twenty travelers where they were going. One Oaxacan couple with a son who looked to be ten years old confirmed that they were going to Chicago. I hesitated to ask if they'd take us, but the father understood my hesitation and offered to take us once we reached San Antonio. They asked for nothing in return, as we were all in the same boat, so to speak. That evening, some of us jumped onto a truck that took us to San Antonio, where a family member of the Oaxacan family waited to take them to Chicago.

We arrived safely two and a half days later. Our aunt's blue house on Kensington Avenue was tiny, like ours. Two houses down, there was a bar and, on the other side of the street, a bread factory with an aroma that immediately called to my stomach. On the next block, there was a pinkish church. Like the first city we had traveled to from the border, this church also shared the same name as the saint of all things lost: San Antonio.

Days later, Tío Porfirio took us to buy an identification and a social security card, so Martín and I could work. To the new world, I was now Carmen Hernández, according to my fake documents. Martín was now Mario de la Cruz. These fake identities helped Martín work in construction with Tío Porfirio, and for me to work at a cookie factory in a nearby city, fifteen minutes away, where I packed cookies into boxes.

Eventually, they gave me a new position as a mixer at the other end of the building. It was a night shift, where I mostly worked with men. The pay was better and the men were nice, but I knew why they showed me any kindness. On slow nights, they proved their motives, hooking up with me in the darkest corners of the factory. Nothing ever got serious, though. I never cared for any man at the factory, or any in the U.S., or any in Mexico, for that matter. They were just a momentary form of stress release from our boring lives.

In June of that year, Tía enrolled me at a college in South Chicago, where every Tuesday and Thursday, I'd take three buses from the factory to the college, and three different buses home. There, I took the ESL and GED classes necessary to enroll in nursing classes. There, I also met Amy, an American girl who I practiced my English with, but most importantly, who helped me realize and accept who I was: a lesbian. With Amy, I explored my sexuality. I opened my heart to her, told her my desires. Through her, I understood why I'd never been in a relationship with any man.

When I told Martín, he expressed how thrilled he felt hearing me finally admit it. "I've always wondered why you never spoke of any boys. I was afraid to ask, though. But..."

There's always a "but". *Why* does there always have to be a "but"?

"Amaya, don't tell Tía. What's she going to think?"

"What does it matter what she thinks?"

"And then Tío will fire me. They'll kick us out..."

"Look, Martín, so what if they kick us out? You're by my side, right?"

"I am, but..." There was my brother's "but" again. Martín sighed. "Just don't say anything."

Martín's response hurt me. Why was he so afraid of what others thought of me? Was he ashamed of having a sister who loved other women? Didn't I deserve to be myself, to love and be loved? Worse, my brother refused to meet Amy, or any woman in my life.

"I'm sorry, carnalita. I really am happy for you, but don't tell Tía, Tío, or Mamá. And please don't bring whoever you're sleeping with around."

Martín broke me, and for a moment I wished the river had succeeded in taking him.

Amy and I broke up shortly after. She was going to leave anyway to study in another state. After our breakup and my conversation with Martín, I couldn't admit my feelings to any other woman. If any man confessed they had feelings for me, I instantly became cold towards them. They respected my decision, though. No one made any advances, except one. He was the worst of them. But that was a few years later.

In 1985, I finally enrolled in nursing classes. *Whatever happened to Sofía?* I wondered after finding her Jane Eyre bookmark one day, which I placed in what I considered my most important notebook. Everything about her was still stuck with me: her brown eyes; the way the light had hit them, matching her face and her arms. Her memory was as fresh as the day we'd met.

Papá remained in my mind and in my heart, too, empowering me to focus on my mission. So, aside from my classes, I quit working at the factory and took a job as a receptionist at a hospital near my aunt and uncle's house. There, I translated for many Spanish speakers. I accompanied these families in their emotional journey and turmoil, navigating halls and past the sick, injured, and dying. I learned where these people—*my* people—came from, what they did for a living, what brought them to this country. We shared so much. Over time, the understanding of what connected us aided me in knowing how to deliver tragic news in a more comforting manner.

It was there too that the past met up with me. And where Death awaited me.

24

AMAYA

ONE COLD NOVEMBER MORNING in 1989, while I waited for my usual bus to arrive, a man parked next to Don Manuel's Mexican supermarket across the street from me.

"Ey, chiquita, where are you going? I'll take you," he slurred. He blinked multiple times, like he hadn't slept in days. He seemed so tired and drunk. I turned from him, extending my neck to search for any sign of my already-late bus. "Psst," the man continued.

"I'm waiting for my bus, thank you."

He insisted. "Ey, mija, don't worry. I'm not like these chamacos around here. I'm a real man." Another car honked and the driver catcalled at me. The drunk man honked back.

If it wasn't for my lateness and the dangerous neighborhood, a part of the city known for gang violence even in plain daylight, I would have continued to ignore the man, but I responded to tell him my job was only ten minutes away.

"You'll be there in five," he said.

Still no bus. "Está bien," I agreed, clutching my purse in front of me as I got into his brown car.

Beer cans littered the backseat and the man smelled strongly of it.

"You like it?" he proudly asked. "Just got it a few days ago." He sped down the busy street, merging onto the opposite side of the road.

Why did I make this stupid choice? I should never have trusted this stranger, who is clearly intoxicated. I wanted to say something, to get out and just walk. Who cared if I would get reprimanded for my tardiness? It was a rare occurrence, anyway.

We reached 111th Street and instead of continuing down Michigan, the man turned right. When I told him he was going the wrong way and that I could just get out of his car and walk the last two or three blocks to the hospital, he ignored my request.

"I just want to show you where I live... eh, where I lived," he said. The drunk eyed me up and down, pursing his lips. I prayed for a red light, so I could run out of this vehicle and get away from him. Why couldn't I have just waited a little bit longer for that bus?

He turned right on Cottage Grove, then left at 114th, and I made mental notes of where he drove in case I needed to retrace the route.

The man placed his heavy hand on my leg and ran his fingers up and down the inside of my thigh. "My name's Ignacio, preciosa. Well, you can call me Nacho."

Pushing his hand away, I asked him to stop and let me out. Ignacio smacked my hand and put his back on my leg. "No pasa nada," he assured. Except, something *would* happen; I knew it. So, when he slowed down at a stop sign, I pulled the door handle to escape, but Ignacio was quick to push the button on his door and lock me inside with him.

"Let me go," I insisted.

Ignacio made an immediate right on Champlain. His hand slid deeper between my legs. My only defense was pushing him off and cornering myself close to the door. When I tried to kick him, the tightness of the space inside the car barely allowed my legs to move. Ignacio sped up on a street that didn't require such high velocity. His left hand held onto the steering wheel, while his arm reached behind my back to pull me closer to him. I clawed at his arm and continued pushing him away, but Ignacio wrapped his fingers around my wrist to stop me. While he tried pulling me to him, the steering wheel jerked, sending the car sideways, left and right. We barely avoided hitting the cars parked along the street.

"Nacho... Nacho... Nacho! El niño," I yelled as a boy crossed in front of us, unaware of the danger that neared him. Ignacio looked up from me and made a quick stop, his car finally scraping on another car. The shrill of the brakes working overtime and the impact against the other car pierced my ears. Then, we hit someone.

The boy. Ignacio hadn't hurt him, right?

"Ignacio, el niño." My voice sounded so small. My chest heaved while sweat trickled down the nape of my neck. The inside of the car fogged up.

"El niño," I whispered again, but the boy was alright. He was lying on the ground to the right. So, who had we hit? The boy turned to us, startling me enough to fall back against Ignacio. I quickly turned to Ignacio, whose bulging eyes told me he knew who the boy was.

"Nacho, we have to get out and help them."

"Damián," he muttered, turning away from the boy. He looked into his rearview mirror as he reversed, scraping against other cars. He backed up on 114th before continuing on to Langley. A block and a half away, he stopped in front of a small park.

"Ignacio, we can't leave them there. We must go back. We have to—"

Nacho's hand slammed on the steering wheel, again and again and again, harder and harder. I was sure he was going to break it.

"Nacho," I said again. Ignacio turned to me and his hand grasped my throat, pushing me to where I'd cornered myself earlier.

"Cállate," he growled. "We're not going to do anything, understood?"

When I tried to speak, his hand tightened on my throat.

"You will do nothing, or I'll find you and break your neck and leave you to rot where no one will find you."

My tears ran down to his hand.

"What's your name?"

"Carmen," I struggled as I lied. My fake identification would be proof enough if he searched my purse. Ignacio squeezed my neck. "Hernández."

"Where do you work? Where was I taking you?"

"At a hospital."

"Let's go," Ignacio said. "I'm taking you in. Make sure you're not a lying bitch. Make something up when we're there. Tell them I'm your father, your brother, whatever the fuck you want."

I nodded.

"But you will stay quiet about this, because now I know where you work. Do you understand?"

I nodded again.

"And I can find out where you live. Already picked you up like a whore off the streets."

Ignacio released me. The pulsing in my neck told me I'd likely get a bruise later. The rest of the way, we said nothing, except for the directions I gave him to the hospital.

Ignacio stayed with me until my lunch break, shadowing me everywhere I went, even to the bathroom. He had asked if we had a private one for employees. Silvia, a girl who'd started days ago, told him where that was. If I needed to go, Ignacio checked to make sure no one was inside, so I wouldn't rat him out.

Ignacio charmed my coworkers. To them, he was a proud father, visiting from Mexico. A puerco and an asesino were what he really was. Silvia, who I'd confided in about crossing the border illegally, asked him if he'd crossed to the U.S. the same way I had. Shit. Why did I have to open my mouth to her? Ignacio eyed me and I knew this was something he could use against me.

Before he left, Ignacio pulled me into one of the unused rooms. He pinned me against the wall of the dark room, closing the door with his other hand.

"I warned you," he said. "If you say anything, I'll find you and I'll kill you."

"Okay," I let out through his hand. And then, unexpectedly, he let something out that made my heart sink.

"That boy, the one I almost hit. He's my son."

Oh my God. What kind of monster had I involved myself with? What kind of father would abandon his son like that?

Ignacio released me. "The other person, the one I hit, that was his mother." Ignacio paused, looking away. But soon, the monster lay his hand on my hurting neck. "But listen, if you say something, not only will I find you and kill you before they put me away, but he'll be homeless too after I open my mouth and report them to immigration. His mother and his sister. I'll send them back to Mexico. Are you willing to risk it for an escuincle you don't even know?"

Fucking Ignacio, hijo de la chingada. What was I supposed to do? I couldn't call the police yet. He'd probably be watching me and attack before they had time to arrive. Plus, he had an idea of where I lived and knew I was in this country without permission. Opening my mouth right away meant risking sending the boy's mother and sister away. Even Martín. No, I couldn't say anything yet. I'd need to come up with a plan.

"I'll be watching you," he threatened, swinging the door open.

LATER THAT DAY, THE past finally caught up to me. The Mexican girl I'd thought lost, still in my mind after many years, showed up. Sofía. She was a woman now, like me. As fate would have it, she was brought to me under dire circumstances. She didn't recognize me, but I did her. My heart, my body, everything in me went numb. My steps faltered as soon as she walked in the room. She was there about her mother, Paloma, who'd been hit by a car earlier.

Clinging to her was a little boy with a face I would remember forever. It was the boy Ignacio almost killed after he forced himself on me. And, because I didn't speak up, I felt as guilty as the man who'd hurt their mother, a cross I'd have to carry for a while.

My heart fluttered as my eyes admired the young woman before me, but I was unable to admit anything to her yet. Instead, I held on tightly to the bookmark she'd once dropped in Mexico, now a faded and damaged relic from our shared past, and stuffed it in my pocket as I opened my work notebook.

IT WAS THIRTY MINUTES past midnight when I waited for my bus at a shelter a block from the hospital. Exhausted and hurt from the long, tiring and stressful workday, I mindlessly played with a glass bottle on the ground, kicking it a few times before it broke. Shards of the bottom half of the glass littered the ground. I sat on the bench. Someone stepped over the shattered bits. Looking up to check, a heavyset man wearing a red baseball cap grabbed me by my already bruised neck and pushed me against the wall. I first thought of Ignacio, but because I knew it wasn't him, I thought perhaps he'd sent someone to kill me.

The man reached for my purse while his other hand squeezed my larynx. With my elbow, I tried to hit him in the stomach, near his ribcage. Wherever, as long as he let me go, but that only made him punch me in the gut. Then, he threw me to the ground with ease. I called for help, but no one listened. The streets were empty and just a whimper came out of me.

I refused to lose this fight, especially after the day I'd had. After Ignacio attempted to sexually abuse me and threatened to kill me, and after not being able to speak up against him to Sofía, I needed this win. I picked myself up to tackle the man, but he was too strong for me, tossing me around like a rag doll. My head hit the metal bars of the bench and my body plummeted to the ground. The other half of the glass bottle slid into my neck like a hot knife slicing through butter.

In my last moments, I watched the assailant rummage through my purse and run away with my cash. Blood pooled around my face. My body felt cold and I shivered as my eyesight faded slowly into darkness.

"WHERE AM I?" I groaned, attempting to stand. There was nothing to hold on to. My arms felt weak against the ground as I picked myself up. Wherever this was—not the bus stop, or the hospital, or home, or anywhere I'd been before. This place was colder than I'd ever experienced and darker than a complete blackout. Wobbling around nothing, it seemed eternal.

"Where am I?" I cried, rubbing my arms to keep warm, which was pointless. My touch was there but wasn't. It was like my body had become so numb that I couldn't even feel the tickling that usually came with numbness. I searched for something or someone that could tell me where I was, but there was nothing. It could've been five hours or five minutes later—time felt endless, stretching in all different directions at once here—that I heard an echoing voice call my name.

"Amaya, you're dead," the ghostly voice said. I couldn't locate it.

"Who... who's out there?" I answered it. A draft of chilly air followed every word and every turn of my neck. I touched the spot where the glass had slid in and it was raw, like uncooked meat. Every touch stung.

I called out again and a horrid creature appeared from the mist. It was an anemic being that grew taller as it came closer, becoming even thinner and more grotesque. Was this Death my wide eyes took in? It resembled the Death I knew, skeletal, with hollowed eyes and rotting flesh, like pieces of an unfinished puzzle. A black liquid oozed from where its eyes should have been. Strands of coarse gray hair, rough and thick, caressed my face. I flinched away. My heart pumped faster than I'd ever experienced. But if I was dead, how could my heart beat so hard and fast?

As if realizing how horrid it appeared before me, its face began shifting, adding lines and curves that brought its appearance closer to what Muerte looked like in Latin American art. Its skeleton arm extended to me and opened its bony hand. Every bone had mold. No, not mold. It looked the way rotting teeth do. Upon the figure's icy hand touching me, I fell back.

"Oh, Amaya, you creatures always cower before us. Is this better?" The creature transformed into a person, androgynous in appearance, for I couldn't tell if it had changed into a man or a woman. "Or this?" it said, and before me, transformed into the woman I'd wondered about forever.

"No, please. Stop. You're not her."

The creature changed back to the ambiguous human.

"Who... who are you? Are you Muerte?" I asked in a quivering voice.

"Yes, Amaya. But I'm not Death as you mortals know me. Humans' feeble minds interpret us in innumerable ways, yet can't comprehend our infiniteness. But yes, I am one of them: Death, Muerte, Yanlou, Yama, Hel. Shall I continue?"

"So, is this what the afterlife is, then? It's so desolate, so vacant."

The same as the Muerte's eyes.

"Oh no, my dear. This is but a realm that will take you to your next journey, be it heaven, as you like to imagine it, or another world, one of immense beauty or insufferable pain. Your father is in one of those. One of beauty."

"Why would I ever choose pain?"

"Some choose it to atone for their sins, a sort of purgatory before they allow themselves peace in their next world. Others, Amaya, don't get a choice at all. The worst ones all go to the worlds of insufferable pain. I deal that hand for them. Fortunately for you, you get to choose your next journey."

What if I wasn't ready to move on? To see the menu of the afterlife? Having seen Sofía a moment ago through the Muerte made me realize I had my own sin to atone for, just not, hopefully, in hell. Or whatever those realms would be.

"Can I go back? There's—"

"Now, Amaya, careful what you ask for? There are conditions if I send you back."

"I've wronged some people... well..."

The Muerte's face shifted back to Sofía's, Paloma's, Damián's. All at once. It knew what I wanted.

"Understood," it said. "But, as I said, there are conditions. You'll help me upon your return."

Surprised by its request, I asked it why, if it was an eternal being and I was a simple creature with a feeble mind, as it had assumed.

"Certainly, you've encountered those who claim to have witnessed miracles, or know of the afterlife, and I can assure you, some have spoken the truth."

But I never believed them. Brujos, healers, and fortune tellers—cheaters and liars, I thought. Is that what the Muerte wanted of me?

"Amaya, I need messengers for the living and the dying. I can't show up before others like I have to you. Well, I have in the rarest of times, and some have claimed to see me, but hardly do I interfere in your affairs. That's why I have messengers."

The Muerte explained that my job would be connecting the unanswered pieces for the living and their dying loved ones. Also, I'd help the dead transition to their next life, the way it would have been with me if I'd not chosen to return. The Muerte pointed to an empty space, where another Muerte stood before its messenger, guiding a new soul through a doorway. The messenger slipped away from that Muerte's grasp as the messenger and the soul disappeared into whatever that realm was.

"The dead also need closure," it said. "And, as I said, we Muertes rarely interfere in your matters. People like you are how we interfere."

I began to doubt my choice, going back, given that chance.

"Amaya, you asked for this. You didn't deserve what happened to you. You lived a righteous life helping others. So, given your request, I'm giving you the chance, *one* chance, to go back. To continue helping them so they have their answers to life's injustices, and, in the end, some peace. You'll help me guide the dead to their next journey. If you refuse, you have a choice to take another path and someone else will guide you there."

Helping the living, like a detective solving an impossible case, that I understood. But what about the dead? Did the Muerte mean I'd take the living's life? That's not what I wanted, not what I signed up for in life. No. My mission was to help save lives because I couldn't save my father from his illness.

How strange and sad that this eternal being was confined in this never-ending void, relying on others to carry each other to different worlds or realms. Did it know what lay ahead? Would it ever rest for eternity?

But going back, regardless of the means, meant helping Sofía and Damián come to terms with what happened to their mother and understand that day's events, once I exposed Ignacio for the devil he was. This was my way of redeeming myself for Sofía, even if Paloma would recover, according to the doctor.

The Muerte saw through me.

"Amaya, you will help that woman and her family get answers to their accident. It'll be your first mission. But I warn you, going back means you're dead to your world."

The Muerte was right. Surely, they'd found my body, so easy to identify being so close to my hospital.

A curious thought came to me when I recalled all the innocent lives lost. All those who were gone forever from the world. Some deaths were unfair. Some people died from preventable diseases or as a result of neglect.

"Muerte, some people don't deserve death. What if I can help them prevent their deaths?"

"Do not meddle with things you do not understand," the Muerte proclaimed.

"But what if they truly don't deserve it?" I countered, louder.

"Amaya, life is unfair. *Death* is unfair. You think I don't want to know what's beyond this emptiness? Alas, that is the nature of life and death."

The Muerte calmed itself, pausing.

"However, *if* you interfere, if you prevent a death, you must exchange it for another life. A life for a life, Amaya."

Was I ready for that? Could I take a life in order to save someone else's?

"Amaya, I sense what's in your heart." It pointed to my heart, then to my head, showing images in my mind of Sofía holding someone's hand as she boarded an airplane. It was encouraging me not to make the wrong choice. Then, the Muerte shook the image out of my head and Sofía withered away.

A glowing entrance appeared. The Muerte needed an answer.

"Muerte, if I go back, does that mean I'll be immortal? What if a car runs me over? Or I fall into a ditch? Or..."

"You'll have one chance, Amaya. That is a condition. You won't be immortal, so make your return count, be it for one day or a thousand. Because when you die, that's it. We'll meet again and someone else will take you there." The Muerte pointed to the glowing doorway. "What happens to you after is not for me to decide."

A new chance at life. Another chance to see Sofía. A chance at redemption.

"Okay," I said. "I'll help you. Tell me what I need to do. Tell me who I have to kill to send to you."

The Muerte laughed and I was relieved that it had gotten the joke.

"No one, Amaya. Whatever brings them to me, that's on them, intentional or not. But come with me and I'll give you instructions before sending you back."

The Muerte waved its boney arm and the glowing entrance disappeared. With its frigid hand around my back, the Muerte guided me through that eternal void.

25

DAMIÁN

THE WHOLE TIME, THIS experience, this emotional journey, was made possible because of her, Amaya. The woman who kept referring to me as "Mr. Vásquez", whom I'd paid little attention to. Nevertheless, she'd been a part of my life, a guardian angel, from the moment of the accident to now. Hell, even before I'd been born.

I should've been angrier at her. I should've cursed her after learning she'd been involved in Paloma's accident, but I had no anger for this angel. I didn't curse her. I understood her silence, understood that Ignacio had had a hold on her.

Her neck radiated where Ignacio had once choked her in the car just as in that hospital room. Additionally, a scar from her death marked the left side of her neck.

"Open your hand," she requested before placing half a bookmark on my palm. I knew instantly that it was Sofía's. When she closed my hand over it, I felt it fold in half. "I'm sorry. Time hasn't been kind to it, but I held on to it as long as I could."

Amaya then looked at me, biting her lip like she couldn't decide whether she should say her next words.

"The Muerte knew that I cared for Sofía from the moment we met. Maybe that's why it chose her as my first mission. But even if it didn't know the love I had for her, I would have chosen her first in a heartbeat. See, the kindness she showed me left an imprint in me even to this day." A tear ran down her face. "Funny, we lived so close to each other in Chicago and I didn't know. But even after many years, I knew her instantly when I saw her with you."

Oh, Amaya. She'd loved Sofía from the moment they met. Would my sister have loved her the same way? Perhaps in an alternate world. In this one, what was certain was that Sofía would have loved Amaya as a genuine friend. Would that have been sufficient for Amaya? Or were they better this way—apart? The bookmark twirled between my fingers as I wondered about what could have been.

"The day of the accident, after your sister handed you to your neighbor while she stayed in the hospital, you left your backpack behind with this movie. After I died, the Muerte said to use... um, alternate methods, if you will, to do my job. So, I remembered the movie you'd left behind and that's how I knew to use it to help you. I just didn't know how."

"Wait, help me? But you wanted to help Sofía," I countered. "Why?"

"I was supposed to help your sister figure out Ignacio was the guilty one, even if I'd been in the car with him. But I didn't know your mother would die shortly after I'd returned to life. Paloma was supposed to return home and recover. The doctor had said that earlier in the day. After she died, I realized you needed this more than your sister. Sofía is a strong woman, but you—you never grieved your mother properly. Your father took so much from you. Sofía had moved on, started her family. You... well, you haven't done it like you and your wife wanted. Ignacio scarred you too much. You needed to realize what your father did and understand that you're not him."

The sun continued beaming down strongly over the city's communal garden. The city's people were still just going about their lives and it all had me wondering what I might've experienced in 1989 had Sofía brought me here to visit after Paloma's death. How often would I have visited after? As I watched the church and those who entered and left, I wondered about Paloma and whether she'd moved on to her next life by now. Was she waiting for Amaya to guide her through?

"Moments ago, you heard your sister pray you find peace and answers to what happened, so I'm granting her that. Well, helping you find those answers and hoping you find peace after this. And, in essence, I'm helping her, too, no?"

I supposed she was right.

There was one more thing I needed to know before we ended our time together. It bothered me still not understanding why Paloma died if she was supposed to recover.

"Damián, I told you that you needed to realize what your father did because it wasn't the accident that killed her."

My heart raced, wondering how else Ignacio played into this story. My stomach turned as I waited for Amaya to fully explain what had happened to my mother.

"When I returned from the dead, I managed to sneak out of the morgue, past everyone, to your mother's room. Your father was there, sitting at her bedside. The door was ajar, but to avoid being recognized by him or anyone else at the hospital, I snuck into the next room and listened from the wall. He confessed to hitting her with his car and swore to her that he had not meant for it to happen. 'But,' Ignacio said, 'you should've given him to me.'"

No, Ignacio. What the fuck were you doing there with my mother?

"Hoping to get a better look and listen, I snuck back out. Your mother had her head covered with her hands, as if she refused to listen anymore. Then, when she reached for the help button, he shoved her hand away. He covered her mouth with his hand and, because her heart was too weak, I knew what could happen. I'd seen it too many times. Your mother writhed in bed. This was too much for her, for her heart. But your father kept shushing her, even when the machines began beeping, alerting him of her condition. His hands tightened around her mouth and nose. When things got worse, when the machines got too loud, he let her go and rushed out, but it was too late. He'd worked her heart too hard. I'm sorry Damián."

"Amaya," I sobbed. "Why didn't you—"

"I hid before he could notice me," Amaya continued. "I hid from the staff that rushed in to save her. But..."

I got off the bench to pace desperately in front of her, letting go of the bookmark. My fingers dug deep, *hard*, into my head as they combed my hair back until my fingers intertwined on the back of my head.

"So, it wasn't the crash that killed her," Amaya said. "Her heart gave out and your father was the reason for it."

Ignacio. You killed my mother.

In all of this, he was a true monster, and to make it worse, he was gone. A guilty man walked away free. I could have killed him at his lowest in the hospital, but I chose not to. I didn't want to become a monster like my father. Was that why Amaya had waited until now to confess this?

Was that also why he asked her for forgiveness in the end? Was that why he looked so shocked when I told him what Richie had said on the day of the robbery? He smiled at me afterwards. There was a satisfied look to him, like he knew I hadn't discovered the whole truth.

Ignacio was dead. Paloma was gone. Would she ever find out the truth?

At that moment, all I could think of doing was falling and striking the ground. I then swung at all the people walking around us, but what good did that do? We were ghosts to them.

"You could've done something," I said, crawling to Amaya. "Stopped him, reported him without giving yourself away."

Amaya claimed the Muerte had warned her not to interfere, but I didn't care to listen to her defense. Instead, I punched the bench, letting out all the pain and rage that had built up inside me. *Goddamn you, Amaya.*

When I could punch no more, I dropped again, facing the sky and cursing my father one more time. "Fuck you, Ignacio," I shouted, and though no person heard, the birds fluttered away.

When my heavy breathing calmed, Amaya helped me up to sit with her on the bench.

"God damn you, Amaya," I quietly said, observing the people that continued entering the church for Mamá's service. Wiping the last of my tears, my eyes red and dry by now, I asked Amaya how the movie played into all of this.

"After your mother died, I consulted the Muerte. It suggested using the movie as a means to reunite the two of you. Bringing her to life for you was not going to happen, but taking you to her through it was. And you got more than I bargained for. You reconnected with her and the people involved in your life. It helped you discover your father and his lies. Plus, a little magic never hurts."

"Amaya," I said, avoiding her eyes and disregarding her last words. "How did you end up working at the hospital near my father's thirty years later?"

"When the Muerte brought me back, I couldn't go home or work at the same hospital. The world thought I was dead. How would the hospital explain a dead body suddenly going missing and coming back alive? So, I ran away until I could figure things out. My first instinct was to reach out to the person who made my fake identification, but I made the mistake of asking him to use my real name. That's something to take care of another day. Anyway, sensing and hoping that we'd eventually meet, I moved around the city until I made it to Pilsen, near your father's house. That's how I got a job there a couple of years ago before he arrived. It was only a matter of time and luck, or coincidence, for our paths to cross."

Thinking back to all that had happened, to all she'd explained and revealed, I wondered about the person in my dream on the way to Chicago. Had she anything to do with the radio interviews? The latter she had no hand in.

"I'm not the only messenger, Mr. Vásquez, and we work in different ways. Some are just more open about it, more honest about their work. But to your dream, yes, that was me. Forgive me if it wasn't clear. Dreams are... messy. Inconvenient. That's why your movie worked best."

"Amaya, you wouldn't let me near my mother and sister," I countered about the dream.

Amaya hesitated before responding, "I'm sorry, Damián. I sure wish I could have done something about that dream. Forgive me for that one. Truly hoped I wouldn't have had to reveal it."

She stood and looked sadly at the church, letting out a deep sigh. "So now, Mr. Vásquez, will you be visiting soon? Like Paloma asked? You must meet your brother."

I promised Amaya like I'd promised Paloma to return. A necessary visit thirty-plus years too late.

As people left the church, Amaya waved at me. "It's time, Mr. Vásquez, for the two of us to part."

"Wait, Amaya—"

"It's been quite a journey, Mr. Vásquez." She bent and picked up the bookmark piece. Asked for my hands; I nested them up for her. "Maybe we'll see each other again."

"But—"

"Oh, and Mr. Vásquez, about your father, don't worry about you leaving him there to die without asking for help. According to his report, your father died of organ failure. Consequences of his own actions. Go on and live your life with your wife. Goodbye, Damián."

Amaya walked backwards a few steps toward the church before turning to it. A flock of birds gathered before me, blocking Amaya from my view. When they scattered, she was gone. It didn't take long for the sound of the birds and the soothing breeze from their fluttering wings to put me to sleep.

PART 3
AFTER PALOMA'S VISIT

26

THE DAY AFTER OUR last encounter, Amaya and I spoke over the phone as I sat across from Señor Pepe at his kitchen table. She wanted to know what to do with Ignacio's body after his death. I told her I needed a day or two to figure it out.

After our phone call, I immediately searched for his family. His wife, Teresa, had died years ago, but their older son, Samuel, lived in Mexico City. I reached out and he agreed to help: I'd pay for Ignacio's body to be sent to Mexico and Samuel would bury him in his childhood home, where his parents had once abandoned him, and where he'd spend the rest of eternity. Abandoned.

That warm and partly cloudy evening, Xóchitl urged her father to pull out their dusty old VCR. Together as a family—Doña Mari, Señor Pepe, Xóchitl and I—we watched the movie whilst enjoying tacos and potato chips, drinking beer and soda pops. I talked fondly of the people I remembered. Yes, even about Jenni's cousin, Carlitos. During this viewing, no one time-traveled, and my in-laws didn't know or find out about that occurrence.

We packed our bags the next day to return to Cincinnati and promised her parents to return the following weekend, because family business is always unfinished business. When we returned to Chicago, Xóchitl and I rented an apartment near Ignacio's, partly to finish my pending affairs after my father's death, and partly to spend a day in the city, something we'd not done since we'd dated. We also wanted to take Jimmy the repairman up on his dinner offer. He and his wife were lovely people. She baked the juiciest Cornish hens with a coffee crust, sides of potatoes, Brussel sprouts, asparagus, candied yams, and to finish, a freshly baked pumpkin pie. It was like our own little pre-Thanksgiving feast.

Before heading downtown, I drove us to Pullman, parked in front of my old house, and pointed to the window of the old apartment Paloma, Sofía, even Ignacio, and I had lived in as a family. We then strolled to my old school. It was amazing how little had changed. My neighborhood. The school. It was as if time had preserved it just for me.

Continuing our walk through the calm and peaceful streets, the sun magnificently shining over them, we went to the McDonald's. That had changed. It was now a replica of all the other ones we'd encountered in Cincinnati, Chicago, and in between. Rectangular and sleek. Plain. The classic design, fun and imaginative, was now in our memories. Still, this particular one, Xóchitl and I recognized it for what it was: the magical place we'd met all those years ago, and the special place where she'd gotten to know Paloma.

In honor of my mother, we each ordered the number one meal. We sat down where we believed Paloma and I had sat, near where we'd once met and played. There, we chatted about that encounter with Paloma. A tall and slim woman with hair up to her shoulders, pushing an older woman in a wheelchair, walked by us.

"¿Damián?" the old woman asked in a frail voice when our eyes met. The younger woman set her food down immediately at the table next to ours and stared at me as if she'd seen a ghost.

"Jenni? Ceci?" I asked. The younger woman nodded and met me halfway after I'd gotten up from our booth. The three of us hugged. Old friends reunited.

"Dami, what are you doing here? Mami and I never thought we'd see you again."

I introduced them to Xóchitl and we sat with them at their table, where I informed Jenni and Ceci that we were visiting so I could show Xóchitl my past. I never mentioned to my old babysitter and childhood friend what my wife and I had experienced. What *I* had re-lived with them at my birthday party, and later.

"Mi hija, she's a teacher there at your old school," Ceci said proudly in Spanish.

Jenni spoke about her first graders and said she and her mother still lived at our old building. Ceci had bought the building years ago, plus a few other buildings in the area.

"We rent some apartments for short periods of time. What are they called, hija?" Ceci tried pronouncing Airbnbs, but it sounded like Arby's.

"Ay, Amá. Don't say that here. He's going to get mad at you." Jenni pointed to the guy at the front counter, then turned to me. "Oh! You'll never guess who rents your old place?" Jenni pointed her finger at my chest. She seemed so comfortable doing it, like we were still close friends.

"Who?" I wondered.

Mother and daughter waved at the guy at the counter, a middle-aged man taking orders, who sported a messy beard. He waved back, rolling his eyes as he pushed buttons on his headset, rushing to pack food orders and looking for missing items.

"Charlie—" Jenni said.

"Carlitos, hija," Ceci corrected.

Jenni apologized as they giggled together. "My cousin's a manager here now."

"I guess he reached his full potential," I joked and Jenni and I burst out laughing, leaving Ceci and Xóchitl confused by our inside joke.

In the hour we spent there, Ceci and Jenni learned about Xóchitl and her parents, and how close they lived, only twenty minutes away. Carlos also joined us for a quick chat, offering us food to take home. I reminded him of when he almost damaged the movie. Carlos remembered spending the day at Jenni's on the day of Paloma's accident, but not how close he'd come to ruining my movie.

As we got ready to leave, saying our temporary goodbyes, Ceci pulled me in and promised to pray for Xóchitl and me. It saddened me to hear her voice like this, so old and wasted, but so loving, the way grandparents speak to their children and grandchildren upon seeing them for the first time in days or years. Ceci was no longer the imposing woman of my childhood and I wondered about Paloma, if they'd still be friends were she alive, and if she'd look just as frail as the woman who'd babysat me so many times. Ceci promised to pray for my mother and sister too, before pulling me in for another hug and a hard kiss on my cheek.

"Seeing you made her... *us* very happy," Jenni said.

"Hijo, when you come back, I'll make you huevitos," Ceci suggested.

"Sí, Ceci. With chorizo," I answered and smiled, wondering if she still saw in me the little boy I once was.

They left before us and Xóchitl and I watched from what used to be our play area as Jenni pushed her mother's wheelchair, disappearing into my old street.

From the McDonald's, we walked back to the car near what was now Ceci's building. Briefly, I stopped near the spot where the car had hit Paloma, but Xóchitl tugged me along. From there, we drove a few minutes down to Roseland, hoping to find any clue that would lead us to Amaya's

We parked at St. Anthony's church. Unfortunately, the blue house she'd mentioned wasn't there. I imagined the smaller, pink one-story building might be her aunt and uncle's house, stacked between two two-story houses and across from a giant lot that I assumed was once the bread factory she'd mentioned. Other than that, there was nothing else that led me to Amaya. After a quick drive around the neighborhood, we left.

The following day, Xóchitl and I met with a realtor to look at Ignacio's house. The house needed to be sold immediately, I requested, and this realtor had no issue with it. Plus, Ignacio having left the necessary documents made the realtor's job easy. She commended the cleanliness of the place, and, as is the way of the world, a cockroach scurried across the living room floor precisely one second later. One woman's shriek followed the other and all I could do was apologize to them, having lost the critter. To play it safe, I hired an exterminator to inspect the house on Monday morning before we headed back to Ohio.

We left useful items out front for anyone to pick up. Everything else, we discarded in the garbage cans in the alley, except for a few personal mementos Ignacio had stuffed in the old boxes. Xóchitl and I ended the day searching for the car keys, which, in the end, we found inside the car. After breaking the driver-side window, I grabbed the keys and attempted to start the engine to no avail. I switched it to neutral, and my wife and I pushed the car out of the garage and into the alley, leaving a note on the window: *Do whatever you want with this car. Burn it, break the windows, destroy it.*

Back at home, the next morning, the realtor called and left a message saying a young couple was eager to buy the house. From afar, via the realtor, Xóchitl and I agreed to sell it to them. Within a week, the house closed. The money cleared in our checking account a couple of days after and we made a plan to use the money to start a couple of businesses: Xóchitl, a marketing agency that, she'd decided, would also educate undocumented immigrants on starting a business; and me, a non-profit helping victims of domestic abuse, emphasizing on emotional maltreatment and mental health awareness.

SOFÍA AND I SPOKE on the phone every week. Moisés was usually busy at his shop, occasionally jumping on for a quick hello before rushing off. When video-chatting became the norm, her children Daniel and Paloma joined in. Daniel looked just like Moisés did on my last time-travel visit.

The younger one, Paloma (or Palomita, as we referred to her), looked like her mother, Sofía. Her face resembled her grandmother's too. That gave me an idea of what my mother looked like when she was young. This Palomita was taller than both, with long, black hair down to her elbows.

"Poor Ángel. None of his children look like him," I joked with Sofía. "Are you sure they're his?"

"Yes." She smirked. "Maybe if we'd had a third one, but he should count himself lucky that our children carried my genes instead of his."

Well, Ángel wasn't *that* bad looking.

On one of those video calls in late April, Sofía, exuberantly joyful, said there was a very good chance she and her husband could visit the U.S. Unable to contain my excitement, I rambled on about how much they'd love Cincinnati and about taking them to Chicago to see Ceci and Jenni. Soon, my exuberance turned to doubt about their visit, my mind grasping at the difficulties and legalities they'd have to field just to visit this country. Too many of my clients, unable to do it the legal way, had no choice but to leave their countries the same way Paloma, Sofía, and Amaya had. There was just no hope for them in the end to get any permit or visa to come, and their economic and political situations only worsened their livelihood. Per my experience with my clients, getting a visa was disappointingly slow, often waiting years... decades to get one. Understanding that struggle, I told myself that Sofía and Ángel shouldn't get their hopes up, which was enough incentive to finally plan a visit to Mexico.

"My brother and sister's birthdays are coming up," I told Xóchitl and she was just as exuberant as I'd been on that call. It would be an amazing surprise for them, Xóchitl declared. I wondered if I should say anything to my faraway family.

"Not yet," she suggested, while I nuzzled the baby bump beginning to grow on my wife. Xóchitl pulled out her laptop, immediately searching for flights to leave in a couple of weeks. With no hesitation, she punched the letters and numbers on the keyboard with gusto.

"We'll be there for your sister's birthday," she declared, and in a matter of minutes, an email notification popped up on my phone.

FLIGHT RESERVED — CVG TO MLM. TUESDAY, MAY 9, 2023. 8 HOURS, 57 MINUTES. 3:30 PM — 11:27 PM.

We'd arrive on the night of Moisés' birthday. I wished she had reserved it for the day before to celebrate with him too, but my wife had done more than enough for all of us and I couldn't be happier.

27

T HE CAB DRIVER AT the Morelia airport in Michoacan, Guanajuato's neighboring state, placed our bags in his trunk, while Xóchitl and I slid into the back of his car. Through the dark roads, the cab driver asked if we'd been to Moroleón, to which we replied it was our first time. The driver, unable to contain himself, went on and on about all the places we must visit.

"You need to go to El Jardín and, while you're there, there's a guy that sells burgers with salchichas on top. Mmm." The driver kissed his fingers one by one. "With a little mayonesa on the bread, a little chopped lettuce, jitomatito, grilled onions... ¡Ay Dios! Heaven on earth."

"We know a little about heaven on earth," Xóchitl said excitedly, reaching close to him, as if she were confessing a secret. The driver smiled, probably reminiscing on the burger he was missing while driving us instead.

Xóchitl lay her head on my arm.

"Xóchi, I dreamt of my mom," I confessed quietly in English, hoping our driver wouldn't listen or understand. The music on the radio played a popular Christian Nodal song. "I'm not sure if it was really her or my mind playing tricks on me, but she held our baby, humming the song she used to hum to me."

"Which one?"

I told her. John Lennon's *Beautiful Boy (Darling Boy).*

"That's a nice one," she breathed.

"Except this time, I was me. No longer a younger version. At one point, when I turned to her, she looked older. Like how she would have looked now if she were alive."

"Hmm. Did you say anything to her?"

"I don't remember. I know I wanted to tell her it was Ignacio who killed her, but it all happened so fast. She just smiled at us and continued humming her song at the baby."

"Hmm. So, we're having a boy?"

I smiled at the thought of a little Damián, or Xóchitl, running around, watching movies with us, breaking stuff, and us laughing about it after scolding them.

We arrived at the rental across from Sofía's close to one a.m. The property owner, Doña Mago, waited outside. Considering the hour and her patience, I figured we'd be safe if Xóchitl and I ever wanted to venture outside late in the evening.

"Buenas noches, jóvenes," the short woman said as she reached her hand up and patted my cheek. That made me feel welcome, like we were a part of her. Or maybe that was just the way the people of Moroleón were. That was how my mother and sister were, kind and welcoming. Doña Mago walked to the cab driver and asked for our bags, but I told her not to worry. I paid the man, plus a little extra for a few of his burgers, and started up the stairs with our bags while Xóchitl walked alongside Doña Mago, arms intertwined, into the home.

Once I returned back down and before going inside to join my wife and our hostess, I stared at the house across from me, the one I had visited on my last time-traveling trip. The world was quiet. There was a certain peace in my family's land.

Despite the hour, close to 2 a.m., Doña Mago insisted we eat, never taking a no for an answer. She served us chilaquiles with chile rojo and refried beans.

"Your wife is eating for two now and you probably haven't eaten anything since before you left."

She was right. We'd boarded our plane around 2:30 p.m. our time, so we hadn't eaten anything in half a day. I was tired, had a headache, and my stomach knew what Doña Mago was up to. I couldn't imagine how my pregnant wife felt despite smiling through it.

Doña Mago spoke to us about her life in Moroleón and I shared that my family was from the city too. I never gave their names and, when she asked, I avoided telling her where they lived, choosing to lie instead. I told her I'd lost the address and someone would text me the address in the morning.

Grabbing a fourth tortilla and cutting a piece of queso fresco with it, Xóchitl glanced at me and gave me a scornful look. It was a look I recognized, the one she had given me many times over whenever I stuffed my face late in the evening.

"What? I'm hungry," I protested in English with a mouthful.

Doña Mago didn't seem to mind and asked about our life in the U.S. We told her about life in Chicago and Cincinnati. She followed with stories about her children's lives in the U.S. and places they'd visited.

"Have you been?" Xóchitl asked her.

"No, niña, never. I've no desire. This is my home. And yours, too."

We finished the night with Doña Mago suggesting places for us to shop at and the best tourist spots. She mentioned her preferred vendors, even the famous hot dog-burger guy, and what nearby stores had what we may need. She said not to hesitate to ask her for anything, even if she had to go out and get it.

As we headed up the stairs, I felt bad for the woman. She seemed so lonely. Her children were away, like Jimmy's, living their own lives. Hopefully, they kept in touch with their parents, because once they're gone, all that "wish I could have" is wishful thinking.

The closed windows in our upstairs bedroom muffled the sounds of outside voices. While unpacking, I searched for my pajamas and chose what clothes I'd wear in the morning. In a zippered compartment of my suitcase—where I thought I'd find only socks and underwear—I also found Sofía's letters and the half bookmark Amaya had given me. Xóchitl must've put them there, because I hadn't. In fact, I realized I had forgotten to put them in at all. Aside they went, to be read while we finished preparing for bed.

While brushing my teeth, I unlatched the metal bars that locked the windows, hoping to still catch the muffled voices outside and wave at them, all neighborly. But when I finally pushed out the hard-to-open windows, I only saw the red of a car's brake lights as it drove away.

Once in bed, as I waited on my wife, I pulled out Sofía's letters from their envelopes, searching for the one she'd written the day of Paloma's viewing here in Mexico. I found it next to a travel agency receipt from July, one of those generic pieces of paper available to buy at any office supply store. Written in the memo was: "Deposit, Ignacio Vasquez," and check-marked "cash." *Hmm. Planning a trip, Ignacio?* It didn't matter. I crumpled it up and threw it near my suitcase to throw away later.

Sofía's letter read:

Damián,

I made it home safely. I pray to God that you'll be well. I've asked Ceci to keep an eye out for you. Please tell your father to let you keep in touch with us and that he should bring you one day, Mijo. I'm sorry for how things turned out, and I promise that one day I'll tell you what happened to Mamá...

Had she known what Ignacio did to her?

I continued reading the letter:

...and why I was sent to Mexico. For now, know that you'll be in our minds and prayers.

Don't forget us, Mamá or me. It won't be hard since she lives inside of us. And know that I'm proud of you, of the kind and helpful little boy that you've become, and I'm confident that you'll grow up to be the most wonderful man. Never change.

Dami, I've included the movie I recorded for you. In it, you'll find,

1. *Your 8th birthday party*
2. *Your return to classes*
3. *Your Halloween with Jenni and Carlitos*
4. *Mamá's funeral in Mexico*

Sorry about that last one, but it'll give you an idea of the family that awaits you. Hopefully, this movie will remind you of how magnificent our mother was. She'll live forever through this.

Love you, Mijo. Take care! We'll see you soon.
Your sister, Sofía Laura Alonso Flores.

I couldn't avoid letting out a few tears. I used my shirt to clean my face before my wife joined me in bed, then stuffed the letter, along with the bookmark, in its envelope and placed it under my pillow.

Finally, my wife came to bed.

THAT MORNING, MAY 10th—Mother's Day—despite only getting about five hours of sleep, I woke up feeling energized. Refreshed. My phone alarm went off a few minutes after I opened my eyes, five minutes after my 8 o'clock one. My phone notified me of the other missed alarms: 7, 7:30, and 7:45.

Xóchitl's clothes were spread out on her side of the bed. Had she been up long? The semi-open window let in the sound of her and Doña Mago chatting downstairs. A truck with a loudspeaker passed by, reminding me of the one I'd seen when I visited with Paloma. The town's voices grew louder. Children's feet pitter-pattered as they laughed and yelled on their way to school. Cars honked. Metal doors slammed. *Las Mañanitas* played nearby from one of the neighboring houses. People were already busy on this Wednesday morning.

I put on a long-sleeved button-shirt that required no tucking, a pair of faded-looking jeans, and a pair of brown shoes that looked like dress shoes, but were really sneakers. Throwing my previous night's clothes next to Xóchitl's, I brushed my teeth and headed downstairs.

"Good morning, Love," I said, kissing my wife on the lips in a shy manner. We were guests in someone else's home; PDA was probably no big deal to Doña Mago, but I was a little bashful in front of others. The TV in the living room played a dubbed version of *La Bamba*. Richie's mom, Connie, played by Rosanna DeSoto, waved her fingers over the white bed sheets hung outside to dry. Xóchitl and I knew what was coming for Connie. For Bob. For Rosie. For Donna.

"Not my Richie," Connie cried to Bob as she threw one of the wet sheets behind her.

"Sofía hated the idea of flying. Hated the end of this movie," I said to my wife.

"Let's skip it then. Come on, Doña Mago is waiting for us in the kitchen."

There, I greeted her with a 'good morning' and wished her a happy Mother's Day. "Sorry we kept you up so late," I apologized.

"Joven, at my age, I'm lucky to sleep all the way through the night. I'm up at 5 a.m. every day, anyway. Apparently, so is your wife or so she tells me. Did you sleep well?"

I confirmed that we did and motioned my head sideways to my wife, closing my eyes and letting out my tongue. Doña Mago caught sight of my silliness and laughed along with Xóchitl.

Doña Mago served us more of her chilaquiles. Xóchitl placed her hand over mine and asked if I was okay. I nodded, though after her question, what little anxiety I carried in me increased a thousandfold as I wondered what Sofía's reaction would be upon seeing me after over thirty years. What would the rest of the family think of me? Dropping in unexpectedly and uninvited.

"Don't worry. Your sister will love it. It's a surprise visit and life's full of them." Xóchitl was right. She'd lived through one of them with me for a few minutes.

As we got ready to leave after breakfast, Doña Mago wished us a good day. She switched on her kitchen TV. Xóchitl waited in the living room, not minding the movie that had followed *La Bamba*, instead focused on the photos on the wall, while I went upstairs for the movie, the flash drives containing the digital versions (thanks to Jimmy), and other gifts for the rest of the family.

Once I was back downstairs, Doña Mago sounded concerned about whatever played on her old TV. Xóchitl called out to her and we saw her holding her towel over her mouth, like she couldn't believe the news. She ignored Xóchitl.

"Let's go, Xóchi. She's just watching the news. Probably something terrible in the area. We'll check on Doña Mago after."

How interesting it was, standing outside of the house, just as it had been with Paloma. The same light gray building with a red metal door stood before me, now with a little rust. Gray hairs had appeared on me over the years. They were my version of rust. They were what told our ages.

The door was ajar. We walked inside to the dark patio where people had gathered to pay their respects to my mother. Was my family home? The place was too quiet. Xóchitl mirrored my walk behind me.

Past the patio was an open area, decorated with green plants that captured the sun's energy. We were a few steps from the inside of the house. I recognized the stairs that had led me to Sofía and Moisés' upstairs bedroom to our right.

My fingers lightly tapped the yellow metal door, one by one, hoping Sofía would be the first one to open the door and invite us in. But no one came. Someone's head did turn to us, then back. I couldn't tell who it was through the frosted glass.

"I hope they still live here," I nervously chuckled at Xóchitl, hoping no one would call the cops on us for trespassing, if a different family lived there. Slowly, I pushed the door open. A young lady sat on a couch. She looked horrified, but not at our sudden appearance. She was watching whatever played on her phone screen.

"Palomita? Hola, mija," I said with a nervous smile. "Where's your—"

I paused when my niece turned to me with a distressed look. What was happening? Was it the same news that had made Doña Mago so distraught? Palomita looked shocked. Maybe we should have said something about visiting, instead of doing it unannounced.

"¿Tío?" the girl asked.

"Sí, hija. Surprise. We came to see you." Whatever joy I had vanished when I saw the red in her eyes.

"Um, Paloma, where's your mother?" I finally asked. My question felt slow, like molasses, unlike the rapid beating of my heart.

"Tío, didn't you see?" The teary-eyed Palomita waved her phone.

Xóchitl gasped. "Dami, check your phone."

I froze. Whatever they'd seen or read, I wasn't ready for it. Xóchitl handed me her phone and only bits of words registered in my brain.

Morelia... plane... Gulf of Mexico... Engine Failure.

It was like being in an alternate reality. Like we were in some twisted Twilight Zone episode.

Xóchitl walked to the TV and picked up a printed piece of paper that looked like a ticket with a blue logo of a man's face below an eagle. She handed it to me. *CONFIRMATION* was printed in bold. I'd seen that logo hours before at the Mexican airport. I snatched it from her and saw that it said the flight had left a few hours after we'd gone to sleep.

Were those... *No*. No! The voices I'd heard outside had nothing to do with this, right?

Two birds landed just outside the window. One, the white one, I already knew too well. The other one, though, was new. It was brown with blue around the black orbs of its eyes and specs of blue that filled part of its wing. That one stared at me, as if it was looking into my soul, cooing that familiar sound. Then, together, they flew away.

"Tío, they went to see you," Palomita cried out, breaking me out of a trance. "She and my dad were going to surprise you."

There were no words from my end. No reaction. I had nothing to give. Xóchitl ran to her instead of me. She held the young girl and they both cried, young Paloma burying her face in my wife's chest.

My body finally reacted. I dropped to my knees, my wife's phone diving on its own after I'd ungripped it. Together, we landed on the hard, cold floor. A stranger's thick and calloused hand grabbed my shoulder, but I pushed it away, wanting nothing to do with this stranger that wouldn't give up trying to hold me. He bent down to wrap his lanky arms around me with great force. I pushed the tall and slender man to the floor next to my niece and my wife. Glancing quickly at the man, I saw that his faded shirt said Mazinger Z and had a robot below the lettering. The robot was a black and silver machine with red wings.

The man crawled to me and I finally let him hold me. When he pulled away from me, we stared into each other's eyes; his were brown and sunken. I saw Mamá in him. He tried to speak, but couldn't. Wiping his mouth and eyes with his shirt, he finally said, "Damián, soy tu hermano Moisés. You finally made it."

As my brother held my shoulders at arm's length, the red metal door out front opened. Palomita turned to see who it was. Xóchitl let her go so the girl could run to them. Whatever they carried, they dropped, and even from that distance, even after hitting the concrete floor, I felt the vibrations. Footsteps hurried to us. Moisés turned to see Palomita enter the living room. He then shook me to look away from him.

"Hijo," the woman following Palomita said. It was like she'd told me in her letter: Sofía had made it home safely.

Epilogue

AMAYA

MOROLEÓN, GUANAJUATO
MAY 09, 2023

*O*NE DAY, *I'LL SAVE someone's life in honor of Papá.*

Sitting across from the Jardín, hours before Damián and his wife would arrive in Mexico for the first time, I thought back to that promise I had made shortly after my father's death. Not long after Damián and Xóchitl's arrival, I'd fly back to Chicago. It was too bad time wasn't on our side. It would've been a nice surprise to run into each other.

The last time I'd seen them was when I visited his city, Cincinnati, for a weekend. Such nice people there. Quaint. Like a mini version of Chicago. There, we dined at the same restaurant before I returned home. Hadn't planned on it. They just showed up. I didn't want to impose on their date. We'd already said goodbye on our last phone call. So, happening upon them as they celebrated the joyous news of their pregnancy was a sweet encounter from afar. I cheered with them, but from a different table.

Sofía's bookstore, *Librería PaloMo*, was only a few feet away, and since arriving in Moroleón two weeks ago, I still hadn't mustered the courage to waltz in and make small talk with her. Since arriving, I'd spent most days sitting outside the paletería or the coffee shop near her store, admiring her from afar and feeding crumbs to the occasional bird that approached. I watched when she opened her store, when she greeted her customers as they walked in, and when she waved them goodbye.

My phone notified me again of my flight check-in, reminding me I only had a couple hours left to be near her. Minutes, actually. She'd soon close her store for the day. Notification swiped. Dismissed. That would be future Amaya's problem, something to take care of once ready to leave for the airport. First, I needed just a bit of courage to walk into her bookstore.

What ever happened to my family? I wondered, drinking my cappuccino. They no longer lived at my old casita. My brother Martín and I hadn't been in contact since just before I died, and I'd lost track of him. Tía Meche and Tío Porfirio were dead. He died in 1995; she in 2002. Mamá was no longer at home and my other siblings had gone their own way. How many of the people passing by had I known? Had any of my brothers or sisters walked by? Maybe we just hadn't recognized each other. Had they seen me and wondered about the woman sitting by the Jardín every day for two weeks?

Each time doves gathered here, I thought back to Damián and all he'd gone through, especially the pain he'd endured that I'd partly been guilty of. And yet, despite the unexpected journey I'd given him to reunite with his mother and find answers and peace, it felt incomplete. Unfinished.

It was 6:30 p.m. Thirty minutes before Sofía closed her shop. My last chance to see her. Otherwise, I may have to walk with her after the fate that awaited her, the one I'd warned Damián about in his dream. I truly wished I could have been clearer about that. I wished I could do something to stop what awaited her.

Now, it was just a matter of time before he became a broken man once again.

The last of my now-cold cappuccino went down my throat, the sediment at the bottom of the cup tickled my throat as it went down. Then, I crushed the Styrofoam cup and threw it in the trash can that was a few steps away. It was time. I was ready to walk into her bookshop.

Don't interfere, Amaya, the Muerte's warning played in my head. *Don't expose yourself,* it had said once, something another messenger had failed to do on the radio.

A little doorbell above the store's door alerted her of my presence.

"Hola," Sofía said kindly. "Can I help you find anything?"

I lifted my finger, as if making a point of what I wanted, but didn't know what to ask for, until I remembered her bookmark. The half I had not given to Damián was still in my purse.

"Hello. Yes. I'm looking for a classic." I played dumb for a moment. "Jane Eyre."

"Ah," she said, walking me to a wall with hundreds of classics. *Don Quixote. The Count of Monte Cristo. The Island of Dr. Moreau.* All displayed facing forward.

"It's got one of my favorite quotes," she said, turning to the chapter of the copy she'd pulled. Twenty-three. "I am no bird; and no net ensnares me: I am a free human being with an independent will," she read for me.

I thanked her. Together, as if we'd been friends all our lives, we walked to her register.

"You... you look familiar," she said with narrowed eyes. When her eyes widened, the evening sun coming in gave them that honey-color I'd noticed all those years ago at the mercado. "Are you friends with my children? With Daniel? Did you go to school with him?"

"No. No. I haven't been to school for a very long time, but people have told me I have one of those faces."

Sofía smiled, but her gaze told me she was trying hard to remember that someone I resembled.

"Well, come back anytime," she said, then paused. "Oh, wait. We'll be closed tomorrow. My husband and I are leaving for a few days." She looked pleased saying that. "My children will open the store this weekend. God, I gotta remember to leave a sign outside."

It broke my heart hearing the excitement in her voice about leaving for a few days. For her husband too and all those strangers joining them, sharing the same sealed fate. Death was a cruel bitch.

Loving our small talk, trying to hold on to this moment as long as possible, I asked about her trip.

"Ohio," she said. She mentioned the brother I'd known and her elation at reuniting with him. "After *many* years," she added, emphasizing how long with open arms.

"I'm sure he's just as ecstatic. Congratulations. All the best," I wished her.

THE CAB DRIVER DROPPED me off at the airport precisely at three in the morning. As he unloaded my two bags from the car, an ambulance rushed past us. *You won't be immortal*, the Muerte reminded me. But it had also told me to make my one chance to return count.

I'd been on this earth only fifty-seven years and I wasn't sure why, but this second chance at life had already exhausted me. I couldn't imagine how many more Damiáns I'd be helping. Would each one drain me more and more until my one chance at a second life expired?

What a strange and cursed miracle, returning from the dead for one day or a thousand, yet still as fragile as any other mortal. For me, assuming I played it safe, how many more days could I endure on this earth? And honestly, I should be grateful for the opportunity. Dead at twenty-three, alive another thirty-four.

There were three hours left before my flight left for Chicago. While waiting to board my airplane, I took out my new book to read. It reminded me of Sofia and forced me to glance occasionally in search of her.

The Muerte wouldn't let my mind rest. *Don't interfere. You're not immortal.*

Sofia and Ángel rushed in, looking for an attendant, hoping it wasn't too late for them to board. The attendant calmed them, assuring them there was still time, as last checks on the plane needed to be done. Boarding for their flight would begin in just a few minutes.

I slouched into my seat, hiding behind the book's pages to avoid being recognized. Silent, I observed my friend afar, reaching for my raincoat over my carry-on. I'd need it once we arrived in Chicago.

The forecast called for rain that morning, or the day after. I couldn't remember or concentrate as I focused on her.

Sofía went to the bathroom and, within seconds, they announced their flight was ready to board. Ángel stood, looking nervous, probably fearing what may happen if his wife didn't hurry. Sofía's large handbag lay next to their carry-ons. Sticking out of her handbag was what looked like a ticket.

A plan hatched in my brain.

I could save a life, redeem myself for not speaking up against Ignacio.

Don't interfere, Amaya, the Muerte warned in my head.

But what if... what if... I could take her place, Muerte?

Don't meddle, Amaya.

Muerte, I can save her. This is my chance at redemption. For her and for Damián.

Life is unfair. So is death.

Yes, but you also said a life for a life.

Your life for hers, Amaya? But what about him? Her beloved.

True. I'd trade my life for hers. I could save her. But who would trade theirs for his?

My two lives. My old one and my new one for theirs. Those would be my exchanges. Chapter twenty-three: "I am a free human being with an independent will."

I wasn't sure if it would work. It didn't fully make sense to me, but I figured it was my best shot. My two lives for theirs.

With my raincoat in one hand, boarding ticket, legal documents, and book in the other—the half piece of the bookmark in it—I headed in his direction, pretending to read, so I could make bumping into him look realistic.

"I'm sooo sorry, sir. Please forgive me. I was completely engrossed in this book." I flashed the front cover in front of his face. "Shit, my ticket. My passport."

"Don't worry, it happens. Oh, and that's one of my wife's favorite books," he said, holding my book while I pretended to pick up my raincoat that covered Sofía's bag. I bundled it all over my chest.

"I've read it so many times. I'm not sure if she has it, but keep it for her. Trust me, this one's very special," I said hurriedly and rushed to the counter.

My old life for his. My new one for hers, Muerte, I begged. *Please.*

Rushing to the attendant who'd just called to board, I quickly took out what looked like Sofía's ticket and her passport. Clumsily, I opened to the front with her picture, covering most of her face.

Lord, please make this work.

"Ay Dios, ay Dios, ay Diosito, I'm so nervous," I uttered. "I just want to get in and sit down. Please!" I purposely dropped my bag and bent down for it, holding the passport I'd just shown the woman. I was hoping to exasperate her enough to just let me in. "Here," I said, quickly showing her the passport with my thumb still covering Sofía, then bringing it back down with me. The woman was giving in, I assumed, as she sighed hard after my desperation.

Ángel shouted for Sofía to hurry and she ran to him. The woman turned to them and I shook Sofía's passport with more urgency, distracting her. It was my way of indicating to her that I was too stressed and just needed to go inside the plane to calm down.

Sofía and Ángel searched for her handbag.

"Ay, *please*, can I go in?" I cried hysterically.

"Sí, sí, ya, go. Go!" she instructed, waving for me to go in, but watching the scene unfold at Sofía and Ángel's spot. They were trying to find what I'd stolen. From halfway down the boarding bridge, I stopped and glanced back, watching them argue with the personnel, including the woman who'd just let me in. They were talking about losing her bag with her ticket, passport, and phone. The already frustrated woman refused to let Sofía board unless she had her ticket and passport. Ángel refused to board without his wife.

A life for a life, Muerte, I reminded it of my terms. *My two lives for theirs.*

Sofía paused and looked in my direction. Our eyes met, her brown eyes with my blue eyes from a distance. She waved and smiled at me as I retreated, taking their place, saving them from the plane that wouldn't make it to Ohio.

Afterword

In my twenties, I read Mitch Albom's *Tuesdays with Morrie*, and, a few years later, after reading Albom's *The Five People You Meet in Heaven*, I looked forward to his book, *For One More Day*, which became an instant favorite.

Many years later, I'd wanted to tell a similar story to *For One More Day;* I, too, wanted to tell the story of a man who re-encounters his deceased mother, because, like my Damián Vásquez and Albom's Charles "Chick" Benetto, I missed my mother, who had passed away many years before.

It wasn't until 2021 when I took a friend's *On Becoming an Author* class (by author Victor Velez) that I began playing with the idea: the story of a man who sees his deceased mother at the house he grew up in. I put aside my idea. In 2022, author J. M. Clark offered writing workshops at his Cincinnati bookstore, and, while taking one of his workshops, it hit me: what if my half-sister hadn't raised me after our mother's passing? What if life ripped my childhood away? Threw me a one-eighty?

That's how and when my story, *When Palomas Visit,* was born.

This novel is a work of fiction, yet it's heavily inspired by what I love and what shaped me; the people I love, like my mother Margarita and my sister Laura; my city, Chicago; the Mexican city my family's from, Moroleón; and my love, my wife Frances, and the life we've built together in Cincinnati.

When Palomas Visit began as a healing journey for me, and it turned into something more. It's a story for the Damián's out there who've their loved ones and want just a little extra time with them. For those wronged by the people that should protect them. It's a story of sacrifices and their repercussions. It's a ghost story. A Day of the Dead and a Mother's Day story.

The next time you see a dove nearby—when palomas visit—, remember that the one person you've missed and longed for will be with you. Their spirit and love will never leave you.

Acknowledgements

The first person to thank is my wonderful wife, Frances, who supports me in all I do, always cheering me on, and who created the amazing cover image. Thank you, Love, for everything.

I'm forever grateful to my editor, Marcelle Iten. Honestly, this story couldn't have been as amazing if it wasn't for her. Marcelle, you made this story a masterpiece. And the book blurb, I couldn't have come up with what you did. Eternally grateful to you.

Thanks to my first set of readers: Elaine Esparza, Jasmine Esparza, Christian Vallejo, Edith Padilla, Manuel Iris, Samantha Fuentes, Brian Taylor, and Dr. Maria Espinola. And, of course, to my Beta and ARC readers.

To my mentors, authors J. M. Clark and Victor Velez. Thank you for the classes and workshops, and the knowledge you shared.

To author Mitch Albom, who started it all for me with his book *For One More Day*, the biggest inspiration for this book. Every time I read your book, my mother's there with me for one more day.

To Beverly Zavala, thank you for keeping my mother Margarita alive through your recording.

And to my family. There's a piece of you in everything good that's in this story. Even Snowball.

About the author

Abel Zavala lives in Cincinnati, Ohio, with his wife, Frances, and their plants (they have no names... rather, Abel forgot their names; if they had pets, it'd be easier to remember their names and include them here). He is a radio personality for a Mexican radio station, La Mega 97.7 FM, and a writer for their Spanish-language newspaper, La Mega Nota.

When Palomas Visit is his first novel.

You can find him on Facebook, Instagram, TikTok, Threads and X under @abelzauthor.